PRAISE FOR *D.*

"Finding our place and following our hearts is the moving theme of *Dare to Dream*, a finely tuned finish to Heidi Thomas's trilogy inspired by the life of her grandmother, an early rodeo-rider. With crisp dialogue and singular scenes we're not only invited into the middle of a western experience of rough stock, riders, and generations of ranch tradition, but we're deftly taken into a family drama. This family story takes place beginning in 1941 but it could be happening to families anywhere—and is. Nettie, Jake, and Neil struggle to find their place and discover what we all must: Life is filled with sorrow and joy; faith, family, and friends see us through and give meaning to it all. Nettie or, as Jake calls her, "little gal" will stay in your heart and make you want to re-read the first books just to keep her close. A very satisfying read." —Jane Kirkpatrick, *New York Times* best-selling author and WILLA Literary Award winner of *A Flickering Light*

"Heidi Thomas's latest novel, *Dare to Dream*, rings of truth. Here is the real West, ranching in the 1940s, women and rodeoing, the heart-rending effect of World War II on the Montana homefront, and great characters who bring it all alive. I loved it." —Irene Bennett Brown, author of the Women of Paragon Springs series and the Celia Landrey mystery series

"Nettie Moser is a strong woman who defies fear, bad luck, and male opposition to pursue her dream of being a champion steer rider. Set in the uncertain war-world of the early 1940s, *Dare to Dream* is a highly readable tale of a resourceful woman who faces life with courage and a daring heart."
—Susan Wittig Albert, best-selling author of *A Wilder Rose* and the China Bayles mystery series

DARE TO DREAM
A Novel

HEIDI M. THOMAS

TWODOT®

GUILFORD, CONNECTICUT
HELENA, MONTANA
AN IMPRINT OF GLOBE PEQUOT PRESS

Names of real cowgirls have been used in the story, but the relationship to the main character is fictional: Marie Gibson, Fannie Sperry Steele, Prairie Rose Henderson, Margie and Alice Greenough, Trixi McCormick, Birdie Askin, Vivian White. All other characters and events in this book are fictional, and any resemblance to persons, whether living or dead, is strictly coincidental.

A · TWODOT® · BOOK

Project Editor: Lauren Brancato
Layout: Joanna Beyer

Library of Congress Cataloging-in-Publication data is available on file.

ISBN 978-0-7627-9700-4

Printed in the United States of America

10 9 8 7 6 5 4 3 2 1

CHAPTER ONE

"Ready or not, rodeo world, I'm back." Nettie Moser inhaled the smell of rodeo—dust, animal sweat, manure—the scent of pure happiness. She strode to the arena fence near the chutes and climbed onto the top rail to watch the color guard parade the flag. A pretty teenaged cowgirl, long blonde curls bouncing under a white hat, led a group of equally lovely, brightly clad ladies through their paces. The rodeo queen and her court.

Nettie shook her head. *Some like the pomp and falderal, but I'll take a rangy steer any day.* She looked around at the crowd. *Wonder where the other women riders are.* She hopped down from her perch and headed for the registration booth where Jake already waited in line. "Here I am, ready to ride."

It had been a long eight years since her dear friend Marie Gibson was killed when her bronc collided with the pickup man's horse. That accident had shattered Nettie's rodeo dream but she finally overcame her fear with the help of her mentor's unforgettable advice: *Live your life, follow your dream.*

"And I'm glad." Jake pulled her into the circle of one arm. "But did you get a look at those steers, little gal? They look pretty big." He winked at her.

Nettie took a couple of exaggerated, swaggering steps. "Never met a steer who could get the best of me." She laughed out loud. It felt so good to be here in Cheyenne. The snorts and squeals and bawls of the rough stock in the pens, the shouts and cheers and curses of the cowboys were music to her ears. Anticipation skittering inside, she could almost feel the steer's rough hide through her denims. She stuffed her leather gloves into her back pocket and leaned over to pull the straps on her spurs tighter. She couldn't wait to be on the back of a bucking, writhing animal, pitting her wiry 102 pounds against its half ton of muscle and bone.

"Hey there, Jake, Missus Moser," a cowboy called as he walked by. Other friends greeted them as they worked their way to the head of the line. Nettie waved to them and danced in place, her boots scuffing up little puffs of dust.

Jake grinned at her antics and swept her into a dance step. "You'll wear yourself out before you even get to the chutes."

Nettie didn't mind his teasing. Once again, she felt the old happiness, the anticipation she'd had when they were first married and looking forward to their dreams. Now, after years of drought and failure and moving from one place to another, she finally had her dream of a home—what looked like an ironclad lease-to-buy ranch at Ingomar, Montana. And she had her first dream again—rodeo. The spring of 1941 was off to a good start.

Jake stepped forward to register. "Jake Moser. Saddle-bronc ridin'." He reached for a roll of bills in his pocket. "Nettie Moser. Steer ridin'."

The man at the desk peered up at Nettie. "No women."

Nettie felt kicked in the gut. "What are you talking about?" Memory flashed: She was fourteen years old again, about to ride in her first rodeo, hearing the old cowpuncher's gravelly voice say, *You can't ride. You're a girl.* She stepped closer.

The cowboy held out his hands, palms up. "This is an RAA-sanctioned event and we ain't includin' women. Sorry."

Nettie clenched her jaw. The Rodeo Association of America. All men. No women allowed. Montana promoters had not joined that group . . . yet.

Twenty years since her first ride. All the rough rides proving themselves, competing with men, the world championships won—and now cowgirls were being erased.

Nettie leaned closer to the RAA man. "I'm a woman, and I'm riding."

"Not today." The RAA man gave no ground. "Them's been the rules the last ten years."

"But not enforced," Nettie argued.

"Then it's about time."

A few of the waiting riders chuckled, one whistled in appreciation, and more expressed the strong personal opinion that Nettie should step aside, at which Jake gave a warning snarl.

"It's for your own good, ma'am," one of the riders called out. "Bonnie McCarroll was killed in Pendleton way back in twenty-nine, and then Marie Gibson got killed in Idaho in thirty-three."

"I was there," Nettie told him and the others. "I lost a friend to a heartless accident. I can't believe that's never happened to you. What about all the men who've been killed? Why, just a couple years ago Pete Knight was killed in Ellensburg, Washington, when his bronc fell on him."

The men stood, humbled to silence a moment.

Nettie stuck her fists on her hips. "In Pendleton, the *men* in charge made Bonnie McCarroll ride hobbled. If your horse somersaulted over you—any of you—while you were tied on, you might not get free either."

"Whoa." Jake held her arm. "It ain't these fellows' fault, Nettie."

"Go tell your troubles to Bob Jones," groused the registration man. "You're holdin' up the line."

Nettie let out a resolute breath and let Jake guide her away. "All right, let's go find Mr. Jones. We've never been to a rodeo where they've enforced those rules."

He stopped. "It won't change things, honey."

"They can't stop us." She spun on her boot heel and walked away, following signs to the rodeo office. Jake was on his own to catch up.

At the office, she knocked on the open door frame. Jake stepped in ahead of her.

"Bob Jones here?" Jake said, holding his arms wide so Nettie couldn't enter.

A sixtyish man turned from the desk with a big smile. "That's me. How can I help ya?" He stood, bow-legged, with the beginnings of a slight paunch, and extended his hand to Jake.

When Jake shook the offered hand, Nettie shoved him aside to face Jones. "Why won't you let women compete?"

Jones' leathery face registered bemusement, peering down at her. "Ma'am?"

Nettie drew herself up to her full five-feet, two-inch height. "Women have been competing for the last ten years at RAA events. Why not today?"

"Now, now, ma'am." The older man reached out to pat her arm. "It's for your own protection. We don't want—"

"That's a pile of horse pucky and you know it. I don't need your protection," Nettie told him, "I want to ride a steer today, and you're not going to stop me."

Jones sobered and picked up the receiver on his desk phone. "Send security," he said before hanging up. "The RAA," he informed Nettie and Jake, "will not be party to any further endangerment of the fairer sex."

Nettie faced the defeat of her dearest dream. "You won't—"

"The RAA is in the wrong," Jake told Jones.

Jones gave no ground. "You can leave the way you came in."

Nettie felt Jake take firm hold of her hand, and he led her out.

She turned abruptly and stomped out of the building, toward the corral. She strode to the chutes, where a group of cowboys fought with a big, feisty steer to get him into the confined space, and shouldered past the young man who was getting ready to ride. "I'm going to ride this one," Nettie declared.

The rider stepped back, a shocked look on his face. The crew stopped their preparations and stared at her. Nettie set her foot on the fence rail to climb over. Halfway up, a pair of hands grasped her arms and pulled her down. A beefy man wearing a deputy's badge leaned close to her face. "Ma'am, you're not ridin' today."

Nettie tried to wrench free of his grip.

"Hey, get your hands off my wife!" Jake had caught up with her. His voice was edged with steel.

The deputy released Nettie and turned, his hand hovering over his holster.

Jake raised his palms. "Just concerned about my wife."

Oh, how she wanted to pummel that officer. Nettie unclenched and tried to speak in a calm voice. "What makes you think you can stop me from riding?"

"Hmmph." The big man pointed at his star. "This gives me the authority, ma'am. This is an RAA rodeo. The rules state no women ridin' rough stock, and I'm here to enforce the rules. Now, I'd advise you to take a seat in the stands and watch."

Nettie ground her teeth. *Like a good little cowgirl.* She looked at Jake. He gestured with his head to leave. Nettie pressed her lips together to prevent her from screaming at the injustice. She turned, but then looked back at the group of gawking men. "This is wrong. You haven't heard the last of it."

"Now, little gal." Jake tried to soothe her with a gentle hand on her arm, but she brushed him away and strode on ahead. His voice trailed after her. "I agree with you, and I'll help you, but I think for today, we'd better head on home."

"You go on and ride. You've already paid your entry fee."

Reluctantly, he left for the chutes.

Nettie studied the crowd in search of cowgirls.

CHAPTER TWO

Behind the stands, she found the group of young cowgirls who'd led the color guard, sitting on a log, smoking, checking their makeup in hand mirrors, laughing, and gossiping. Just like Nettie, Marie, and the Greenough sisters used to do.

Nettie drew a deep breath. "Howdy, gals. Nice parade this morning."

The blonde girl, still wearing her "Rodeo Queen" sash over a bright red satin shirt, stepped forward to shake Nettie's hand. "Hello. Mandy Jacobs. And you're—?"

"Nettie Moser." She scanned the cowgirl's perfect look, from her glittery eye makeup to the sharp creases in her denims. "Listen, ladies. I'm incensed. I started riding steers in 1920, along with the best of them. And today, I come to sign up, and they tell me 'No women's events.'"

The girls stared at Nettie with blank looks.

"What do you think about that? Are we going to let the men do that to us?" Heat rose from Nettie's core and her voice went up a notch. "After all we've done? Lucille Mulhall beat all the men in steer roping, Marie Gibson, Alice and Margie Greenough won national bronc-riding championships at Madison Square Garden—" She broke off, realizing that her audience hadn't a clue. *Oh my gosh, they're too young.* "You don't even know who I'm talking about."

A brunette who looked a little closer to Nettie's age stood. "Hi, I'm Trixi. I know the Greenoughs."

Nettie eyed the younger woman's beaded and fringed shirt and silver-conchoed gauntlets, white Stetson, and matching boots. "Are you a rider?"

"I'm a trick rider. But I do know about Alice and Margie riding broncs and Marie Gibson. I'm from Montana too."

Nettie raised her eyebrows. "Great. So am I. So, they're allowing trick riding?"

"Yes, just exhibition riding by the ladies." Trixi picked up her rope and twirled out a loop, playing it in and out amongst their legs. The other girls giggled and stepped back out of the way.

"Listen, we cowgirls need to support each other. Marie Gibson was a great bronc rider, right alongside the men. She helped me when the men made fun of women riders. She always said, 'Follow your dream,' and my dream has always been to ride bucking stock."

The young women looked at her intently. Trixi nodded. "I know. Montana women have always followed their own path. Why are they stopping you from riding today?"

Nettied repeated the RAA's rules and how this rodeo's promoter was enforcing them for the first time in her experience.

The blonde girl's eyes widened. "I do remember my grandmother talking about women bronc riders. That's so keen. But it's also dangerous. I love riding my horse, but I don't like getting bucked off."

Nettie shook her head. "Women are just as capable as men. We've already shown them that."

"That's right." Trixi swept her curls away from her face. "So, you ride broncs?"

"I've tried a few, but mostly I'm a steer rider. But now they won't let me." Nettie's eyes stung suddenly and she shook her head to clear the childish emotion. "But, you know what, I'm not going to let them stop us."

Mandy, the blonde, stared at her a moment. "Mrs. Moser, I admire you for that. Good luck." She and the other girls headed toward the bleachers.

Nettie blew out a frustrated breath. "Looks like we have our work cut out for us, reeducating the younger generation about real rodeo."

Trixi stood. "I'd like to help. I'm up to ride in a little while. But let's stay in touch. I do get over to Miles City once in awhile for their rodeos."

Nettie watched the cowgirl stride away, pretty and confident. For a few minutes, she felt encouraged. She wasn't alone.

Smiling, she walked to the bleachers to watch the trick riding. Although Nettie had never mastered the skill, Marie had done some of that and showed her a few of the moves.

Following a flowery announcement, Trixi's palomino galloped into the arena, Trixi standing upright on its back. She twirled a rope above her head, gracefully spinning the loop down the length of her body and back up. The loop grew wider and encircled the horse, then Trixi passed the twirling rope under the horse's galloping hooves. He didn't miss a step. Nettie applauded along with the crowd.

Trixi tossed the rope to a cowboy standing by the fence, and smoothly went to a handstand atop her horse, her fringes fluttering in the breeze. More cheers accompanied Trixi's antics as she held her body straight out to the side of the horse, then upside down. Her silver conchos flashed in the sunlight as she vaulted up across the saddle, touching the ground on the other side and springing back up again.

Nettie stood, yelling at the top of her lungs. What strength that took and what grace Trixi showed! Trick riding took its own measure of courage.

She ran down the steps to the chutes to greet Trixi with a hug. "That was spectacular. You are a talented rider."

"Thanks. It's taken a long time and a lot of practice to get to this point." Trixi took off her hat and mopped her brow with a handkerchief. "You know, trick riding is one of the few things women are still allowed to do. I'm teaching a couple of girls from Ovando. At least that's keeping the rodeo tradition alive."

Nettie nodded. That was a start. But what could she do?

Nettie waved good-bye to Jake as he drove off in their old truck to town to pick up Neil from the high school dormitory. He would be home for the weekend and soon be home for the summer, and she could hardly wait. She hated being away from her sixteen-year-old son, but it seemed they'd always lived in places far from town.

Nettie ambled down the slope from the house to the barn, a coffee cup in her hand. The spring sun shone warm on her back and she stopped to listen to the meadowlarks trill. It was always good to come home again. Even though this rodeo trip had been a bust as far as her riding again. With a rueful smile, she continued to make her way to the small pasture next to the barn. How ironic, after wasting all those years being afraid to ride, now that she was ready to go again, they'd banned women's rough stock events.

As Nettie approached the fence, the old Hambletonian mare pricked her ears forward, rumbled a greeting, and trotted toward her. Nettie set her cup on the ground and clicked her tongue. "C'mere, Tootsie." She rummaged in her pocket for a lump of feed cake, held it out, and let the horse lip it out of her palm with her velvety mouth. Jake's wedding gift to Nettie. The mare was getting up in years now—had to be close to nineteen—but Nettie could never bring herself to sell Tootsie, even though she hadn't ridden her in years.

"What a beauty you are." Nettie smoothed a hand over the horse's face and down her neck. "You're my special girl." The mare bobbed her head up and down as if she agreed with her owner's assessment. Nettie laughed. "So, what am I going to do to get women back into the rodeo arena, other than as beauty queens?"

Nettie patted the horse's neck, picked up her coffee cup, and went on to the chicken coop to refresh the hens' water and scatter some grain. She looked up at the sun overhead. Nearly noon. Better fix some dinner in case the men came home soon.

Back in the house, Nettie went to her desk. *I'll write Alice and Margie Greenough. They'll be with me on this.* She rummaged around in the drawers, found the addresses, took out paper and pen, and sat down to write.

The pickup chugged to a stop outside. Nettie looked up at the clock. *Oh my goodness, it's three o'clock and I never got dinner going.* Hearing the deep rumble of her men's voices, she rushed out onto the porch to greet Neil with a big hug.

"Hey, Mom, you're squeezing the life out of me." Her six-foot, four-inch son laughed above her.

Nettie stepped back to hold him at arm's length. "My heavens, I think you've grown even taller in the last two weeks." She studied his long, lean frame. "And skinnier too. I'd better get some food in you, get you fattened up a little."

Jake guffawed. "Yeah, we're gonna be working off any fat you got left this weekend and more come summer." He picked up Neil's suitcase and stepped inside.

"Are you hungry? I'll scramble some eggs and bacon." Nettie linked her arm in her son's.

He shook his head, his black hair slicked back from his forehead, glasses winking in the sunlight. "Naw, we had a bite in town. So I hear you took on the RAA men in Cheyenne. Pretty soon you'll be making us cook our own supper."

Nettie scoffed. "Yeah, that would go over real slick, about the way my riding did. Well, have a slice of pie anyway. It's apple. Your favorite." She bustled into the kitchen and opened the cupboard.

"Okay. Can't pass up pie." Neil sat at the table. "Want some, Dad?"

"Sure." Jake came in and tossed the mail on the table. "Got any coffee goin'?"

Nettie dished up pie and poured coffee, sat down, and riffled through the mail. "Oh, a letter from my sister." She carefully tore the end from the envelope and pulled out the stationery. Her older sister, Margie, still lived in the Cut Bank area and she wrote a newsy letter about their parents and her family's goings on. Nettie stopped reading, blinked, and went back over the last paragraph:

> . . . *Gary turned eighteen and is talking about enlisting in the Army or even the Canadian RAF. He seems to think the US will get involved in the European war. I have to say, I'm not happy about this . . .*

Nettie's heart chilled. Her favorite nephew. He always seemed to understand what she was feeling without her having to say a word. Just like her big brother Joe.

She shook off the bleak feeling, forced a smile, and put an arm around Neil's shoulders. "So, what have you been up to since we saw you last?"

"Band practice. Getting ready for the music festival competition." Neil took another bite of pie. "Mr. Sorenson says I'll be playing first trumpet next year."

"That's great, honey. I'm proud of you."

"Oh yeah." Neil took an envelope from his shirt pocket. "Here's my report card."

Nettie opened it to see A's, straight down the list. Pride swelled her heart. She gave her son a kiss on the cheek. "I'm *so* proud of you." She glanced at Jake. "Can you believe this? Our student."

"Yeah, yeah, it's great," Jake mumbled around a mouthful. "But I wanta know, how will all this book learning help runnin' a ranch?"

"Oh, Dad." Neil stood up, took his plate to the sink, and picked up his hat. "I'm going down to the barn." The screen door slammed behind him.

"Jake." Nettie frowned at her husband. "Why do you always have to give him a hard time about being good in school? I wish you could be happy for him."

Jake sighed, leaned back in his chair, and reached for his tobacco pouch. "I am proud of him, little gal. He's already far ahead of either one of us in schoolin'." He held a cigarette paper troughed between his fingers and shook tobacco into it. "Just wonderin', is all." His voice trailed off as he pulled the string taut on the pouch with his teeth and rolled the cigarette.

"You're afraid he doesn't want to be a cowboy."

Nettie searched her husband's wind- and sunburned face.

Jake shrugged, struck a match on the seam of his denims, and lit his smoke. He stood. "Better get to the chores."

CHAPTER THREE

An almost giddy excitement buoyed Nettie from her worry over her men's relationship as their pickup crested the last hill above the Yellowstone River Valley. The annual Miles City Roundup brought people from throughout Montana and Wyoming for a raucous, rip-roaring good time. It was a chance to buy or sell bucking horses, to compete in the arena, and most of all, to reunite with old friends.

Jake shifted gears to slow their descent into town. Colorful May wildflowers polka-dotted the hillsides and spring-greened cottonwoods lined the river banks.

Even after nearly twenty years, the awe and excitement of her first big rodeo away from home washed over Nettie. At sixteen, she'd been with her friend and mentor, Marie Gibson, drinking in the pageantry of the parade, experiencing the thrill of watching the Montana greats, like Bob Askin, ride with such grace and skill. She still remembered his advice: *Ridin' broncs is just like dancin' with a pretty girl. Just get in step and the rest comes naturally.*

Jake drove through town, past the Range Riders Café and the Miles City Saddlery where Nettie'd bought her first pair of new gloves. She remembered the pungent leather smell she still thought better than the finest perfume. They continued outside of town to the fairgrounds and rodeo arena where dust swirled from the animals in the pens.

This was where she had come to heal from her little sister's death from influenza and her mother's indifference from profound grief. It had been a rite of passage, an opportunity to prove herself as a rodeo rider. But she'd been thrown from her steer and snapped her wrist.

Nettie shook her head ruefully. *So much for my big dreams of fame and fortune.*

They pulled up and parked in the huge lot behind the arenas. Jake looked around. "Not as many rigs here as I thought there'd be."

Only about half-full. Usually by this time, it was nearly impossible to find a parking spot. "Sign of the times, I guess." Nettie got out.

Neil jumped from the back, grabbed his trumpet case, and waved back over his shoulder as he strode off.

"Want me to sign you up to ride or rope or something?" Jake called after him.

"Naw. Gotta go meet the band, practice for the parade."

Jake took a drag on his cigarette and exhaled from between his teeth.

Nettie squeezed his arm. "Let's go get signed up for our rides. See if the locals have joined RAA and if they're banning women from Montana events yet." She winked at her husband.

Jake laughed then. "They'd better not be, if they know what's good for 'em." He stubbed out his cigarette butt in the dust with his boot. "You go get 'em, little gal. I'm right behind ya."

At the rodeo office, Joyce Rudyard, a woman with laugh lines deeply embedded around her eyes, greeted them. "Mosers! How the heck are ya?" Joyce had been a fixture at the Miles City Roundup ever since it started in 1914. She came out of her booth to hug Nettie. "Good t' see you. You gonna ride?"

Nettie nodded. "If you'll let me."

"You wanna ride, you bet I'll take your money," Joyce said.

"They wouldn't in Cheyenne," Nettie told her, glad to count out the ten dollars for a steer event that night and a saddle-bronc ride on Saturday.

"It's a sad day for rodeo, turnin' ladies away." Joyce efficiently recounted the bills before tucking them into the money box. "We got half the ticket sales as last year, why be fool enough to cut riders too?"

Jake paid for his events and tickets to the barbecue for the family later that evening, and they stepped outside. "Well, little gal, looks like you're set. Let's go get checked into the hotel." He paused, scanning the arena and parking lot.

"Neil will find us," she assured him.

Nettie clenched her jaw to keep her teeth from chattering as she looked at the big red steer who snorted like a freight train. Its kicks at the sides of the chute ricocheted inside her head. *Why am I doing this? I'm thirty-six years old, for heaven's sake. What am I trying to prove?*

She took a deep breath. *This is what you wanted, Nettie Moser. I am a woman and I can do this.* She pulled her high-crowned Stetson tight on her head, and climbed down from the railing to settle on the steer's back. *You don't scare me, you wild brute. I've ridden bigger and badder steers than you!* Smoothing the glove tight on her left hand, Nettie wrapped it under the surcingle, and nodded to the cowboys at the gate.

She felt the raw power of the animal's flesh beneath her. The beast exploded from the chute like a stone from a slingshot. Nettie's body flew backwards on the steer's back, then forward toward its head. Her right arm flopped in the air as if it were a separate entity, waving at the crowd. *Rhythm. Gotta get my rhythm.* The steer twisted and spun. Nettie slipped to one side and then to the other. *The dance. Get in the rhythm.* Her knees tightened. She forced her torso to relax. Gradually, as if a fiddle had struck up a tune in her head, she felt the beat, and rolled with the steer's raging gyrations. The sounds of the world around her faded, except for her own breath keeping the rhythm in her head.

The whistle split the silence. Nettie heard the crowd cheer. She felt the pickup man grasp her around the waist, pull her from the steer's back, and carry her to safety at the fence as cowboys herded the steer back to the holding pens. Nettie scrambled onto the lower rails and looked up to see Jake's tanned, weathered face grinning down at her.

"Great ride, little gal." Jake reached a hand down and pulled her to the top. "You did it!"

Nettie sat beside him and expelled a breath. "Whew. I did, didn't I?" The thrill of all her past rides united with today's triumph. She felt as if she could take off from that top rail and soar through the sky like an eagle.

Later that evening, they loaded their plates with barbecued beef and beans and wandered among the crowd, greeting old friends. Many of the cowboys had a compliment to offer, a friendly slap on the back.

"Good ride."

"Nice to see ya ridin' again."

"Keep it up, Miz Moser."

Nettie glowed.

"Hey, Mosers, come join us," Bob Askin called from a nearby picnic table.

"Howdy, Bob." Jake set his plate down.

Nettie sat across from the rangy, leather-faced cowboy and a young girl, about eight, with dark braids. "And who is this with you?"

"This is my daughter, Birdie. Honey, meet Mr. and Mrs. Moser." Bob nodded from one to the other.

Birdie grinned from under a tall-crowned hat. "That was a great ride, Mrs. Moser."

Nettie smiled back. "Thank you, dear. Are you a cowgirl too?"

The girl's braids bounced as she nodded. "I'm gonna be a trick rider. Just like my grandma."

Nettie nodded. "I remember her from my first Miles City Rodeo back in the twenties. She sure wowed the crowd with her backward handstand. You look a lot like her." She turned to Bob. "And I've always kept your advice from then. 'Get into the rhythm.'"

"At first, I wasn't so sure you were gonna make it to the whistle," Askin told Nettie. "But then I could see you settle in. Good job."

"Good advice," Nettie told him, then turned to Birdie. "A girl can do a lot worse than listen to wisdom from a great cowboy."

Birdie looked at her dad and grinned.

They all dug into their beef and beans as conversation about ranching, rodeoing, and riding flowed between bites. Nettie looked up when she felt a touch on her shoulder. "Neil, hi. Did you get something to eat?"

Her tall, lanky son nodded. "I'm going with the guys to get something now."

She turned to the Askins and introduced them.

Bob offered a hand. "You ridin' tomorrow too?"

Neil shook his hand. "No, sir. I'm playing in the band. In the parade."

Birdie gazed up at the tall teenager. "I'll be in the parade too."

"Oh. That's great. I'll probably see you there." Neil turned back to Nettie. "Ah, I was wondering . . . Art, you know, from band, he's invited me to stay with him tonight. Is that okay?"

Jake cleared his throat, but Nettie jumped in before he could object. "What about Art's folks? Do they know about this?"

"Oh yeah, they say it's fine with them. They have a keen tent trailer. May I? Please?" Neil addressed Nettie, his face averted from his father.

"I was hoping you'd do some team roping with me tomorrow." Jake spoke in a low, controlled voice.

Neil looked at him then. "Dad, I don't think that's such a good idea. We haven't practiced together since last summer. I don't want to drag you down in competition."

"Are you just givin' up on rodeo?" Jake's voice was taut now, his lips thin.

Neil sighed.

Nettie put a gentle hand on Jake's arm. "Let him go make music with his friends. He can work with you all summer."

Jake yanked the Bull Durham sack from his shirt pocket, stood, and walked away from them into the evening darkness.

Nettie kept her voice light and put an arm around her son. "Have fun. We'll see you in the parade tomorrow."

"G'night, Mom. Thanks." Neil strode off.

She picked up her plate. "It was good to visit with you again, Bob, and nice to meet you, Birdie. See you tomorrow."

A tight binding constricted Nettie's chest as she walked the grounds, looking for Jake. This issue with Neil was not going to go away. *Well, I've discouraged Neil all along from getting involved in rodeo.* On one hand she was glad her son wouldn't be risking life and limb in riding, but on the other . . . she shuddered. *I've helped create this rift between Neil and his dad.*

She finally found her husband, passing a bottle with a group of men behind the chutes. Squatting down next to him, she leaned into his side. "Think it's time to head for our hotel?"

Jake took another pull from the bottle. "Reckon so." He stood and helped her up. "Well, gentlemen, see ya in the mornin'."

Jake drove to the hotel, smoking silently. Nettie glanced over at him, bit her lip, and took a breath. "Neil's just trying to find his way. He'll come around."

Jake waved her words away like the smoke from his cigarette.

In their hotel room, Nettie lay awake, fidgeting, wondering, and worrying, until the pastel light of dawn slanted under the window shade.

All too soon, Jake woke her with a "Rise and shine, little gal! We got parades to watch, broncs to ride, and people to see."

Nettie rubbed her gritty eyes. *Just like Jake to ignore what happened last night.* She kissed him on the cheek and went to get washed up and ready for the day.

As they drove downtown, Nettie stole a look at Jake. Although he turned to grin back at her, his jaw remained tight. She reached over to rub his shoulder. "Do me a favor?"

Jake's grin turned to a grimace. "Let it go, little gal. It's fine."

But she knew something had to give in the war of wills between her men. She had to get Jake and Neil to watch each other today, to have the chance to understand one another better.

At ten o'clock they joined the crowds lining the sidewalks of Main Street to watch the rodeo queen lead the parade with the Stars and Stripes and Montana flags. Fire trucks and cowboys showing off their rope tricks were interspersed with high-school marching bands, Model Ts trailing streamers, and colorful floats. Every time she heard music from down the block, she craned her neck to see if it was Neil's band coming.

Finally, she spotted their orange and black uniforms and heard the rousing "Beautiful City of Miles." She grinned and tapped Jake's arm. "Hear that? They were chosen to play the official city song."

"Yeah, ain't that somethin'." Jake nodded.

Nettie gazed up at his lean face. He seemed calm, maybe even pleased at the sight of their son.

The band members marched in intricate formations, weaving in and out. Neil walked tall, playing his shiny brass trumpet. Nettie turned to a woman next to her and pointed. "That's my son there, the tall one."

"He's a good-lookin' kid," the woman said. "They're the best band here."

Nettie wanted to climb to the highest point and shout. She marched in place along with the rousing music until it faded down the street and the next group of honking cars and tractors crawled by.

Back at the rodeo arena, Nettie and Jake watched the team ropers and the steer wrestlers and cheered on old friends. Saddle-bronc riding would be coming up next, so they walked down to the chutes.

"Hey, Jake, who you draw?" someone asked.

"Black Diamond."

"That outlaw? Not too many of us have ridden that son-of-a-gun to the end," one cowboy remarked.

Nettie swallowed her fear. Jake was a good rider. He'd be okay.

Jake lowered himself onto the snorting bronc. Even from her perch on the fence, Nettie could see its nostrils flare, its muscles quiver. The gate opened. The horse Jake straddled vaulted through the gate, his back arched like a cat, and landed on all fours with an audible thud.

"Ride 'im, Jake!" Nettie screamed, fists clenched at her sides, adrenaline sending thrills through her body.

Black Diamond kicked toward the sky with his hind legs, then pawed the air with his front hooves. Jake spurred forward and back, riding as if he'd been born on the back of that demonic horse, melded to its muscular back, absorbing the blows like he had springs in his body.

Before Nettie realized the time had passed, the whistle blew and the stand erupted in a roar of applause. She ripped off her hat and waved it wildly. "He did it. He rode Black Diamond!"

A cowboy next to her clapped her on the back. "Whooee, what a ride."

Nettie ran to the corral fence, where Jake climbed over. She wrapped him in a tight hug. "That was the most spectacular ride I've ever seen."

He grinned down at her. "I beat that black devil." He spun her around in a jig.

Bob Askin appeared beside them and shook Jake's hand. "That oughta put you in the money."

Nettie paused in her victory dance. Jake might very well win a nice purse, maybe up to fifty dollars or even a hundred. That would be swell! It could go toward their lease payment. Or maybe some new tack.

"Good ride, Dad."

Neil stepped up and offered his hand to his father. Behind him, several band members stood and clapped.

Jake took Neil's hand in a strong clasp. "Thanks, son." He smiled. "Nice job in the marching band. You were the best of the bunch."

Neil flushed. He turned toward Nettie, and she threw her arms around her men. She barely felt the ground beneath her.

They watched a few more rides where the cowboy was thrown almost before the horse cleared the chute or the bronc crowhopped a few times and quit bucking. Then it was Nettie's turn. With nerves tickling her stomach, she climbed to the top of the chute to meet her destiny with White Lightning.

"You want the stirrups hobbled?" asked the cowboy saddling the bronc.

"Absolutely not." Nettie shook her head. Some of the cowgirls liked riding that way, because they weren't thrown as easily. But that had been Bonnie McCarroll's fatal mistake at Pendleton. She wasn't able to get her feet out of the stirrups.

Nettie pulled her hat tight to her head and eased herself down onto the bronc. She thrust her boots into the stirrups, adjusted her seat in the saddle, and took a deep breath. *Remember the dance.* She nodded to the cowboy at the gate. The horse burst forth, rising up on his hind legs. At the same time he twisted and swapped ends. The next thing Nettie knew, dirt plowed into her nostrils, her eyes. For a moment she lay there, unable to catch her breath. Then slowly she sat up, sputtering. She rubbed her shoulder. *That's going to bruise for sure.*

The pickup man rode up and jumped down. "You all right?"

Nettie shook her head to clear it. "I'm fine. What happened?"

The cowboy chuckled and helped to her feet. "You got bucked off. Glad you ain't hurt."

Neil loped to her side. "Mom, Mom!"

Jake knelt beside her. "Nettie. You hurt?"

Nettie let out a disgusted sigh. "Just my pride." She patted Neil's arm and grasped Jake's hand. "That sure happened fast. Guess I won't be winning any money on that ride."

CHAPTER FOUR

Nettie carried the bundle of mail into the house and flipped on the radio to hear Gene Autry singing "Back in the Saddle Again." She grinned at Jake. "That's me—back in the rodeo saddle again." She hummed along as she thumbed through the mail.

She gave Neil the *Miles City Star.* "Here, honey, see if there are any pictures or a story about the rodeo." Jake got the *Hoofs & Horns* magazine, a farm periodical, and a bill from the Oasis bar.

As Jake picked up the magazine, an envelope fell out. "From Alice Greenough."

"Finally." Nettie eagerly tore open one end and fished out the letter. She skimmed through the "thanks for writing" and "how are you's" to read aloud:

> *Well, my dear, I'm sorry to hear of your experience at the Cheyenne rodeo. Unfortunately, that seems to be the way women's rodeo is going—mostly exhibition riding and the "Ranch Glamour Girls." I've been talking to my good friend Joe Orr about getting into the rodeo business ourselves. He has a few head of bucking stock and we hope to buy more.*
>
> *I wish you luck in your endeavors, but I'm afraid I can't offer much help for change at this time.*
>
> *Sincerely,*
> *Alice*

"Aarrgh." Nettie threw the letter on the table. "What is wrong with Alice? Is she giving up on riding?"

Jake shrugged. "Well, she is a few years older than you."

Nettie grimaced. She stood and went to the stove to put on water for tea. "Yeah, that makes her almost forty. I guess she's hanging up her spurs. If things don't change, maybe I should too."

Neil walked over to drape a long arm around her shoulders. "You're not too old to ride, Mom. Sure, you got thrown from the bronc, but you made a nice steer ride. And won that nifty silver compact."

"Oh yeah, some prize." Nettie snorted. "They're not even giving women money any more. What's this world coming to?" She measured out tea leaves and poured water into the teapot. "There are some oatmeal cookies in the cupboard, honey. Would you get them out?"

After carrying the tea to the table, she sat next to Jake. "So Alice and Joe are going into the rodeo stock business."

Jake shook his head. "I dunno. We didn't have a lot of luck doin' that."

Nettie sighed, remembering the drought of the thirties and trailing their horses to Idaho, not being able to sell any, even for enough to buy food.

"Course, they do have contacts with Madison Square Garden and the bigger rodeos, so maybe they'll do all right." Jake picked up the *Hoofs & Horns* again.

Neil set a down a plate and grabbed a cookie, poring over the newspaper. "Hey. Look, here's a picture of our band."

"Oh my goodness. Look at you." Front and center of the photo was Neil, holding his trumpet to his lips, one knee raised in a marching step with the other band members. Nettie hugged him. "We gotta cut that out, get it framed."

Jake's voice rumbled close to their heads. "Good picture. Shows off those fancy boots you had to have. Can't even wear 'em for riding."

Nettie frowned at him over Neil's head. She read the caption aloud. "'Forsyth High School Marching Band wins Competition.' Hmm, you didn't tell us you won."

Neil ducked his head. "Yeah, well, no big deal. You were both winning your rides."

Nettie kissed him on the head. "You should have told us." She lifted her tea cup high. "Here's to our prize musician."

Jake shook his son's hand, and Neil's face flushed.

Nettie breathed easier. They both were making an effort, and that made her happy, for now.

~~~

Jake pushed back his breakfast plate and stretched. "Think I'll go over to Forsyth and check on some bulls for sale. Wanna ride along, little gal?"

Nettie stacked their dishes and glanced at Neil, mopping up the last of his syrup with a bite of pancake. "Um. Well, I'm mucking out the stalls today. Take Neil." This would be a good chance for the guys to be together, maybe even talk.

Jake shrugged. "Sure. Wanna go, son?"

"Yeah, Dad. I'll go." Neil picked up the plates, pecked Nettie on the forehead, and took the dishes to the sink. She heard them laughing as they strolled outside.

After the men roared away in the old pickup, Nettie ambled down the slope toward the barn. Their saddle horses trotted up to the fence and stretched their necks out, waiting for a treat. *Hmm. Tootsie's not with them.* Her old mare was usually the first one to arrive. Nettie stepped inside the barn door, scooped up a handful of feed cake, and walked over to the horses.

Blue, Neil's roan, shoved his head into her outstretched hand and grabbed the pellet from her palm. Jake's horse, Stranger, arched his proud Arabian neck toward her politely, lipping his treat with a soft, gentle mouth. Nettie stepped aside and whistled to her saddle horse, Windy River, who stood back from the others, eyeing them all suspiciously.

She whistled and held out her hand. "C'mon, Windy." The thoroughbred cross pranced forward a bit, then stopped, raised his head, and blew a fluttering breath through his nostrils.

"Come get your treat," Nettie coaxed. Finally the horse came to her, looking her over as if he suspected she had a bridle hidden behind her back. He nuzzled the treat from her palm, then skittered back, out of reach.

"Playing hard to get, huh, boy?" Nettie laughed. It was always a challenge to catch Windy for a ride. But she loved his spunk.

"So, guys, where's Tootsie today?" She climbed through the barbedwire fence and walked toward the nearby coulee, calling and whistling. "Here, girl. Tootsie, where are you?" The other horses trotted behind her.

The early June day gave promise of the warmth of summer to come. A meadowlark warbled; another answered. Nettie walked through the greening pasture grass, breathing in its fresh aroma. Yellow buttercups nodded their heads in the slight breeze. A beautiful day for a walk on the prairie, but she scanned the hills and hollows with apprehension.

At the edge of the washout she peered down. The horses gathered around behind her. No Tootsie. She whistled again and walked farther along the coulee. Amid the sound of the horses' hooves, the birds twittering, she heard a faint whinny. She stopped to listen. Windy River tossed his head up, ears pricked forward. He rumbled a whicker. Blue and Stranger joined in, and they trotted off toward the south.

Nettie followed them, heart thudding in her chest. When the horses stopped, she looked down into the shallow coulee, and her heart broke. Tootsie lay in the bottom, one leg bent at a sickening angle.

"Oh no!" Nettie plunged down the steep embankment. "No, no, no." The mare uttered a weak whinny and struggled to rise. A bone protruded from her left front cannon. Acidic bile rose in Nettie's throat. She bent double, vomiting up her breakfast. Panting, she untied her bandanna and wiped her face and mouth. Then she took a deep breath and turned back to her beloved Hambletonian.

"Tootsie, Tootsie girl." Nettie spoke softly to soothe the frightened horse as she stroked Tootsie's neck and ran a hand along her back and hindquarters, checking for other injuries. "What are we going to do?"

Nettie would have to ride eight miles to Ingomar and use the phone at the Oasis Bar to call. If the vet was there and willing to come, it would take him another two hours to make the seventy-five-mile trip. If he'd even come for a broken leg.

Nettie looked at the terrible wound, sinew hanging from the protruding bone, blood oozing from the hole. The sky swirled around her and her hands were icy. She was fooling herself if she thought it could be fixed. "I can't leave you to suffer."

She stroked the mare's neck and brushed the mane back from the forehead, moving her hand down the beautiful chestnut face to her velvety mouth. The horse's breathing became more labored and her struggles less frantic.

Nettie swallowed hard. Only one thing to do.

Biting her lip until it bled, she climbed the bank and ran back to the house. *Blast it! Why did this have to happen when Jake and Neil are gone?* Muttering curse words under her breath, she opened the bedroom closet door and took out Jake's Winchester 30.30 rifle. With shaking hands, she checked to see that it was loaded and walked back to the coulee, her steps faltering as she drew near.

The other horses milled around the top of the bank, whickering softly as if to soothe their injured comrade. Nettie stood at the brink and gazed down at the horse, her favorite of all, the one she'd had since she and Jake were married. When the mare got too old to work, Nettie couldn't bear to give her up, but chose to let her graze through her retirement years in contentment.

Nettie slid down the bank once again and knelt beside her beloved Hambletonian. Clasping her hands together, she looked up into the clear sky. "Oh, God, help me. I don't think I can do this." She wrapped her arms around the horse's neck. Tootsie groaned, a desperate, heart-wrenching sound.

"Dear old girl, I'm so sorry." Nettie stood, worked the lever to chamber a round, and aimed the rifle at the star on Tootsie's forehead. The mare looked at her with liquid chocolate eyes. Nettie's eyes blurred and her arms shook. She lowered the barrel. *I can't do this.* Her breaths came in gasps. *I have to do this. Help me.*

The old mare rasped a breath and attempted to lift her head. Nettie took a deep breath, wiped her eyes, and brought the rifle up again. Her finger tightened on the trigger as if it belonged to someone else. Numb to the world around her, she didn't hear the shot or feel the recoil.

Nettie stood frozen for a moment, then dropped the rifle to the ground. Leaving the gun where it lay, she crawled to bury her face in Tootsie's mane, tears mingling with the familiar scent of horse sweat.

It was nearly dark when Jake and Neil found Nettie, her arms still wrapped around the mare's neck.

"Mom! Are you hurt?" Neil knelt beside Nettie and rubbed her shoulder.

She looked up at him and shook her head. "I had to do it." Tears flowed again, hot against her cold, dry cheeks.

"C'mon, little gal. It's okay." Jake set down the lantern, took off his coat, and draped it over her shoulders.

"No. It's not." Nettie got to her knees and began digging in the earth with her fingers. "I can't leave her here like this." She scrabbled furiously in the dirt, trying to dig a hole, pain from rocks and broken fingernails a welcome sensation. "I've got to cover her."

"C'mon, now. We'll come back and do that later." Jake lifted Nettie to her feet and wrapped her tenderly in his arms, patting her back as she hiccupped sobs. Neil picked up the rifle and they helped her walk back to the house.

"I had to shoot my pal." Nettie's body shook as if she'd been out in sub-zero temperatures.

Jake cradled her in one arm and stroked her face and hair. "I know, honey. I'm so sorry we weren't here."

Back at the house, Jake settled her into her rocker and tucked a blanket around her. Neil got busy in the kitchen.

"Here, Mom, drink some tea." Her son set a steaming cup in front of her. "I'll make you some toast. That'll make you feel better."

Nettie gave him a wan smile. That's what she always fixed him when he was not feeling well. She reached out and squeezed his hand. "Thanks, hon."

The next morning, Nettie dragged her feet into the kitchen where Jake was busy fixing breakfast. "Good morning, sweetheart. Here's some flapjacks for ya." He set a heaping plate in front of her. Neil poured her coffee and patted her arm as he walked by.

Nettie gulped past a lump and tried to eat and drink what they had fixed her.

When Jake finished, he pushed back his chair. "Neil and I are going out to check on the cattle. Now, you just stay here and take it easy. Will you be all right?"

She nodded. "I'll be fine. Tootsie had a good life. We had a good ride together." She tried to smile. "You guys run along."

Jake gave her a peck on the cheek and Neil squeezed her shoulder.

After they'd ridden off, Nettie threw herself into cleaning out the stalls, raking up old straw and manure with furious strokes. She dumped bucket after bucket of water and scrubbed the walls, as if she could scour away her pain and grief.

Then, to her surprise, she easily caught Windy, jumped on his bare back, and rode out into the pasture. She let him have his head and together they thundered over low, rolling hills and through shallow coulees. Nettie shook out the pins in her hair and let it blow free, crouched low on Windy's neck, and urged him on, faster and faster.

Finally, he slowed and she reined him in on the top of a flat butte overlooking the ranch. Nettie tried to avoid looking toward the coulee where Tootsie lay, but hawks and crows circled the sky above. A shuddering sigh escaped. How ridiculous and desperate she'd been last night, trying to cover the horse. This was the natural way. Tootsie would feed the carrion eaters and fertilize the ground, her gift to nature.

Off to the west, their small herd of red-and-white Herefords grazed. She saw Jake and Neil riding along the outskirts of the pasture, checking on the young calves who frolicked in the sun. For miles around, she could see no other signs of civilization. *Just the way I like it.*

Nettie dismounted, let Windy's reins drop to ground-tie him, and sat on a sand rock. The spring breeze cooled her sweat-soaked denims. She sat, gazing into the blue horizon, mere wisps of clouds scudding by. Losing a horse she'd had for seventeen years was like losing a child. Sure, she'd had other horses she loved—Toby, her first horse, for one—but they had either died peacefully or Papa had quietly taken them to a neighbor's when their time came. She'd never had to put down an animal herself. The vision of looking down the rifle barrel at Tootsie's star blurred her eyes again and her hands shook, feeling the pull of the trigger.

The sun climbed high into the sky, insects whirred, and birds chirruped. Nettie simply sat, letting the sounds and warmth soothe her. At last, her grumbling stomach let her know it was dinnertime. The guys would be at the house, wondering what happened to her.

She stood, walked over to Windy where he grazed nearby, and gathered up the reins. "Okay, ready to go home?" He bobbed his head. Nettie swung up onto his back and nudged him into an easy lope toward home. It would take time to get past this hurt, but she had to keep moving, keep following her dream.

CHAPTER FIVE

Nettie heard the low rumble of a big engine and gears grinding. She looked out the kitchen window to see a truck roll up the lane and park near the corral. It was Chet Miller, one of their neighbors, with a bull Jake had bought for breeding. After driving all that way to Forsyth, he'd met Chet who lived about five miles away and raised prime bulls.

Nettie walked down to join Jake and Neil. Chet stepped from the truck, and a girl in her early teens jumped from the passenger side.

"Hi, Neil," she chortled.

Neil blushed and nodded at her.

The girl, wearing her red hair in pigtails, turned. "Hi, Mr. and Mrs. Moser. I'm Ruthie Miller."

Nettie smiled. "What a nice surprise. Ruthie, why don't you come on up to the house and help me put on some coffee while the men unload this bull."

The bull snorted and kicked at the stock rack.

The young girl chattered away as they walked up the slope and into the kitchen. "I know Neil from school," she volunteered. "I'm taking clarinet lessons so I can be in the band too. I'm only a freshman though."

Nettie nodded, bemused. The girl acted like she was about ten years old.

"Dad says you're a steer-ridin' cowgirl and you've won lots of prizes." Without prompting, Ruthie opened cupboard doors, searching until she found cups and the plate of oatmeal cookies. "I wanna

30

do that too, but Mom says it's too dangerous for girls, and that people would talk about me behind my back."

She set the cups and cookies on the table. "Is that true? Have you ever been hurt bad? Do people talk about you? Do they think cowgirls have a bad rep-repu-tation?" She paused in her litany to sputter out the word.

Nettie laughed. "Well, little Ruthie, you certainly are a chatterbox."

The girl gave an impish grin. "Yeah, I know. That's what Mom says too. She says I need to slow down and listen." She paused for a breath and sat, her chin on her hands. "So, Mrs. Moser, tell me about being a rodeo cowgirl."

Nettie took a seat across the table. "Gosh, how to begin. I was just a little older than you when I rode my first steer in a neighborhood rodeo and I stayed on him until he stopped bucking." She paused to remember the cheers and the feeling of triumph. "What a thrill that was. I felt like I was on top of the world."

Ruthie's eyes were wide. "What then? Did you go right to another rodeo and start winning?"

"No, it didn't happen quite the way I planned." Nettie laughed. "My mama was a little like yours. She was afraid I would get hurt and she didn't want to think about 'what the neighbors would say.' So it took a lot to convince her to let me go. Marie Gibson finally showed Mama that cowgirls could ride broncs and still be good wives and mothers too."

"Wow." Ruthie was uncharacteristically quiet for a minute. "Do you think . . . I wonder if you could talk to my mother. You're a cowgirl and you're a mom and—"

"Now, let's not get too far ahead of ourselves," Nettie interrupted. I've never met your mother and I can't just talk her into letting you ride rough stock. You'll have to show her you are responsible and won't neglect your chores and schoolwork and everything she wants you to learn."

The girl looked thoughtful. "Yeah, I guess so. She does get kind of mad at me when I go riding instead of cleaning my room."

Nettie smiled. Certainly sounded familiar—just like her when she was young. "Another thing you should be aware of—cowgirls aren't being allowed to compete on broncs and steers as much anymore."

"They're not? Why?"

Nettie told Ruthie the history of how rodeo evolved from just the neighbor cowboys getting together to see who could stay on the longest or rope the best to the big organized rodeos with rules and regulations and how the Rodeo Association of America had formed, leaving women out.

The girl's mouth dropped open. "No women's competition?"

Nettie shook her head. "I'm afraid not. Now, your best bet is being beautiful and trying out for rodeo queen or trick riding."

Ruthie wrinkled her freckled nose. "Well, I'm no beauty queen, that's for sure. Trick riding might be fun." She tossed her wiry pigtails. "But I've been riding calves out in Dad's pasture. I'd still like to try steer-riding."

The sound of the men's boots on the porch interrupted their conversation. "But in the meantime, we have to take care of the men," Ruthie blurted.

Nettie laughed and stood to get the coffee pot, and Ruthie found the sugar and cream.

Nettie leaned against the fence to watch Jake and Neil as they sharpened the sickle blades on the mower and tinkered with the old Ford tractor. "Looks like we'll have a good hay crop this year."

Jake looked up from his task. "Yeah. We're gonna start on that crested wheatgrass field tomorrow. The alfalfa will be a week or two yet."

Nettie smiled. "Maybe we won't have to buy hay this year." She thought back on all the hard winters when they'd had to scrounge for straw or thistle-laden hay to feed their cattle and horses. She hated watching the animals grow skinnier day by day as the cruel below-zero wind drifted snow over any grass they might find.

She turned toward the barn. "Well, I guess I'll go straighten out the tack, see if anything needs oiling."

As she walked away, she heard Jake's low voice. "So, son. You up to a little team ropin' at the July Fourth rodeo in Miles?"

Around the corner of the barn, Nettie stopped to listen, hope lifting her heart.

A moment passed before Neil spoke. "Uh, well, Dad, I'll be playing in the band for the parade."

"Your mother and I will be riding in the parade, and competing too." Jake's voice had its steely edge.

Nettie's heart plummeted. Her guys had been getting along pretty well since school let out, Neil riding, helping out wherever he was needed. Of course, they hadn't discussed those sore subjects: rodeo or band or school. Nettie certainly understood Neil's love for music and learning, but on the other hand, she knew Jake wanted Neil to share his love of rodeo and ranching. She started back toward them. *I'm getting sick of this conflict. Just going to have to knock some sense into their mule heads.*

"Sure, I guess I could do both."

Neil's reply stopped Nettie before she'd rounded the corner.

"All right, then," Jake said. "When we get this hayin' equipment ready, what d'ya say you and I do some practicing?"

"Okay, Dad. Sounds good."

Nettie heard the reluctance in Neil's voice and the happiness in Jake's. She could kiss them both for trying, at least.

Red, white, and blue streamers and banners fluttered in the breeze as Nettie lined up with Jake to join the parade. Windy pranced beneath her, nervous and eager. Nettie tugged at the sleeves of her blue satin shirt, reset her tall-crowned gray Stetson, and snugged her denim-clad knees tighter against the saddle.

"What's holdin' up the show?" Jake, in his matching shirt, grumbled beside her. "We been waitin' for half an hour already." He touched his heels to Stranger's flanks and trotted around the other riders and floats ahead.

Nettie heard a band play Miles City's theme song. Her heart swelled. *Probably Neil's band.* Car horns honked, horses whinnied, and the lineup moved slowly forward. She urged Windy forward and he trotted down the street, bobbing his head and pulling against the reins. She soon caught up to Jake and he took his place beside her, waving to the bystanders as they rode past.

Even after all the years of riding in Fourth of July parades, Nettie still felt the thrill of excitement to be a part of the pageantry, the flags, the speeches, and the competition. The crowd looked smaller this year though. Empty spots showed along the streets, not the usual two- or three-deep lineup, and fewer elaborately designed floats rolled down the parade route. The economy definitely had affected them all and rodeos were fewer and farther between.

At the end of the parade, they rode into the fairgrounds and dismounted at the corral. Nettie heard a high-pitched voice. "Mrs. Moser. Mrs. Moser. Over here!"

She turned to see Ruthie Miller jumping up and down and waving. "Hi, Ruthie."

The girl let her horse's reins drop to ground-tie him and ran to Nettie, giving her a big hug. "The parade was fun, wasn't it? Did you hear Neil's band? Weren't they good? I'm going to play in it next year." Her red braids bobbed in time to her hurried words.

Nettie laughed. *Hard to believe this girl is thirteen, the way she acts.* "Yes, yes, and yes, to answer your questions." She patted Ruthie's shoulder. "And I'm glad you'll be in the band next year. I'm sure you'll enjoy it."

"Mrs. Moser." Ruthie stopped her frenetic activity. "There's a kids' calf-riding exhibition this afternoon, and—" She broke off and looked up at Nettie with wide green eyes.

"Yes?"

"And I want to ride in it."

"That's great. I'm sure you'll do just fine." Nettie turned to loosen Windy's cinch.

"But my mom's here. And and she doesn't like the idea."

Nettie sighed. "As much as I'd love to tell you just to go ahead and ride, I have to tell you to respect your mother's wishes." She faced away from the girl and rolled her eyes. *I can't believe I'm talking like this. Is this what happens when we get older and have kids of our own?* She'd been just a little older than Ruthie when she defied Mama's wishes and rode in her first rodeo. The excitement of that ride had her walking in the clouds for days afterward.

"Aw, Mrs. Moser." Ruthie's voice took on a whine.

Nettie turned back, still feeling the thrill of all her successful rides, and studied the young teen's drooping face. "Introduce me to your mother." Seeing Ruthie's sunny transformation, she added, "But I'm not making any promises, you understand?"

Ruthie bounced on tiptoes again. "Yeah, yeah, I understand. C'mon, Mom's over there."

She took off toward the grandstand.

"Wait. Ruthie." Nettie pointed at Ruthie's horse.

"Oh." The girl's face flushed and she walked back to grab the reins, her head down. "Sorry."

Nettie grinned, helped Ruthie unsaddle her pinto, and released both horses into a small pen. "All right. Now let's go find your mother."

Mrs. Miller sat at one end of the bleachers, dressed in a denim skirt, red-and-white-striped blouse, and a white straw hat, holding a baby.

"Mom! Mom!" Ruthie bounded up the steps, two at a time. "I want you to meet Mrs. Moser. She's a rodeo cowgirl and she rides steers and broncs and—"

"Whoa. Slow down, young lady." Mrs. Miller frowned and glanced at Nettie. "I'm sorry. Has she been bothering you?"

"Not at all. Ruthie is a delight." Nettie sat down beside the woman. The woman's weary face lit up. "Gee, thanks."

"Ruthie, why don't you run over to the concession stand and get your mom and me a cup of coffee." Nettie fished in her pocket and gave the girl a dollar bill. "And get yourself a soda if you'd like."

The girl grinned and took off at a run down the bleacher steps. Her mother shook her head. "She's a handful. Nothing like her older sister was. Ruthie's headstrong and overactive and—" She stopped and clapped a hand over her mouth. "I'm sorry. Here I am, blabbing family business to a stranger."

Nettie leaned back. "No, that's okay. I heard much the same thing from my mother when I was growing up. I guess that's why I'm drawn to Ruthie. She reminds me of myself at that age. It would have been nice to have a daughter, even though she might have been as difficult as I was for my mother."

Mrs. Miller's eyebrows shot up. "Gosh, I didn't think there was another one like Ruthie in the whole world."

Nettie laughed. "Oh yes, there are actually quite a few of us. I was just like her when I was her age. I loved to ride, I never listened to my mother, I dreamt of being a rodeo star."

"Mrs. Moser, I—"

"Please, call me Nettie."

"I'm Zelda." She offered her hand and Nettie grasped it, solid and warm.

Ruthie carefully ascended the bleacher steps with the coffees and a soda.

"Thank you, dear." Her mother smiled and patted the bench beside her. Ruthie gave Nettie the change and sat.

The announcer bellowed into his bullhorn. "And now, ladies and gentlemen, for your entertainment pleasure, we present the ladies' trick-riding exhibition. Our first rider is Trixi McCormick from over west of the mountains."

Nettie sat up straight. "I've met her."

The rider stood on the back of her galloping palomino, her body arched, arms reaching for the sky. Dressed in a beaded buckskin top, fringed pants, and a white Stetson, she waved at the cheering audience as the horse circled the arena. Then, the horse slowed to a gentle gait. Trixi uncoiled a rope and encircled herself and the palomino, whirling it around, under the horse's feet, and back up over her head. Soon a second rope twirled from her other hand. At that moment, a brown-and-white dog ran out from the chutes.

Nettie gasped along with the crowd. That dog would tangle the ropes and trip the horse.

But as Trixi again twirled the longer lariat around the horse, she spun the shorter one close to the ground and the dog jumped through the loop. It ran around the horse and jumped again, and again. The crowd shouted, whistled, and clapped.

Nettie and Ruthie leaped to their feet, applauding. Zelda sat with her mouth agape.

When Trixi exited the arena, Ruthie shrieked. "Wow. Wasn't that keen? Oh my gosh, I thought the dog was gonna bite the horse. I thought there'd be a big wreck. Oh my!"

Nettie laughed. "I thought so, too, for a minute."

"That looks like so much fun. Did you ever trick ride, Mrs. Moser?"

Nettie shook her head. "No, not really. My good friend Marie Gibson used to do that and I tried a few moves, but it wasn't my strength. I always thought it looked fun though."

The rodeo announcer broke into their conversation. "Next up is today's youngest trick rider . . . ten-year-old . . . Birdie Askin!"

"She's only ten?" Zelda remained wide-eyed.

A shiver of excitement raced through Nettie. "I've met Birdie. I know her father too."

The young girl, dressed in a red satin shirt and denims, also entered the arena standing on the back of her black horse. She twirled blue and white silk scarves, swooping the sashes up and around in a colorful dance through the air. Then, almost before Nettie could blink, Birdie dropped to the horse's back, down along its side, swooped under the animal's belly, and back up the other side. The crowd roared.

"Neato-keeno!" Ruthie jumped up and down, pumping her arms in the air. "Did you see that, Mom? Did you? She's just a little kid. I could do that. Mrs. Moser, Mrs. Moser, I want to do that. Can I, Mom? Can I go meet Birdie?"

Zelda put a hand on her daughter's shoulder. "Ruthie. Calm down. Now."

"But Mom. Did you see that? I could learn to do that, don't you think? Could I? Could I?"

Zelda turned to Nettie and rolled her eyes.

"I'll take Ruthie down to meet Birdie and Trixi, with your permission, Mrs., uh, Zelda."

The woman sighed. "You sure you don't mind?"

"Not at all. I'd be happy to. Would you like to come along?"

Mrs. Miller shifted the sleeping baby on her lap. "Thanks, but I think I'll just stay here and relax."

"Aw, c'mon, Mom. Please?"

Zelda smiled. "Okay, Ruthie, let's go meet these trick riders."

They found Trixi and Birdie in the pen behind the chutes, hanging up their saddles. Their horses rolled in the dust and then trotted around, happy to be free.

Another girl stood off to one side watching, a look of yearning on her face.

"Hi, girls. I'm Nettie Moser and this is Mrs. Miller and her daughter Ruthie. We sure enjoyed your performances."

"Nice to meet you, Mrs. Miller, Ruthie." Trixi put out a hand to shake, then turned to Nettie. "Oh yes, I remember you from Cheyenne. They wouldn't let you compete."

Ruthie shifted from one foot to the other. "So you're only ten?" she asked Birdie.

Birdie stretched up on her boot toes. "Almost."

"I want to learn how to trick ride." Ruthie grabbed Birdie's hand. "Is it hard?"

Birdie shook her dark braids. "Not really. But it takes lots of practice, right, Trixi?"

"You got that right." Trixi grinned.

Ruthie leaned closer to Birdie. "Please, show me."

The other girl stepped forward hesitantly. "Could you show me too?"

Nettie turned to her. "Oh, hello. I'm sorry. We haven't met. I'm Nettie Moser."

"Lilly-Anne Scott." She shook her blonde curls. "I've been trying to teach myself how to trick ride."

Ruthie bounced over to her and introduced herself. "Are you the new neighbors, over on Froze-to-Death Creek?"

Lilly-Anne nodded. "We just moved there a few weeks ago."

Birdie smiled. "C'mon, I'll let you meet my horse."

The girls went skipping through the corral toward the horses.

Trixi grinned at Nettie. "Birdie is showing a lot of potential. I've been coaching her some, when I can get over here. And I'd be glad to help the other girls too."

Nettie put a hand on Zelda's arm. "It would be a great opportunity."

The baby whimpered and Zelda patted his back. "Gosh, I don't know."

Trixi looked at the girls gathered around the horses. "Let me see how well Ruthie rides and then we can talk some more."

Nettie found Jake at the chutes, pacing, smoking a cigarette, and hissing the smoke through clenched teeth.

Nettie bit her lip. Uh-oh. "What's wrong?"

Jake exhaled a whoosh of smoke. "Team roping is next, and that boy hasn't bothered to show up. That's what's wrong."

Nettie's chest caved inward. "Oh dear." She turned and looked around to see if she could spot Neil.

The announcement of the first team ropers thundered across the arena. Jake threw his cigarette butt down and ground it into the dirt with his boot heel. He strode to where Stranger was tied, patiently standing with his back leg cocked.

"Might as well give it up," Jake muttered and began to loosen the cinch.

Nettie walked over beside him and put a hand on his arm. *Dear Lord, help me find the right words to say.* She swallowed hard. "Did he know what time—?"

Hearing hooves pound the hard-packed earth, Nettie glimpsed a rider loping toward them. She turned to see Neil pull Blue up short and slide off the horse's back.

"Sorry, Dad. Got held up. Hope I'm not too late." Neil panted his words as if he'd been galloping.

Jake swiveled his head around, his lips taut. "Well. Nice of you to show up." He turned his attention back to tighten the cinch. "We're up after this next team."

Nettie's shoulders relaxed. Another family disaster averted. "Okay, guys. I'll head back to the grandstand now to watch you. Rope good now, you hear?" She patted both men on the back and left before anything else happened.

Nettie went back to where Trixi and Zelda were watching the girls ride. "Lilly-Anne already has some of the fundamentals down." Trixi grinned. "And Ruthie is a natural on a horse. Mrs. Miller, I think your daughter has potential as a trick rider."

Zelda shifted the baby to her other arm and sighed. "But it's dangerous going under the horse's belly like that."

"It can be. Like everything else." Trixi shrugged. "Just going out for a pleasure ride, the horse could step in a gopher hole and throw you."

"It's a mother's natural reaction." Nettie nearly burst out laughing, remembering a similar conversation between Marie Gibson and her mother. She patted Zelda's arm. "I understand how you feel. Even though I took some pretty crazy risks when I was young, when Neil started talking about rodeo, I said, 'No, you can't do that, it's too dangerous.'" Nettie did laugh then.

"Ruthie would start out slow," Trixi said. "If you folks are willing to take her over to Ismay on occasion, Birdie will be a good influence. Even though she's just ten, she is more like a grown-up in so many ways. And Lilly-Anne also seems to have her feet on the ground— unless she's doing a trick, of course."

Zelda chuckled. "Well, maybe that would be good for Ruthie, help get rid of some of that excess energy. She's just so obsessed with rodeo. I suppose it would be good to have a couple of friends like that. I just can't fight with her anymore. And her dad doesn't see the harm in it." She looked at Trixi. "I'd feel better if an adult was in charge of her training. You don't live in this area, do you?"

"No, I live over on the west side, at Ovando. But Birdie's dad is a rodeo man. I think he can ride herd on a couple of young gals for a day at a time."

"But Ismay is a hundred fifty miles from Ingomar." Worry lines creased Zelda's forehead. "I don't know how she would get there. Chet is so busy with ranch work all the time, and I . . . " She trailed off, looking down at the baby.

"Let me take Ruthie and Lilly-Anne a couple of times to get some basic training." Nettie stretched her legs.

"Why would you go to so much trouble for us?" Zelda asked.

"Because riding is pure happiness, the essence of freedom, something that makes you feel like you can accomplish anything. That's what draws your Ruthie, too. Believe me, I know. I've been riding since I was two."

Zelda stared out at the prairie beyond the corrals, a half-smile on her face. Then the baby gave a sharp cry, and Zelda turned her attention back to the child, shushing and cooing. "You're right. Girls should have their dreams." She gave Nettie a wistful smile. "Okay, I'll let Ruthie give it a try."

Nettie reached out and squeezed the woman's arm.

Then the announcer's voice called out, "And next up is father-and-son team, Jake and Neil Moser." Nettie climbed up on the corral fence to watch. "My men," she told Zelda and Trixi.

Cowboys had herded a steer into a chute, and Jake on Stranger waited to the left side of the chute, with Neil and Blue on the right. Jake gathered his lariat loop, adjusted his boots in the stirrups, and nodded.

The man at the gate released the latch and the steer burst from the chute. As soon as it crossed a white line etched in the dirt, Jake spurred his horse forward, rope twirling. He threw the loop.

Nettie held her breath. As if in slow motion, the loop dropped toward the steer's head. Would it settle over the neck or both horns? If it caught only one horn, they would be disqualified.

Yes! The rope tightened around the horns. Jake dallied his end around the saddle horn and reined Stranger to the left to turn the still-running steer.

At that moment, Neil was there on Blue, throwing his loop to catch the steer's hind legs. The rope fell short. The crowd hushed.

"Oh no!" Nettie moaned. But before she could think of the consequences, Neil snatched up the slack and threw another loop.

A good catch! Nettie leaped to her feet, yelling at the top of her lungs. "Woo-hoo!"

Both horses backed up to tighten the ropes and the steer flopped on its side, stretched out and unable to move. The rodeo official waved a flag.

"E-leven seconds!" bellowed the announcer. "Pretty quick on the rebound there, young feller." The crowd whistled and applauded.

Nettie let out a pent-up breath. Not as fast as Jake would've liked, she was sure, but with luck, they might still be well within the time to place. Maybe at least win back their entry fee.

Trixi whooped beside her. "Fantastic recovery. Your boy has great reflexes!"

Nettie grinned with pride. "Yeah, he did good, didn't he?" She slid off the fence and ran around to the other side of the arena to congratulation her men.

Back at the pens, she found Jake and Neil unsaddling and putting away their tack. "Hey, quick recovery, honey. That was great."

Neil looked down and scuffed his boot in the dust. "Nah. Not great. I missed."

Jake reached into his shirt pocket, pulled out his tobacco fixings, and silently rolled a cigarette.

"You missed the first loop, but you got it on the next try, and you did it in good time." She looked over Jake's shoulder at the arena where another team raced out to rope their steer. The header caught the steer by one horn, and the heeler rushed in to snare its hind feet and threw the animal.

"No time," called the announcer.

Nettie turned to her men. "See, they only caught one horn and they're disqualified. You guys did better than that. Now, be happy about it!"

Jake took a drag and hissed out the smoke.

Nettie waited. "Both of you," she repeated.

Then Jake threw down his cigarette butt and smiled at Neil. "You were pretty quick on the draw, son."

Neil looked up from under his hat brim and fought a grin. "Yeah, I was, wasn't I?"

Nettie walked back to the corral where she'd left the young girls earlier. Trixi and Bob Askin were there talking to Mrs. Miller, the baby on her shoulder. He touched his hat and grinned at Nettie. "So you've found yourself a couple little cowgirls?"

Nettie raised her eyebrows. *My cowgirls? Hmm.* "Well, I don't know about that, but Trixi thinks they have potential."

Trixi nodded. "I sure do."

"I've never really done trick riding," Nettie said, "so I can't help her with basics, but I could bring them over a few times to have you and Birdie give them some tips. And if Lilly-Anne's folks are on board, the girls could practice together. They're close neighbors."

Bob leaned back against the corral fence. "Birdie pretty much taught herself."

"Yeah, me too." Trixi glanced over to where the girls brushed Birdie's horse. "You watch other riders and then try things yourself and practice till you have it perfected."

Nettie glanced from one to the other.

"Sure, you're welcome to come over any time." Bob moved a toothpick from one side of his mouth to the other.

Zelda still had a pinched look on her face. "I'd sure hate to turn Ruthie loose on your family, Mr. Askin. She's kind of a wild one."

"Well, Birdie can hold her own and she'll keep your girl busy practicin' tricks. That'll tire her out purty good." Bob laughed. "If she needs more, I can put her to work in the corrals and barns."

Zelda nodded and Bob shook her hand.

Ruthie let out a loud whoop and ran to the other girls, yelling, "I can do it! I can ride with you!" They all hugged and jumped up and down, then raced to get their horses.

Nettie breathed a sigh of relief. *Good. If Lilly-Anne gets permission now, that's taken care of.*

CHAPTER SIX

Nettie saddled Windy for a ride to the pasture to check the cows. The August sun beamed its white-hot rays on her back. The hills and coulees rolled out a golden-brown carpet to the clear blue horizon. She breathed deeply. God's creation never ceased to fill her with awe and peace.

A grasshopper whizzed through the grass nearby and Windy side-stepped, eyeing the place where the noise had come from.

Nettie urged him forward. "C'mon now. You can't let a little insect scare you."

She found their red-and-white cows lazing around what was left of the water in the small reservoir. Some stood in the muddy water, switching their tails against the flies; others lay nearby, chewing their cuds. Even the calves seemed lethargic in the heat.

Counting, Nettie decided not all were at water and rode up the hill to look for the rest. Windy threaded his way through the sagebrush. Nettie loved these solitary rides. Even though she was aware of the tractor in the hayfields where Neil and Jake were stacking hay, it seemed just another pleasant buzz, along with the flies and other whirring insects.

Too bad Ismay was so far away. She'd driven Ruthie and Lilly-Anne over a couple of times to learn from Birdie, but it was just too far to go very often. Oh well, at least the girls had each other to practice with at the Millers or the Scotts.

She reined Windy up at the top of the rise and surveyed the pasture below. The rest of the cattle were down at the bottom of the meadow near the fence. Okay, that looked like all of them. Satisfied with her count, Nettie had started to turn her horse around to head home when she heard a plaintive bawl and caught a glimpse of a calf running along the fence line.

"Oh, drat. It's on the other side." Nettie pulled Windy around and trotted down the hill toward a gate at the corner of the pasture. If she could get the calf headed in the right direction, she could easily put him back in.

At the gate, she dismounted to unhook the wire from around the post and left it open. Remounting, she rode a wide berth around the calf to come up on his other side. Nettie came up closer behind it and clucked. "Okay, little feller, let's go back to our side."

The calf moved forward, with its mama trotting along on the other side of the fence, lowing anxiously. A couple of times, the cow stopped and the calf tried to get through the fence. Nettie urged him onward, hoping he would find the open gate and not run off over the prairie in the opposite direction, as calves often did.

Fortunately, Mama found the opening and came through it to reunite with her baby, and Nettie shooed them back into their own pasture. The calf immediately began suckling, its mother giving soft little moos.

Nettie slipped out of the saddle to close the gate. She hadn't seen any wires down on the fence, but sometimes calves just got rambunctious and went right through.

"All right, Windy, time to go home and take some iced tea out to the guys." Collecting her reins, she stuck her boot into the stirrup and started to swing her leg over to mount up.

At that moment a sage hen fluttered out of the brush. Windy snorted. Nettie grabbed for the saddle horn. The gelding threw up his head and bolted.

As Nettie hit the sun-baked ground, she felt her shoulder pop.

Lying still, trying to draw in a breath, Nettie heard Windy's hoofbeats galloping away. Her chest felt like the horse had sat on it. When she could at last catch her breath, she rolled to one side and tried to rise. Pain in her shoulder radiated down her arm and up into her head. Bright spots exploded in her vision and her head spun. She lay flat again, groaning.

Time drifted by like a wispy cloud. How long she lay there, she couldn't tell. Nettie opened her eyes. The sky was clear. No more bright spots. *Home. Gotta get home.*

Slowly, holding her left arm steady, she rolled to her right side. Pain shot through her shoulder. Bile rose in her throat. Taking deep breaths to still the pain, Nettie lay in that position until the nausea passed, then gingerly sat up. Dizziness threatened again and she fought to stay upright. *Jake, help.*

The afternoon sun drummed on her head, seared her eyes. *Gotta get up.* She looked around for a stick, something, anything to help her rise. A large sagebrush loomed just out of reach. Nettie tried to scoot her body toward the brush, but the pain washed over her again. Reaching down, she unbuckled her belt and inched it from her belt loops, grunting with the effort. She clumsily rebuckled it, eased it over her head, and slipped it under her forearm to cradle the arm close to her body.

With her right arm free, Nettie scooted closer to the sage until she could grab hold of a sturdy branch. She rested a minute and pulled herself to her knees. Then with a heave and a yell she stood. The amber hills seemed to sway against the sky. Her legs shook. Sweat poured down her back. *No, not going down again.* Holding on to her sage lifeline, she took deep draughts of air until the horizon righted itself.

Nettie took a step. Stopped. Let go of the brush. Took another step. Breathed deeply. Cradling her left arm close to her body, she tottered forward. Only a mile to the house. *Home,* she repeated in rhythm with her halting steps.

Stopping every few feet to catch her breath, she used her red bandanna to mop her heated face. *Jake, Neil, where are you?*

The relentless sun continued its descent from directly overhead. Nettie kept putting one foot in front of the other. Home, home, home. Her heart pounded with the effort. Hours seemed to pass by, maybe even days. . . . *Home.*

As Nettie finally turned up the rise toward the house, she heard a shout.

"Mom!" Neil came running from the barn with Jake close behind. They caught her just as she let herself crumple.

"My shoulder," she groaned.

"You're as pale as new snow. Neil, get a couple pillows." Jake picked her up and carried her to the pickup. "We gotta get her to the hospital."

Neil was back in a minute with a jug of water and the pillows. Jake mopped her sweaty face and Neil tipped the container to her lips.

Nettie moaned as the men situated her on the seat between them with pillows to cushion her arm. Jake ground the gears, and a rooster tail of dirt spun up behind the tires. As Jake wrestled the steering wheel, he glanced over at Nettie. "You awake? You okay?"

Nettie groaned. "Um-hmm." She gritted her teeth against the shots of pain whenever Jake rounded a corner a little too fast. This was going to be a long forty miles to Forsyth.

Neil took her hand and cradled it in his. "You're going to be okay, Mom."

"When you didn't come out to the field with our tea, we decided to come in for a break." Jake shifted. "I saw Windy racing around the yard, still saddled. Didn't see you." He gunned the engine. "We were just saddling our horses to come look for you. Oh my gosh, little gal, I was so scared. What happened?"

"At the gate. Getting back on. Sage hen spooked him." Nettie closed her eyes and tried to will away the pain. She dozed and woke every few minutes. Neil periodically held the water jug to her lips and helped her drink.

Finally, after what seemed like hours on a medieval torture rack, she felt the truck careen into the hospital entrance.

Neil jumped out. "I'm getting help."

Jake got out, came around, and opened her door, trying to help her sit up. Neil came running back with nurses carrying a stretcher. Nettie nearly screamed when they lifted her onto it, but clamped her lips tight to hold it back.

The doctor poked and prodded, while Nettie squeezed Jake's hand. "Well, Mrs. Moser, I can't find anything broken. Looks like you've got a dislocated shoulder." He looked at Jake. "Hold her steady. I'm going to pull it back in place." Gripping Nettie's hand and forearm, he paused. "This is going to hurt for just a moment."

Nettie braced against Jake. The doctor pulled. She heard someone yell, and the room faded away.

When the men's faces came back into focus, the excruciating, piercing pain was gone. Nettie sighed. "That's better."

The doctor applied an ice pack. "Yes, that relieves the immediate pain. But you've probably torn some ligaments, so I'd expect you to be pretty sore for several weeks." He reached for a square of muslin and fashioned a sling. "You'll want to keep that shoulder immobilized. Probably won't be able to do housework or cooking for awhile." He winked at Jake.

The trip home didn't seem as long as the ride to the hospital. Nettie was drowsy from the medicine the doctor had given her, but at least the pain and nausea were gone.

Back home, Jake and Neil walked on each side of her, holding her upright. They helped her up the steps onto the porch and into the house, and settled her into the rocking chair in the living room. Neil put pillows around her and propped her feet up on a footstool. "I'll make tea, Mom."

"I'll scramble some eggs for supper," Jake volunteered.

Nettie leaned back and closed her eyes, listening to her men banging pans in the kitchen. She didn't remember the last time either of them had waited on her.

But after a few days of sitting around, doing nothing, even being taken care of chafed at Nettie like a wrinkle in a saddle blanket. Holding her arm in the sling close to her body, she put a few carrots in her pocket and walked down to the horse pen near the barn to visit the horses. Blue and Stranger nuzzled the treats from her palm, but Windy watched from the other side of the pen. He finally approached warily. He stretched his neck out, then pulled back abruptly, blowing through his nostrils.

"Windy, Windy." Nettie reached out again with a treat. "What am I going to do with you?"

He came forward then and lipped the carrot with his velvety mouth. As he crunched, his liquid brown eyes seemed to hold her gaze.

"You're sorry, aren't you? I know you didn't mean to throw me. I should've been able to stay on. I've ridden worse broncs than you." She rubbed his forehead. "That bad ol' sage hen just scared you, didn't it?"

The gelding bobbed his head and nuzzled her hand again. Nettie took another carrot from her pocket and fed him. She would have to get back on him soon. Couldn't let this accident keep her from riding. Or give him the idea that he could throw her again.

She visited the horses every day, yearning to be up on Windy's back, galloping over the prairie. As long as she didn't move the arm, the shoulder didn't bother her too much. After a week of this, she looked around and, not seeing the guys, grabbed a bridle from the barn and a handful of feed pellets.

Nettie whistled. "C'mere, Windy. Here, boy."

After dancing around her, playing shy, he finally came to get his treat. Nettie lifted the bridle, one-armed, to place the bit in Windy's mouth. He clamped his teeth and wouldn't take it. Instinctively, she raised her left arm to grasp his lower jaw and encourage him to open his mouth. Pain shot through her shoulder. "Ahhh!" Nettie dropped

the bridle and rubbed her upper arm. "That wasn't such a great idea."
Besides, how did she think she would get a saddle on him?

She hung up the bridle.

Another week passed and she asked Jake if he would saddle and
bridle Windy for her.

"What? Are you loco, little gal?" He stared into her eyes. "Can't let
you get thrown again before you're even healed up."

"I'm going crazy around here with nothing to do. How about on
Sunday we take Ruthie and Lilly-Anne over to Ismay and watch them
practice trick riding?"

CHAPTER SEVEN

Nettie scratched her left arm under the hot muslin and winced. This shoulder was taking much too long to heal for her liking. She adjusted her arm in the sling and leaned against the fence. Inside the corral, Birdie, Ruthie, and Lilly-Anne made last-minute adjustments to the straps and footholds on their saddles. They were dressed like sisters in plaid shirts, denims, and boots.

"Okay, Mrs. Moser, are you ready?" Ruthie called out. "Here's what I've learned so far."

"I'm ready. Let's see what you got." Nettie waved her hat.

The girls mounted and urged their horses into a gentle lope around the corral, dust flying in the wake of their hooves. First Birdie, then Ruthie and Lilly-Anne thrust their feet into footholds on the saddles at the top of the withers and stood upright on their horses' backs. With her red braids bouncing, Ruthie grinned and waved as she galloped past Nettie. For a second, the girl's balance wavered and she bent at the waist to recover.

"Looking good," Nettie yelled. "Concentrate." A shiver of envy shot through her. These girls didn't have to hide their passion like Nettie did as a girl.

Back in the saddles again, while the well-trained horses continued their gallop around and around, the girls each slid to the side with one foot in the stirrup and one hand hanging on to a strap. They held themselves straight out at a ninety-degree angle to the running mounts. Birdie then released her foot from the stirrup, bounded down to touch the ground, and leapt back up onto her horse's back, first on one side, then the other. But when Ruthie tried it, her foot slipped from the stirrup, she lost her handhold, and she fell in a heap on the ground.

"Ruthie!" Nettie scrambled over the fence, ignoring the pain from her shoulder. *She can't be hurt! Please don't let her be hurt!*

Birdie reined in her horse, skidded to a stop beside her, and jumped off, Lilly-Anne right behind. "Are you all right?"

"I'm fine." Ruthie sat up and glanced at Birdie. "What did I do wrong?"

Birdie shrugged. "I guess you lost your balance."

Ruthie stood up and turned toward her horse. "Here, Ginger."

Nettie grabbed Ruthie's arm. "Honey, wait a minute. Let me check you out. Are you hurt?" She wanted to help the girl, not let her put herself in danger.

"No, no, course not." Ruthie whistled for the horse. "I've been dumped lotsa times. Gotta get back on. But what did I do wrong?"

"It seemed like you lost your center, Ruthie. Riding bucking stock, you have to feel the rhythm. Right here." She pointed to her midsection.

"I was trying to do the moves at the exact same time as Birdie."

"We both want to learn that." Lilly-Anne nodded.

"Not yet," Nettie counseled. "That takes lots and lots of practice. Perfect one thing at a time. Birdie, go through these moves and let us watch you."

"Yeah, Mrs. Moser is right about the practice." Birdie remounted and galloped her horse around the corral before executing the trick.

Beside Nettie, Ruthie intently studied the other girl's moves. "Do it again, Birdie."

After another couple of times, Ruthie climbed back on Ginger.

"Relax, Ruthie," Nettie said.

Ruthie rode Ginger around and around, as she increased speed. Nettie could see her relax as she was caught up in the horse's rhythm. She slid to the side, one arm and leg straight out.

"Relax, relax, relax," Nettie murmured.

Then, as graceful as an antelope, Ruthie bounced to the ground and back up into the saddle, across to the other side, down, and back up again.

"Woohoo!" Nettie hollered as Ruthie reined up in front of her. "Very nice riding."

Ruthie jumped down from her saddle. "Did I do good? Did you see me? This is so fun. I love it."

"I saw all that. You did a great job, Ruthie." Nettie turned to Birdie. "You're a good model."

Birdie dismounted more sedately than Ruthie had, but she was grinning just as wide. "Guess what, Mrs. Moser. We're going to be in the Madison Square Garden rodeo."

"You are? How is that going to happen?"

"Well, Birdie's dad is going, and we're going along," Lilly-Anne said.

Nettie raised her eyebrows. Bob volunteering to take three young girls to New York?

"Yeah, we're ready to compete." Ruthie jumped from one foot to the other. She glanced at Birdie and added, "Well, I have to practice a little first, but I wanna go."

Nettie brushed a palm over her mouth to hide her smile. Leave it to Ruthie to jump ahead. "So did your dad say he'd take you, Birdie? Have you asked your mom, Ruthie? Or your dad, Lilly-Anne?"

Birdie nodded. "Dad's okay with me going."

The other girls ducked their heads. Then Ruthie looked Nettie straight in the eyes. "Mrs. Moser. We were hoping you would help us."

"Help you get permission?"

"Yes, please, please, please." Ruthie persisted.

"He might agree to let you go as spectators," Nettie said. "But to compete?" What she would have given to go to the big New York competition when she was Ruthie's age. How could she ignore the girls' dreams?

"You can talk my mother into it," Ruthie chimed in.

Nettie smiled at their eager faces. "Well, I can give it a try, and you'll have to ask your dad if he'll take two more along, Birdie." Marie had talked Mama into letting Nettie go to a big rodeo. Now it was Nettie's turn to do right by these aspiring rodeo girls.

They found the men at the barn, where Jake and Neil sat on a log watching Bob oil his saddle. "Hello, ladies," Bob called out. "You all done with the exhibition?"

Nettie sat down next to Jake. "These girls sure are showing promise. I was impressed."

Bob grinned at his daughter. "This little squirt's been wriggling around all over the back and sides of a horse since she could walk. She thinks she's the next Tad Lucas."

Birdie's face turned pink and she shuffled her boots in the straw.

"She already is!" Ruthie cuffed her young friend's shoulder. "And she's a keen teacher. I'm gettin' really good, too."

Everyone chuckled at the girl's enthusiasm.

"I hear you're planning to go to the Garden this fall." Nettie brushed dust off her denim pants. Ruthie fidgeted beside her.

"Yup." Bob studied a spot on his saddle, then rubbed at it again. "Figure I'm gettin' a little long in the tooth for fightin' these broncs. Might be my last opportunity to compete there."

"Would you be up for some company?"

Jake and Bob both turned to look at Nettie. "You wantin' to go?" Bob asked.

"Me?" She paused, surprised. That actually had not occurred to her. "No, no. I was just thinking, this might be the chance of a lifetime for these young gals to go see the big rodeo. See how the stars do it." That old yearning rose up inside again. Oh, to be in the games at the Garden. A pain shot through her shoulder. She winced. With her injury, it would be a long time before she could do anything, let alone ride.

"Yeah, Dad, what d'you think?" Birdie sidled up next to him and put a hand on his shoulder.

Bob looked up at his daughter, then burst into guffaws. "Well, by golly, I knew something was up. Didn't know quite what it'd be this time." He turned to the other girls. "I wouldn't mind takin' you gals along—"

Ruthie squealed and jumped up and down. "We can go! We can go!"

"If you can get your folks to agree," Bob said.

Nettie turned to Jake. "Well, I guess we'd better get Ruthie home, so we can talk to her mom."

Ruthie leapt into the air. "Yippee!" Then she took on a more stately pose. "Thank you, Mr. and Mrs. Moser." She jumped into the back of the pickup, Jake and Nettie said their good-byes, and they headed back to take the girls home.

"Those girls sure have you twisted around their little fingers, don't they, little gal?" Jake glanced over at her with a bemused smile.

Nettie shook her head. "I guess they do." She turned to look at Ruthie bouncing in the pickup bed. "She just reminds me a lot of me when I was that age. Course I wasn't a flibbertigibbet like that. Lilly-Anne is a little more shy."

Jake reached over and squeezed her arm. "You were pretty shy when I first met you, as I recall."

Her skin tingled and Nettie remembered the confusion she'd felt the first time he touched her. She smiled at him. The thrill never went away.

They dropped Lilly-Anne off first and talked to Buck and Mrs. Scott, who promised to think about it and see if they could come up with some money. When they reached the Millers, Ruthie jumped out almost before they came to a stop. "Ruthie! Slow down," Nettie called out the window as the girl dashed toward her house. Nettie took a deep breath and followed at a much slower pace. Jake headed to the barn to talk to Chet.

Zelda Miller opened the door. "Nettie. What a surprise. C'mon in."

Nettie entered the tiny kitchen, which smelled of burnt toast and stale coffee, and looked for a place to sit. Every chair held a pile of clothing, dirty dishes littered the cupboards and the table, and a saddle sat in the corner. A dirty-faced toddler waddled into the room, wearing only a diaper, and the baby screeched from another room. Another four- or five-year-old peeked around the doorjamb. Nettie's skin crawled. This was the kind of nightmare she was thankful to have avoided. On other hand, Mama always kept her eight kids and house clean. A pang of guilt shot through Nettie's chest. This woman needed help. Mama had her older daughters to lend a hand.

Zelda's face grew pink and she gave a short laugh. "Excuse the mess." She turned and called out, "Ruthie, would you pick up the baby? Please? Where is that girl?"

"Coming, Mom!"

Nettie heard footsteps clatter and finally the baby stopped wailing.

Zelda sighed. She swept a pile of clothes off a chair and motioned to Nettie. "I'm sorry. Would you like some coffee?"

Nettie looked at the brown-stained enamel pot on the stove, wondering how long it had been there. "No, thanks. I'm fine. Sit with me for a minute. You look like you could use a break."

Zelda sank into a chair as if she couldn't bear the thought of standing any longer.

Nettie stood up. "Here, let me pour you a cup." She grabbed a lone clean cup from the cupboard and poured the muddy brew. "Cream?" At Zelda's nod, Nettie added some from the icebox and handed the cup to her.

Tears glistened in the woman's eyes as she accepted it. "Thank you. You always seem to catch me at my worst. And here you are, serving me with your arm in a sling." The toddler came over and clutched at her skirt. Zelda lifted him onto her lap. "So how did the trick-riding lesson go today?"

Nettie laughed. "They are really catching on quickly."

Zelda rolled her eyes. "Ruthie sure seems to love it."

"She really does and she shows great potential. Which brings me to something I'd like to ask you."

Zelda cocked her head.

Nettie took a deep breath. "Bob Askin is taking Birdie to the games at Madison Square Garden this fall, and he's invited Ruthie and Lilly-Anne to come along."

Zelda jerked as if Nettie had slapped her. "No! Absolutely not. If she'd stay home more often, maybe this house wouldn't be such a mess." She looked toward the door into the other room, where Ruthie quickly ducked out of sight.

Nettie swallowed. Oh dear. She hadn't expected such an adamant response. She reached out and put a hand on Zelda's arm. "I'm sorry. I don't want to add to your problems. But this opportunity may not come again. Bob is talking about retiring, and this is probably his last trip to a big rodeo."

Zelda's lips thinned into a straight line.

"I always dreamed of competing in the big arena, but never was able to. Riding seems to calm Ruthie, and I think having this to work toward would focus her."

Zelda blew out a breath and looked away.

Jake's and Chet's voices came from the yard as they approached the house and their boots made scraping noises on the porch.

"Looks like Jake's ready to go." Nettie stood. "Please, just think about it for a few days."

"I'm still not convinced. But I'll talk to her father."

Nettie smiled. "Okay, that's all I ask. It was nice to see you again, Zelda."

"You should come for dinner next time. The house will look better, I'm sure." Mrs. Miller set the toddler down.

"That would be nice." Nettie turned to go and caught a glimpse of Ruthie in the other room, her mouth and eyes wide.

"I'll see you later, Ruthie." Nettie waved and stepped outside to join the men.

Before long, Ruthie bolted out of the house, the baby bouncing on her hip. "Mrs. Moser!" She stopped in front of Nettie, tears streaming down her cheeks. "How could she say no?"

Nettie took her arm and led her around the side of the house, out of earshot of the men. "Honey, I know how badly you want this. But after seeing how much work your mom has with the house and the little ones . . ." She closed her eyes and took a breath. "You're the only one she has to help."

Ruthie let out an explosive breath. "But I gotta go! I just gotta. It might be my only chance, ever, in my whole life!" She took a step forward. "I'll help Mom more, I promise! I'll do the laundry, I'll wash the dishes, I'll clean the kitchen, I'll—" She stopped suddenly, out of breath.

"I know how much you want to go and I know you want to help," Nettie said. "But if you're serious about competing, then you'll have to spend a lot of time practicing, and you already know that doesn't leave time to help your mother."

Ruthie whimpered. "Aww, Mrs. Moser." She seemed to shrink inside herself. "I wish my sister hadn't died. She liked housework."

Nettie blinked. Oh dear. A child who'd died. What hardships Zelda had to endure.

Ruthie shifted the baby in her arms. "I try, I really do. But I can't stand to be stuck in the house with all the chores and the dirty diapers and snotty noses and crying." Tears glistened in her green eyes. "I'm never gettin' married. Maybe I'll just run away. Then I can do whatever I want."

Nettie took a step back. That's exactly how she'd felt at that age. She had sneaked out to avoid chores and to go riding every chance she had. And she'd run away once. Oh, gracious!

"Ruthie, please promise me you won't run away." She rested her hands on the girl's shoulders and peered into her eyes. "Give it a few days. Let's try to find a solution. Okay?"

"Okay." Ruthie cast her eyes downward.

"You 'bout ready to go, little gal?" Jake's voice came from around the corner.

"Coming." Nettie ached at the sight of the girl's slumped shoulders and dejected expression. "Don't give up, honey. Your mom did promise to think about it." She hugged Ruthie. "I'll see you next week. Keep practicing those tricks."

Back in the pickup, Jake glanced over at her. "Well? What did Mrs. Miller say?"

"She said no." Nettie sighed. "Jake, you should've seen that place." She described the Millers' living situation. "I understand why Ruthie wants to get out, but I can't take away Zelda's only help. And then there's the money."

Jake shrugged. "Well, maybe things'll get better for them. Chet's doing pretty good, selling his bulls. They throw good-quality calves and he's gettin' to be known all over the country."

Back home, Neil had finished the chores, so Nettie fixed supper and went out to sit on the big front porch. She rocked; thoughts and ideas flickered through her mind like a movie reel. How to get Zelda some help. The Millers certainly weren't well off enough to hire someone. They lived too far away for Nettie to help. She smiled. *I hate doing my own housework. Not going to do someone else's.* If Ruthie were to follow her rodeo dream, she needed to work at it now. Maybe this younger generation would break the ban, and women's participation in rodeo would get better again.

As the violet dusk settled over the sun-baked prairie, Nettie got up and ambled to the pasture to visit the horses, no closer to a solution than she'd been at the Millers'.

CHAPTER EIGHT

A week later, Jake drove Nettie over to the Scotts' to watch the girls practice. Ruthie and Lilly-Anne came running to meet her.

"Mrs. Moser! Mrs. Moser!" Ruthie bounced up and down as if she had springs on the bottoms of her boots. "Guess what! I gotta tell you. I gotta tell you!"

"Yeah, wait'll you hear," Lilly-Anne chimed in, not to be outdone in the excitement department.

"Slow down, girls." Nettie shut the pickup door. "One at a time now. What?"

Ruthie took a breath. "Lilly-Anne and I are helping Mom. We spent a whole day cleaning and washing and ironing and whew!" She wiped the back of her hand across her forehead. "And we're going to help out every morning too, and then in the afternoon we can practice our tricks."

Nettie raised her eyebrows. "Wow. That's wonderful, girls. Lilly-Anne, what a kind, generous thing you're doing."

The girl glanced down at her scuffed boots and shrugged. "I want to help Ruthie. I want her to come with us to New York."

"What a great solution. I'm proud of you." Nettie looked into Ruthie's face.

"Mom's invited you to stay for supper tonight," Ruthie told her. "The house is all clean and we put a chicken in the oven and even baked a pie. And maybe . . . if you talk to her again she'll change her mind."

Nettie put a calming hand on Ruthie's shoulder. "I'll do my best. What time is supper?"

The Millers' kitchen sparkled in contrast to the last time Nettie had seen it. The toddlers were clean and the baby cooing in a basket in the corner of the kitchen where the saddle had lain previously. Tantalizing smells wafted from the chicken browning in the oven and a fresh rhubarb pie sat cooling on the window sill.

Zelda greeted them with a smile. "C'mon in. I'm ready for you this time." She wiped her hands on her lacy apron. "Sit down. We'll be ready to eat shortly."

Nettie gave her a hug. How nice to see her friend looking more energetic, even dressed up, with a tortoiseshell comb in her freshly waved hair.

The men gathered around the table, and Zelda took the chicken out of the oven. Ruthie went straight to the cupboard to get plates and silverware to set the table. She poured coffee and lemonade, helped her younger siblings into their chairs, and dished up their plates.

Chet bowed his head. "Father, for what we are about to receive, we give thanks to your bountiful goodness. Amen."

The clatter of silverware against plates kept a rhythmic beat to the conversation about horses and cattle, dry weather, and news of the war in Europe. Nettie and Zelda exchanged small talk about the kids and recipes, and Ruthie jumped up to refill cups, take away plates, and serve the pie. Zelda watched her with an eyebrow raised. Nettie smiled to herself. It was nice to see Zelda more relaxed.

Chet pushed his chair away from the table with a groan. "You gals outdid yourselves tonight."

"Mighty fine vittles." Jake rose and followed Chet outside, rolling a smoke as he went.

Ruthie's face flushed as she gave Nettie a wink. "C'mon, kids, let's go get the pie washed off your faces." She herded the little ones out to the pump just outside the kitchen door.

"This was very nice of you, to have us over." Nettie took a sip of her coffee.

Zelda gave a little laugh. "Well, I was so embarrassed last week when you stopped by. But, my goodness, Ruthie and her little friend volunteered to help out, and they've done wonders, as you can see." She swept an arm out, with an expression of disbelief on her rosy face.

"They sure did," Nettie agreed.

Zelda chuckled. "Of course, they negotiated this work in exchange for Ruthie taking time to practice with Lilly-Anne."

Nettie nodded. "That was a very good idea. Shows initiative and dedication."

Zelda blinked, her eyes suddenly shiny. "I am really proud of Ruthie. I'm afraid I've tried to push too much responsibility on her after . . . her older sister died of an infection two years ago."

Nettie's heart contracted. "I'm so sorry to hear that." She laid a hand over the other woman's. "I lost a baby sister to influenza when I was young. I know that was terribly hard on my mother." She cleared her throat. "But you know, I see so much of my younger self in Ruthie. I was so much like her. All I wanted to do was ride, and once I'd ridden a steer and stayed on till the end, I was utterly hooked on rodeo. Much to my mama's dismay, of course."

"Yes. Us protective mothers." Zelda sighed. "I just hate to see her doing something so dangerous, especially after—"

"I know."

"But I guess I can't lock her up in the closet until she's twenty. And she's terribly headstrong and gets extremely unhappy when she isn't out riding." Zelda smoothed stray hairs from her face.

"Have you seen her trick riding? She's getting very good."

Zelda stood up and turned to stare out the kitchen window. The house was silent except for the Seth-Thomas clock ticking from the mantle in the living room. Nettie wondered if she should say anything more. How could she reassure Zelda, comfort her, ease her burden?

After long minutes, Zelda wiped her eyes with the edge of her apron and picked up the coffee pot to pour more for them both. Easing slowly into her chair, she looked into Nettie's eyes.

"Who am I to deprive her of a little pleasure in her life before ..." Zelda's eyes flickered to the baby's basket.

"You'll let her go?" Nettie held her breath.

"Yes," Zelda said. "Her father and I will let Ruthie go. If you chaperone."

Ruthie burst into the kitchen, unable to stay in hiding. "Oh Mom, Mom, Mom! You are the best, the best mom in the whole wide world. I can go! I can go!" She danced around the room, clapping her hands and squealing, which prompted the baby to start crying.

Shaking her head, Zelda got up to retrieve the child. "Ruthie. Calm down, now. Mrs. Moser must be willing to chaperone."

"Please, Mrs. Moser, will you, please, please?"

Nettie hesitated. Could she really do this? "Well ... goodness ... I don't know."

"You would be perfect! You're already helping us, and you said you've always wanted to go to Madison Square Garden." The girl's eyes were wide pools of expectation.

Nettie chuckled. "I'll have to talk it over with Mr. Moser first, but yes, I would be honored to chaperone you, if we can swing it."

Ruthie continued her dance around the kitchen and jigged her way out the door.

Zelda shook her head with a wry smile. "You were right. Having something to focus on has made such a difference in her this past week. Thank you for helping her."

"Thank you for believing in your daughter and letting her have her dream. I never had a daughter, but if I did, I'd want her to be like Ruthie."

"Now *that* might be a mixed blessing." Zelda giggled.

"It just might indeed."

Nettie and Zelda collapsed with laughter.

~ ~

The next day, Nettie wrote a letter to Trixi, explaining the situation and asking if she was planning to go to New York and if she could help Nettie make the proper arrangements. Neil took it to the post office in town on his way to play for a dance.

Jake watched him drive away. "I'm glad he's back to playin' the good ol' fashioned fiddle instead of that horn." He scuffed out the door toward the barn.

Jake hadn't minded Neil playing cowboy fiddle music, but he'd always had an inner flinch about Neil's trumpet-playing in the band. Nettie turned to the sink to do the supper dishes. She didn't really know why, unless he thought it was too "sissy." But there were lots of men who played brass instruments and made a living for themselves, to boot. Just look at the popularity of the Big Bands: Dizzy Gillespie, Cab Calloway. She flicked on the radio to see what might be playing and hummed along with the Dorsey Brothers' "Lullaby of Broadway." She liked that kind of music.

After she'd cleaned up the kitchen, Nettie turned off the radio and took a walk in the cooling evening to visit the horses in the pasture. She stopped at the barn, where Jake was puttering away at some chores, to grab a pocketful of feed pellets. "It sure is exciting that the girls are going to Madison Square Garden. And guess what. They've asked me to chaperone them!"

Jake gave her a sharp glance. "What did you say?"

"I said yes! Oh, honey, I've always wanted to go to the Garden."

Scowling, he reached for his cigarette makings. "You didn't think to ask me first?"

Nettie felt her neck stiffen. "I wanted to talk to you about money and arrangements, but I didn't think I had to ask your permission."

Jake tapped tobacco into the paper, twirled the ends, and jabbed it in his mouth.

"What are you objecting to? Me being gone? The money?"

He swiped a match across his denims and lit his cigarette, taking a deep drag and letting the smoke hiss out from between his teeth. Long seconds passed as he took another inhale.

"Sometimes you can be so exasperating! Why can't you just talk to me?" Nettie turned on her boot heel.

She stomped out to the pasture and stopped at the fence, watching the horses grazing peacefully. Nettie took a deep breath to calm herself and whistled. Neil's roan, Blue, was the first to raise his head and came trotting over to get his treat. Stranger arched his neck, stood to assess the situation for a moment, then joined the roan at the fence. Nettie let them nuzzle her pocket, gave them another treat, and rubbed their faces. Characteristically, Windy River held himself back. She chuckled. He wasn't about to let himself get trapped into being bridled.

"C'mon, Windy. No bridle tonight. See?" She held her arms out wide.

The high-strung thoroughbred cross jigged forward, then stopped just short of Nettie's outstretched hand, sniffing the air. He came closer, almost touching her fingertips, then shied away.

"Fine. If you don't want a treat, just go away then." Nettie shook her head. "You're as stubborn as Jake."

She hadn't ridden Windy since her shoulder injury, and every time she mentioned it, Jake looked at her like she was crazy. "I'm not so sure he's the right horse for you." Of course, that raised her hackles. If she could ride bucking steers in rodeos, she could certainly ride a spirited horse.

Windy finally stretched his neck out and took the pellet, letting Nettie stroke his soft nose for a second before he whirled away. The bay kicked up his heels and galloped over the prairie, his black mane and tail flowing in the wind.

Nettie itched to go for a ride. *It's been long enough. I'm getting better.* Maybe she'd take Blue for a little jaunt. He's calmer, maybe easier to ride at this point. She grabbed a halter left hanging on a nearby fencepost. The roan was docile, allowing her to catch him. The heck with a saddle, she decided, and swung up onto his bare back, using the strength of her right arm to pull her aboard.

The horse trotted out toward the hills, then settled into a gentle canter. Nettie gripped his sides with her knees, pleased that her shoulder didn't hurt. The sun was just sinking into the hollow on the horizon like a prayer, leaving the sky ablaze with orange and gold. A calm settled over her. Nothing like a nice ride to take away her frustrations. The other two horses followed along, as if happy to be running free. Nettie loosened her hair from its bun and let it float in the cleansing breeze. The burn in her clenched thigh muscles felt good. She needed to get back to riding. She urged Blue into a gallop. Windy and Stranger ran ahead.

Out in front, a rabbit startled out of the brush just inches from Windy's hooves. The horse snorted, stopped in midstride, and spun around. Right into Blue's shoulder.

Blue turned sharply to the left.

"No!" Nettie grabbed his mane.

He stumbled. Nettie tried to tighten her legs, but lost her balance. The prairie whirled around her. Her arms windmilled. Branches of spicy sage whipped at her face as she fell into the brush.

For a minute, she just lay there, afraid to move. Blast it! What damage had she done this time? Finally Nettie wiggled her fingers and toes and tested the movement in her left shoulder. It twinged, but it didn't feel worse than before. She sat up slowly. The sagebrush had broken her fall and she'd landed more on her right side and back.

Blue fluttered his nostrils. Nettie looked up to see him standing next to her, his big, liquid eyes searching her face, as if to ask, "Are you all right?"

"Oh, Blue. You are a dandy." She stood up. The other two horses were long gone. She flexed her arms and legs. Just a few scrapes from the brush, but none the worse for wear. Boy, was she lucky. "C'mon, boy. Let's go home before Jake discovers we're missing."

Nettie tried to mount, but found the muscles in her arms shaking and weak. She led Blue toward a rock outcropping, where she could stand and get on his back.

The roan carried her back home at a gentle walk.

Jake stood just outside the pasture gate, his cigarette a bright glow in the deepening dusk.

Nettie reined Blue in, slipped off his back, and removed the halter, avoiding Jake's gaze. The horse trotted away a short distance, then dropped down and rolled in the dust.

Her husband leaned forward and plucked a piece of sage from her hair. "Are you all right?"

She ran her hands through her hair, trying to finger-comb it back into its customary bun. "I'm fine."

Jake exhaled. "Man, I was worried." He put an arm around her. "I'm sorry. I do want you to go. We'll work things out."

"Really? You don't mind?"

He shook his head. "Sometimes I worry that you're sorry you married me, that I wasn't able to give you the rodeo life you dreamed of."

Nettie opened her mouth and closed it a couple of times. "Never." She leaned into his side. "I want both—you, and a chance to ride. And to help the girls with their dreams."

"My wife, bronc-buster, teacher, mother hen." He chuckled then. "Can't keep you down, can we?"

Nettie giggled. "Nope. Never could. Never will."

Arms intertwined, they walked up the incline to the house.

CHAPTER NINE

One Sunday as Nettie, Jake, and Neil sat on their porch drinking coffee and enjoying the afternoon sun, an old beat-up Ford turned into their drive. Jake frowned. "Wonder who that is?"

Nettie didn't recognize the car as one of the neighbors'. She stood when the men rose to greet the visitor.

A tall young man emerged from the vehicle and pushed his hat back from his forehead.

"Gary!" Nettie rushed down the steps to give her nephew a big hug. He picked her up and twirled her around, then shook hands with Jake and Neil.

"What brings you to this neck of the woods?" Jake asked.

Gary scuffed his boots in the dirt. "Well, I'm going to head up to Canada in a few days to enlist, and I wanted to come visit you guys first."

Nettie drew in a gasp. Oh no. Margie's fears were coming true. "Oh, Gary, really? You're really going to do this?"

He looked down, a flush rising up his neck. "I know, Aunt Nettie. Mom's pretty upset with me too." He put a gentle hand on her shoulder. "But I feel very strongly about this. I need to go."

Neil nodded and Nettie gulped. Jake clapped Gary on the back. "Well, son, good to see ya."

Gary reached back into his car and with a flourish presented Nettie a huge bouquet of store-bought flowers.

"Gary. Thank you." Her disappointment melted. Always the thoughtful one. This must have cost him a pretty penny. "Such a rare treat. Where on earth did you get these?"

"Aw, made a stop in Billings. Wanted something special for my favorite aunt."

Nettie gave him a hug. "You are such a sweet boy. C'mon in and have coffee with us."

They tromped up the steps and settled on the porch again. The boys cuffed each other on the shoulders and then Gary grabbed Neil in a bear hug.

Nettie brought out fresh coffee and oatmeal cookies. Gary grabbed two. "Oops, they stuck together." He grinned. "I've missed you, Aunt Nettie. It's been a long time. We used to have some good times."

"Yes, we did." She patted his arm. Aw, Gary, the softy. He couldn't just take off without saying good-bye.

They sat until dusk, reminiscing about growing up around Cut Bank, the neighborhood rodeos they'd ridden in, how things had changed since Jake and Nettie were newlyweds and raising draft-crossbreds, how mechanization and drought had put them out of business.

Gary helped Jake and Neil with the chores, and after supper, he helped Nettie with the dishes. "You don't need to do that," she protested.

"Sure I do. We used to have some good visits over dishes when I was a kid."

Later, Jake brought out a bottle of whiskey, and they talked some more, into the wee hours. "Ya know, nephew." Jake poured himself another drink. "I gotta admire you. Takes a lotta guts t' go fight them Huns."

"Thanks, Uncle Jake. Wish my folks felt the same way."

Nettie sat up straight. As much as she loved Gary, anger rose up at the example he was setting for her son. "Yes, you know I respect you too, but this is not the path for most." She looked at Neil. "You are not to get any ideas, young man. You'll be finishing high school."

Neil squirmed in his chair. "I know, Mom."

As Nettie headed off to bed, she prayed that he did know.

The next morning, Gary was up early. He squeezed Nettie in a bear hug. "I just had to come see you again. Don't worry about me. I'm doing the right thing."

Nettie could only nod and hang on to the embrace a little longer.

The Ford left a cloud of dust behind as Gary drove away. Nettie felt as if she were losing a son. How much longer would it be before Neil followed Gary's footsteps?

One Saturday evening, as Neil headed off to play for another dance, Jake came out of the bedroom with a clean shirt on. "Let's go in to the Oasis. I'm a mite thirsty tonight."

Nettie sighed, weary from a day of drudgery, cleaning house. "I don't know, honey. I think I'd like to just sit on the porch and watch the sun go down."

Jake leaned in close to her face, a twinkle in his blue eyes. "I'll buy you supper. You won't have to cook."

"You ol' devil." Nettie swatted his arm and laughed. "You know exactly what to say, don't you? All right. Let me get cleaned up a bit."

He gave her a quick kiss on the cheek. "Don't take too long now. You're purty enough the way you are."

Brushing a stray tendril of hair from her face, Nettie shook her head and went in to wash up and change clothes. They could always check the mail while they were in town. Maybe there'd be a letter from Trixi.

Dust swirling behind the pickup, Jake pulled into the little town of Ingomar. He drove past the railroad depot, the wood-frame elementary school, and Bookman's General Store and parked in front of the Oasis Bar.

Nettie stepped inside the cool, dim building behind Jake and inhaled the yeasty aroma of beer and acrid cigarette smoke.

"Afternoon, Mis-ter and Missus Moser. What'll it be?" The proprietor leaned on the bar twirling his handlebar mustache.

"Howdy, Mis-ter Easterday." Jake touched his hat in a mock salute. "I'll have a whiskey." He kept walking to the round table in the back of the room where a group of men sat, playing poker.

"Deal 'im in, boys," Easterday called out. "What'll you have, Nettie?"

"Just a lemonade, Clyde." Nettie paused. "But I'm going to run over to the post office first and check our mail."

Clyde reached for a bottle and poured Jake's drink. "Sure. I'll have a cold one ready when you come back."

"See you in a bit." Nettie strode down the wood-planked sidewalk, her boots clunking with every step. Inside, Si the postmaster was finishing his daily chores. He greeted her and handed her the mail. Nettie frowned. Nothing but the *Hoofs & Horns* magazine.

Back in the Oasis, she perched a hip atop a stool and sipped her icy lemonade, flipping idly through the magazine. Nettie watched Clyde pour a round of drinks, set the glasses in a tray, and carry them to the poker table.

She got up and wandered over to watch Jake play. Looked like he had a good hand. Maybe he'd win tonight. She patted his left shoulder twice, their signal of good luck.

He looked up at her. "Might as well order us some beans and beef."

She nodded. Might as well. Looked like they'd be here awhile. It was hard to get Jake to go home when he started gambling. *Oh well, he needs a little entertainment once in awhile. Just hope he doesn't lose.* Nettie went back to the bar and ordered food.

Clyde set the steaming plate in front of her. The sweet and spicy aroma tickled the back of her throat and her mouth watered. "Thanks. Looks good."

The bartender grinned. "Yup, 'tis, even if I do say so myself." He picked up his rag and polished the dark cherry back bar, its mirrored shelves lined with colorful bottles, a contrast with the building's rough-hewn floor planks and bare-wood walls.

"That's sure a beautiful piece. You don't see something like that very often in Montana."

"Nope." Clyde leaned against the counter in front of Nettie and surveyed the massive back bar. "Came all the way from St. Louis by boat, early 1900s."

"That's a long trip." Nettie took a bite, savoring the beans swimming in their tangy sauce. Mmm. Better than cooking at home.

"Yup. It was in storage in Forsyth during Prohibition. I just bought it a few years ago. There was another one like it, but it burned in a fire."

"Hmm." Nettie nodded. *Why did I ask?* Clyde could drone on for hours about anything. Interesting, but she just wanted to enjoy her supper and mull over getting to New York.

As the evening waned toward midnight, Nettie asked for paper and a pen to write a list of options for raising money. What could she do? Sell eggs or milk? She sighed and rubbed her eyes, more than ready to go home.

Shouts from the table in the corner nearly caused her to fall off her barstool. She turned to see Jake raking a pile of greenbacks toward him. The other men tossed their cards into the center of the table and stood.

"Doggone, you ol' cuss, you won my last dollar," one fellow complained with a good-natured chuckle.

"See ya next week," another said as he headed out the door.

Jake scooped up his money and came over to the bar, waving it. Clyde chuckled. "Fifty bucks, huh? You are one lucky saddlebum."

With a big grin, Jake threw an arm around Nettie's shoulders. "See this green, little gal? I think it's time to make a trip to the Miles City Saddlery."

Midweek, Neil drove into Ingomar and brought home some groceries and the mail. Nettie flipped through the envelopes, newspapers, and circulars, not really expecting anything at this point. But there it was—an envelope with Trixi's name in the corner. Anticipation shivered through her. Nettie smiled at herself. She was just as excited for Ruthie to go to the Gardens as she would have been for herself a few years ago.

She ripped the end off the envelope and slipped the sheet of paper out. Trixi wrote enthusiastically about her riding and upcoming appearances.

> *Yes! I'm going to the Garden in October. In fact, there's a group of us traveling together. I was thinking, if your young friends are going, we could find a job for them to do—earn their way.*

At that moment Neil banged in through the door. "Mom, have you seen my new leather gloves?"

Nettie looked at him over the top of the page. "What? No. I haven't seen them, honey."

Her son left again, letting the screen door slam. She returned her focus to the letter. What did Trixi say? She reread the letter. Jobs for the girls—fantastic!

> *I'm glad you are going as a chaperone. I'm going to be very busy with my own events, so if you could help me out with my girls, that would be great. The train fare is about $20 to $25, but I'll bet the group would be willing to chip in a little to pay for your hotel or we might be able to find someone to stay with.*

"Yeehaw!" She jumped to her feet and, without thinking, lifted her arms into the air. Pain shot through her shoulder. "Ow!" Nettie grabbed her left arm and held it close to her body. When would this shoulder heal?

She waited a minute until the throbbing subsided. No, this was not going to stop her. She wanted to go to Madison Square Garden. And take Ruthie with her.

Nettie sprinted out the door to find Jake and tell him the news.

Jake was in the barn, repairing tack. He looked up as Nettie entered and ran his hand through hair beginning to show a little gray around the temples. "These straps have seen their best days. Guess it's time to go spend that money I won the other night."

Nettie stopped in front of him. "Uh, yeah. About that . . ." She handed him Trixi's letter.

Jake squinted as he read. "Mmm. Good. The girls could work. That's just dandy." He raised his eyes to Nettie's.

"Now I have to figure out how to pay my own way. I have about ten dollars in egg money, but I'm going to need fifteen more for the train, and then if we do stay at a hotel . . ."

Jake handed the letter back to Nettie and reached into his pocket for his tobacco and papers.

She glanced at the pile of old saddles, bridles, stirrups, and cinches and sighed. There was always an additional expense to ranching and farming. Never seemed to be able to get ahead. "I know, you had your heart set on replacing a bunch of our tack." How could she let him work with worn-out equipment when they had the money he'd won?

Jake nodded and took another drag on his cigarette. "Yeah. Some of that stuff is gettin' a little long in the tooth." He dropped the butt and ground it out in the dirt with his boot heel. "There's a poker game at the Oasis every Saturday night. I could win enough for you and for new tack."

Nettie forced a smile. "Oh, honey, that's too risky. You could lose what you already won and we'd be farther behind."

Jake chuckled. "What? You don't have any faith in my ability to win?"

"Of course I do, sweetheart. But let's think about the options a little more. Sleep on it."

She walked back to the house, her steps dragging. How could she let the girls down? Zelda wouldn't let Ruthie go unless she had an adult chaperone and Trixi said she'd be too busy.

Jake came in for supper later. Neil followed. "Got that buck rake fixed, Dad."

"Good, son. Thanks."

The men washed up at the basin while Nettie dished up their plates. "So, school starts again in a couple of weeks, huh?"

"Yup. My last year, then on to college." Neil grinned.

Jake frowned. "Thought you'd come work for me."

Nettie glanced at her husband. *That old conflict raising its ugly head again.* She patted her son's shoulder. "Where do you think you'd like to go, honey?"

He shrugged. "I don't know yet. Maybe Bozeman. Or Missoula. I don't know which one has the best music program."

Jake snorted. "Music? In college? What would you do with that?"

Neil looked down at the floor. "Probably teach."

"No. You're not doin' that!"

"Well, I think I should be able to do what I want when I'm an adult." Neil's eyes blazed behind his glasses.

"C'mon, guys. Sit down and eat." Nettie plunked the steaming plates on the table. Her men simply did not see eye to eye on Neil's future. "Honey, if you would be happy teaching music, then why not?"

Jake dug into his venison stew. "But he's a rancher. We raised him to be the best durned cowboy around."

"Yeah, Dad. But I can never be as good as you." Neil took a bite, then set down his spoon. "Besides, I love music. I've been giving some of the younger kids lessons. And I like it. I think I'm good at it."

"Well, how're you gonna pay for such a fancy education?" Jake barked.

"I s'pose I'll have to get a job." Neil pressed his lips into a thin line.

"Sure. And leave me and your ma here alone to run the ranch. Maybe have to pay some hired hand to come help." Jake's tone turned acidic.

Nettie grimaced. The issue of money again. "All right, all right. Let's just eat. We don't have to figure this all out tonight."

Later, as they got ready for bed, Jake continued his grumbling about "my son who doesn't want to be a rancher."

"Jake, just leave it be. It's his life. You can't dictate what Neil is going to be. I won't let you!" Nettie glared at him. "My mother tried to force me to be something I didn't want to. And you were on my side then. Why can't you understand the same thing about Neil?"

Jake shook his head, growled goodnight, and turned away from her.

That night she tossed and turned. When she dozed, dreams of Neil and Jake facing off mingled with the roar of a train, hoofbeats, and the applause of a rodeo crowd.

Nettie awoke before dawn and slipped out of bed to make a pot of coffee. She sat down to write a letter to Trixi.

Sorry, Trixi, I just can't afford to go this time. If you know of another woman to serve as chaperone for the girls, I would be ever so grateful. I'd sure like to see them get the chance to go.

CHAPTER TEN

Jake wandered out of the bedroom, yawning. "You're up early, little gal." He poured himself a cup of coffee and sat at the table with her.

"Didn't sleep very well." Nettie rubbed gritty eyes. "I'm writing to Trixi. Telling her I can't go."

Jake frowned. "Why not? I thought we'd talk about that some more. Here's the fifty I won." He put the money in front of her. "I want you to go."

"Jake, we can't afford it." She picked up the bills and slapped them back on the table in front of him. "You won't give Neil money for college. I'm not taking this for a trip to New York."

Nettie stood and stalked into the bedroom to get dressed.

That afternoon, when Nettie came back from a ride on Blue, she walked toward the barn to hang up her bridle. She heard voices and stopped just outside the door.

"Son, this family always finds a way to accomplish things, thanks to your mother. I really want her to go to Madison Square Garden and I'm going to buy her a train ticket. And the next time I win a few bucks at poker, I'll put it in a college fund for you. How does that sound?"

Nettie nearly dropped the bridle. That didn't sound like Jake, at least not the Jake of late.

After a pause, Neil spoke. "Thanks, Dad. I think Mom ought to go too. I have a few dollars from playing for dances. I'll pitch in for the ticket."

Nettie stepped through the big barn door. "Guys! You can't do that! Use your money for new tack, Jake, and put yours toward college, Neil."

"Ah, heck, little gal." Jake leaned against a stall. "We'll get new stuff when we need it. But Madison Square Garden . . . that doesn't come along every day. That money is yours."

Neil came over to give her a hug. "Yeah, Mom. You go. We both want you to."

━━◆━━

Nettie got out of the pickup at the corral where Ruthie and Lilly-Ann were saddling their horses. She stretched in the warm September sunshine. "Guess what, girls?" Nettie grinned as she told them the news about the money.

"Oh . . . oh. Oh!" Ruthie was uncharacteristically speechless for a moment. Then she squealed, jumped up and down, and grabbed Lilly-Anne's hands. "We're going to Madison Square Garden!"

Lilly-Anne whooped and the girls swung each other around, giggling and shrieking. Amused at their youthfulness, Nettie shook her head. *Was I ever like that?*

Ruthie broke from her whirling and twirling. "Mrs. Moser. Oh, I'm so excited! Thank you, thank you, thank you!" She and Lilly-Anne ran to Nettie and threw their arms around her.

Nettie laughed and hugged them back. "Now, girls, you have your work cut out for you. Lots of practice in the next few months."

Ruthie looked up at her with huge round eyes. "Oh, yes, yes, yes!" She squealed again and hugged Lilly-Anne. "I can't wait. It'll be so much fun."

The girls ran off to find Lilly-Anne's dad and tell him the news, then Jake and Nettie took Ruthie home.

Ruthie jumped from the pickup and burst into the house, Nettie following close behind. "I'll have enough money to go to New York! Mom, I can go!" She jumped up and down. "Miss Trixi said we could work and earn our way and oh my gosh, Mom, I'm going!" She stopped. "I still can, can't I?"

Zelda simply rolled her eyes and sighed at her daughter's antics. She laid the baby in his cradle and looked at Nettie. "Are you sure you're up for weeks of this?"

Nettie laughed and waved off Zelda's question. "I think we'll manage just fine."

Chet and Jake came into the house, poured cups of coffee, and sat at the table. "So what will all the expenses be?"

Nettie pulled out Trixi's letter and turned it over to where she'd written down the details: the train ticket, shipping the horses, room and board.

"Bull sales have been good, so we can swing the train ticket. But seventy dollars to ship her horse, huh?" Chet picked up a pencil, chewed on it for a moment, then scribbled numbers on the back of an envelope.

Ruthie's dad looked at his wife. "This gal of ours is going to be an expensive one."

"In more ways than one." Zelda's face held a rueful smile.

Chet nodded. "But rodeo seems to be the only thing that settles her down, and that's worth a lot right there."

Zelda smiled. "I'm in favor of that."

"There's always a chance the girls might win a prize." Jake took out his tobacco and shook it into a paper.

"I think we can swing it." Chet got up to pour more coffee into Nettie's cup. "And you're sure—absolutely sure—you want to take this on?"

"I am." Nettie took a deep breath. "When I was their age, Marie Gibson took me to my first big rodeo in Miles City and I knew rodeo was my dream. I want to help these girls." She nodded decisively. Ruthie and Lilly-Anne were the future of women's rodeo.

◆◆◆

The next month was snatched up in a dust devil of getting ready for the trip to New York. Neil went back to high school and so did Ruthie, but on weekends she was at Lilly-Anne's, practicing for hours. Jake occasionally drove Nettie there, but sometimes she wrestled the pickup over the rutted roads herself, wincing at the shoulder pain when she hit a bump.

Not being able to ride Windy frustrated her, but she knew it wasn't wise. When she absolutely couldn't stand it anymore, she rode Blue. Jake would often saddle up Stranger, mumbling about her stubbornness, and ride with her.

"You don't need to babysit me," Nettie complained. "I've been riding since I was two and rode my first steer at fourteen."

He just grinned. "I know, but you're not fourteen anymore. I don't want my best girl getting hurt again."

Nettie would never admit it to Jake, but she appreciated his care and the company.

"I do wish I could take a horse to New York, but I know, I know." She held up a hand to stop the objection she knew was coming.

Jake sat easy in the saddle. "You're going to be busy enough, ridin' herd on those girls and watching all the events. Man, what a shindig that's goin' to be."

Excitement tickled Nettie's insides. "I can't wait! But I wish you could go too. You'd get to meet some of the greats."

"I know. But I gotta be practical about this." He reached over and squeezed her arm. "You can tell me all about it."

"I will." She wet her lips. "Thank you."

Toward the end of September, Nettie received a letter from Bob Askin, saying he'd been laid up after being thrown by a horse, so he and Birdie wouldn't be able to go to New York. A quick visit to the Scotts with a bottle of whiskey and Buck finally agreed to go along. "Aw, heck, I might as well ride one more time before I get too old."

The fall days shone warm and bright, gradually cooling into crisp October nights.

Finally the day arrived. Nettie woke early, repacked her suitcase twice, cooked breakfast, but couldn't eat. She stood out on the porch until Buck drove up in a 1935 Carryall Suburban with Lilly-Anne, Ruthie, and their horses in a trailer. He loaded Nettie's bag. "Ready?"

Nettie took a deep breath. She turned to Jake and he took her into his arms for a crushing hug. "Have fun. I'll miss you, little gal." His blue eyes shone bright and wet.

"I miss you already." She kissed him good-bye, got in the car wiping her eyes, and they headed for the train depot in Miles City.

Ruthie was in character, bouncing in her seat, her red pigtails whipping up and down. Lilly-Anne giggled and started to bounce too. Buck jerked his head toward the backseat. "Girls! Settle down, now." He glanced at Nettie. "It may be a long two weeks."

"Yup, it sure might be." She bounced in her seat a bit, then laughed and looked back. "I'm as excited as you are, but remember your manners. This is a good opportunity to practice being ladies." She turned and sat demurely in her seat, her hands folded in her lap.

"Yes, Mrs. Moser." The girls quieted and sat up straight. They rode in relative peace the rest of the eighty-six-mile trip, an occasional giggle breaking out, followed by "Shhh" and serious faces.

Nettie leaned back in the seat. She couldn't blame the girls for being wound up. This would be the biggest event they'd ever attended. Nettie, too, for that matter. The old familiar flutter in her stomach brought back memories of that first "big" rodeo in Miles City she'd attended with Marie. Oh, the dreams she'd had then—visions of the huge crowds' applause while she accepted championship saddles and buckles—before she'd had to adjust them to be a wife and mother.

❦

Smoke and steam billowed around the locomotive like a dragon belching. Buck took the horses to the corral to be loaded on a freight train leaving the next day. "Travel easy, Buster," Lilly-Anne whispered.

Ruthie stroked Ginger's neck. "Will they be all right? What if nobody puts them on the train? Who's going to feed them?"

"They'll be just fine. Mr. Scott talked to his friend who works here and he'll keep a special eye on your horses. C'mon, we've got to get on board." Nettie and the girls dragged their bags to the passenger car, where a porter helped them board.

"Mrs. Moser, look at all these seats, all the people." Ruthie's eyes were great pools of green against her freckled face. Cowboys, women and children, and uniformed soldiers lined the rows of seats up and down the car. Conversation buzzed.

Nettie searched for empty seats. "Won't this be fun, girls? Let's find a place to sit."

"Hey, cowgirls!" a voice came from behind her.

Nettie turned. "Trixi. Good to see you." She hugged the young woman. "You remember Ruthie and Lilly-Anne."

"Of course. From the Miles City Roundup last spring." Trixi shook the girls' hands. "C'mon, I'll show you where we're sitting." She led them into the next car where she introduced them to Thelma and Margaret, her trick-riding cohorts, who appeared to be in their late teens. The younger girls settled in with them, giggling and asking non-stop questions.

"Have you been to New York before?"

"How long is it going to take?"

"Where are we going to sleep?"

"When can we eat our lunch?"

Nettie settled onto the scratchy upholstered seat and rested her feet on a metal footrest that stretched out from beneath. Tempted to join their excited chatter, she hugged herself to contain her own giddiness.

After a while, Buck found them and settled across the aisle. He picked up a discarded newspaper, its headline blaring news of the European war.

Nettie sighed. Gary was probably there already. Goosebumps prickled along her arms. She didn't want to think of that right now.

"Dad, were the horses okay?" Lilly-Anne called across the aisle.

"Yup. Settled in the corral and chowin' down, last I saw."

Ruthie had a frown on her face. "I hope they don't get in a fight with other horses."

Buck shook his head. "Naw, they'll be fine. Don't worry about 'em."

The porter called the final "All aboard," the engine roared, and the station drifted by.

"We're moving!" Ruthie pressed her nose against the glass.

Outside the window, the town disappeared as the train picked up speed. Memories of past train rides danced with reflections on the glass. How Neil had run up and down the aisles, exploring and making friends on their trip eight years ago to Idaho Falls when—her smile faded—that's when Marie had been killed. The reflection blurred into a cowgirl atop a bucking bronc, her hand waving high. Memories squeezed her heart. Marie, deep in conversation with Mama, convincing her that Nettie should be allowed to rodeo. Marie consoling when Nettie was bucked off and broke her wrist.

Marie. Such a good friend. Wish she could be here with us. She gave me her best. She would want me to do this.

Nettie breathed in an oily metallic smell, mixed with the odor of stale cigarettes, and coughed. She leaned her head back on the white linen cloth draped over the headrest.

Another train, another adventure. The rhythm of the car, murmur of voices, and clickety-clack sounds lulled her. Her first train ride was when she was six and moved from Idaho to Montana. Her second, when she was not much older than Ruthie and Lilly-Anne, had taken her to her first big rodeo with Marie. Then, another train ride with Jake to Great Falls when they got married, the dining car, holding hands. Such bliss. Trains brought good things into her life. She closed her eyes and dozed.

CHAPTER ELEVEN

New York City. A medley of discordant sounds—honks, engine roars, bicycle bells—assailed Nettie's ears as they disembarked onto the platform. Outside the train station, traffic whizzed by, more cars in one spot than she'd ever seen in her life: not only the familiar black Fords, but taxicabs and blue Buicks and red Hudsons and black Cadillacs with leather upholstery. And she'd thought Great Falls was a busy town. Nettie breathed in vehicle exhaust mixed with sausage aromas from sidewalk vending carts. This was so far from her Montana world.

A muscular young cowboy friend of Buck's met them inside the depot waiting room. "This here's Fritz," Buck made the introductions.

Fritz shook hands with Nettie and Trixi. "Let's get you all loaded up."

They gathered their bags and loaded them into Fritz's Suburban, similar to the one Buck owned.

"All right. Hop in. I'll take you to your lodgings, show you the Garden on the way." Fritz grinned at his passengers, ground the gears, and shot out into traffic. Horns blared as several taxis swerved around them, drivers leaned out of their windows and cursed, pedestrians and bicycles moved in masses across the multi-laned streets like the locusts of the '30s. Ruthie shrieked. Lilly-Anne giggled.

Nettie clutched the seat fabric. "We're going to be killed! How in the world can you drive in this mess?"

"Aw, you get used to it." The cowboy shifted and drove forward as the traffic light changed to green ahead of them.

"So you're from around here?" Nettie asked.

"Naw. California. But I been here plenty."

Buck chuckled. "Fritz, you're too modest."

"Fritz Truan?" Nettie asked in awe. She'd read about him in *Hoofs & Horns* magazine.

"Yup," Buck confirmed. "Madison Square Garden's World Champion bronc rider last two years running."

Nettie caught a glimpse of Ruthie's wide eyes and open mouth that mirrored her own thoughts.

"It's an honor to meet you," Nettie said.

Buck reached over and clapped his friend on the shoulder. "Yup, and he prob'ly won't mention it, but he was the youngest cowboy ever to be crowned."

Fritz chuckled. "Well, I hope I'm still ridin' when I'm as old as you."

Buck cuffed his shoulder and laughed along with him.

After what seemed like hours of dodging other vehicles, veering around corners, stops and starts, Nettie caught a glimpse of the brightly lit marquee:

MADISON SQUARE GARDEN, HOME OF THE WORLD CHAMPION RODEO, FEATURING SINGING COWBOY GENE AUTRY

A lump rose in her throat. "We're here."

"We're here," Ruthie echoed. "Mrs. Moser, we're here. I can't believe it. Can you believe it, Lilly-Anne?" Both girls leaned toward the window.

"We'll come back here tomorrow, after we've picked up your horses, and you can look around. But let's get you ladies settled in your digs." Fritz drove on past and up the street a few blocks to the YMCA.

Trixi checked them in at the desk, the men helped carry their bags up the stairs, and the women selected vacant bunks. Nettie looked around at the large, communal sleeping room. This would be a different experience.

After a sleepless night, listening to others' rustlings and snores, to Ruthie and Lilly-Anne whispering, Nettie got the girls up early. Fritz and Buck took them to the freight train depot. Various sized pens held bawling cattle and milling steers, ready for shipping.

Ruthie's eyes were wide. "Oh my gosh, how are we going to find Ginger and Buster in all that?"

Buck chuckled. "Oh, we'll just have to climb to the highest point and whistle, see if they'll come runnin'."

"Oh, Dad!" Lilly-Anne rolled her eyes.

The men checked in at the depot and found out where the horses were being unloaded, and then went back to the stock car to collect them. Lilly-Anne and Ruthie ran to their mounts as soon as they clopped down the ramp. Ruthie buried her face in Ginger's mane. "Oh, I was so worried about you!"

"They're just fine. None the worse for wear." Buck led the procession back to the vehicle where he and Fritz loaded the horse trailer.

Fritz maneuvered them back through the maze and din of the traffic once again to the Garden. He drove past the grand entrance and turned into a huge doorway on a side street. Nettie blinked as they left the bright daylight and bustle of the city street and headed down a long tunnel, dimly illuminated with electric lights. They met a stream of empty trucks and horse trailers heading back out.

Ruthie gripped the seat in front of her. "Where are we going?"

"The barns and holding pens and everything's underground," Buck explained.

Nettie's heart tripped. "This must be huge."

"It is," Buck said. "It surely is."

Fritz drove into a monstrous underground area with corrals and stalls all around.

Nettie gaped. "Wow, if I didn't know we were in the middle of New York City, I'd think I was back at the Miles City Roundup."

Trixi nodded. "It's amazing, isn't it?"

"Yup, kinda like the ol' Bar X itself." Buck opened the door and got out. Nettie, Trixi, and their young charges followed.

The familiar smell of sweat, dust, and manure greeted Nettie's nostrils. *Gosh, Jake and Neil should be here to see this.* Calves bawled and bulls snorted in corrals, horses whinnied, and hooves pounded on stall doors. Cowboys in bright shirts, shiny boots, and ten-gallon hats milled around, organizing tack, brushing horses, saddling up. Nettie felt as wide-eyed as Ruthie. *Must be hundreds of head of livestock down here.*

Fritz pointed to a ramp that led upward from where they stood. "That's where they take the stock and we ride up into the arena at street level."

A tall, rangy man approached, doffed his hat to the ladies, and shook hands with the men. "Good t' see ya again, Fritz. Howdy, folks. I'm Dan Hines, arena director. You can unload your horses and get checked in over there." He waved a hand toward an office building.

After Buck and Fritz unloaded the horses and tied them to a fence by the horse trailer, the adults walked over to stand in a long line in front of the office. When they finally got inside, a huge hulk of a man stood to greet them, crushing Nettie's hand in a firm shake. She winced. *He must weigh three hundred pounds.*

"Foghorn Clancy," he boomed. C'mon in, we got some paperwork for ya." He directed them to the counter where several clerks worked. "Hey there, Fritz. You gonna defend your title?"

"You bet." The young cowboy touched the brim of his hat. "Bring 'em on."

"That's the spirit." The big man guffawed, his jowls jiggling. "Ladies, I'd be happy to show you 'round when you're done here."

Once they all made it outside, Foghorn greeted the younger girls with exaggerated charm, bending over their hands with a mock kiss, and ignored their giggles at his name. Then he escorted them to the stalls, where they took care of their horses.

Later that evening the big man came back to check on them, rested a hand-tooled leather boot on the lower fence rail, and tamped his pipe. "Now, Fritz and Buck know the ropes, but Mrs. Moser, you and the young ladies, this here's your first time ain't it?" His gravel-filled voice boomed.

"Yeah," Ruthie spoke up. "It's my first time. It's so big. So many horses and bulls and people! Do you do this every year?"

"Yup, we sure do. Tex Austin started this rodeo in 1922. Prize money that year was twenty-five bucks. We've hosted the World Championship ever since."

Nettie leaned forward. "Tex did the rodeos in London, didn't he?"

Foghorn nodded and drew on his pipe.

She swallowed hard. The ones Marie had invited her to, the ones Nettie'd had to forego when she became pregnant and again after Marie was killed.

Foghorn tapped his pipe on the rail to empty it and stuffed it back in his shirt pocket. "C'mon, I'll show you 'round the pens."

They followed him to another large corral. "Now those are the out-law buckin' horses." Blacks, bays, and duns milled around, some eating, some dozing. "They don't look 'specially mean, do they?"

"No, I have to admit, they don't." Nettie had expected biting, kicking, and fighting, but the horses seemed almost docile.

"Well, they are. I've seen 'em in the chutes reach 'round, grab a would-be rider by the arm, and shake him like a cat playin' with a mouse."

Ruthie and Lilly-Anne hurriedly stepped back from the fence, quickly joined by Margaret and Thelma. Nettie and Trixi exchanged bemused glances.

Foghorn flourished an arm toward the pen. "Did you know they're descendents of Coronado's horses?"

Nettie wracked her brain, trying to remember what little history she'd learned in grade school.

"Who's Coronado?" Thelma asked the question Nettie didn't want to.

"Ah, he was a Spanish conquistador. Came to Mexico to conquer the mythical Seven Cities of Gold."

The girls leaned toward him, as if eager to hear what came next. "How do you know all this stuff?" Ruthie asked.

The big man roared. "Well, they call me chief statistician and publicity drumbeater 'cause I been around so long."

"Anyhow, those cities didn't exist, of course, but his horses, they were big, bred to carry a man wearin' full armor. He turned 'em loose 'stead of takin' 'em back to Spain, and they roamed the prairies, wild, for centuries." Foghorn paused. "What you see here's what's left of the wild outlaws. Gettin' scarce now, though. We have to keep on the lookout for 'em all the time."

Ruthie yawned, Lilly-Anne joined in, and Nettie suddenly felt the weariness of the past several days fall heavy on her shoulders. "Well, Mr. Foghorn. This has been most interesting. It is getting late, though, and we'd better go turn in for the night."

Trixi, Margaret, and Thelma echoed their thanks, and they all said good night, joined Buck and Fritz back at the stalls, and climbed back into Fritz's car.

—•—

Nettie crawled onto the hard, lumpy cot at the "Y" and pulled the blanket up to her chin. A great longing overwhelmed her. She missed Jake's reassuring warmth beside her, even his snorts and snuffles. How were her guys managing by themselves? Would they get enough to eat? Oh dear, maybe she shouldn't have come. *Oh, come on now, Nettie Moser*, she chided herself, *you wanted this more than anything in the world.* She grinned. *Well, almost anything.* And the men could take care of themselves just fine.

All around, other women snored, coughed, and murmured. The heat radiators banged and hissed. She turned on her side and tried to pound the pillow into a more comfortable shape.

"Mrs. Moser?" Ruthie's whisper came out of the darkness nearby.
"Yes?"

"I can't sleep. Can I come sit by you awhile?" Rustlings told Nettie
that Ruthie was already on her way.

She smiled to herself. "Sure, c'mon over." She reached out and took
the girl's hand. Ruthie sat next to Nettie. "Everything's so . . . big. So
many people. So noisy."

Nettie patted Ruthie's arm. "Yes, it certainly is. I'm feeling a little
of that too. We're not used to all this. But isn't it exciting at the same
time?"

"Yeah, I'm excited." The voice was tiny, not so convincing. "But, I
guess I'm scared."

"You don't need to be. I'm right here with you all the way." Nettie
sat up. "You're you no matter where you go. And you love riding, don't
you?"

"Oh, yes, I do."

Wrapping her arms around the girl, Nettie rocked her until she fell
asleep. Then she lay down beside Ruthie on the narrow cot. This was
what having a daughter might have been like.

— ❦ —

Nettie and Trixi walked into the massive indoor arena, elbowing their
way through the jostling crowd to find their seats for the opening
ceremony. The younger girls followed, their faces shiny and round
with wonder, eyebrows arched, eyes wide, and mouths open. For once,
Ruthie was speechless. Even Trixi looked starry-eyed. Nettie turned
in a circle, gazing up at the row upon row of seats that reached to the
high-domed ceiling, filling with a steady flow of rodeo fans and par-
ticipants. An usher showed them to their seats, and a medley of Glenn
Miller Big Band sounds interspersed with Gene Autry hits blared
from loudspeakers.

Then the opening notes of the "Star-Spangled Banner" rang
through the stadium and the audience rose as one, hats removed, hands

over hearts. Below, a cowgirl dressed in shiny blue satin rode out to the center of the arena, carrying the Stars and Stripes. An entourage of women riders followed, their horses "bowed" on one bent knee while the National Anthem played. Nettie felt stinging behind her eyes. The threat of the European war seemed far away at this moment. If only life could go on with this splendor.

"And now, ladeees and gentlemen, to begin our program tonight . . ." the announcer's voice boomed through the speakers. "With eight Garden rodeos under their belts at the tender ages of eleven and twelve, we have the veteran roping and trick-riding act . . . the McLaughlin Brothers."

Beside Nettie, Ruthie straightened her posture and Lilly-Anne leaned forward. "They're younger than us," Ruthie whispered.

Two horses dashed into the arena, the boys' ropes twirling. Simultaneously, they stood up on the backs of their mounts, spinning huge loops. In perfect unison, they jumped through the loops, landing upright again on the running horses.

Ruthie gasped. Lilly-Anne clapped and turned to Trixi. "Did you see that?"

With a wry smile, Trixi nodded. "They're good, all right. I still have trouble with that one."

With each new death-defying trick, the crowd roared, coming to its feet in a final ovation.

Nettie hooted along with the rest. Those boys were good. She glanced over at Ruthie and Lilly-Anne. Ruthie caught her lower lip in her teeth and took rapid, shallow breaths. Nettie reached over to pat the girl's shoulder.

"Mrs. Moser. I can't." Ruthie's lips trembled.

Oh dear. Nerves. Nettie put her arm around Ruthie's shoulder. "Sure, you can. You're just as good as they are."

Nettie rested her boot on the lower rail of the chute as she watched the next cowgirl mount her snorting bronc, tensing her legs in the saddle and nodding to the gate keepers. The horse burst through, crow-hopping and sunfishing. Nettie tightened her shoulders and winced at the momentary stab of pain. *If only I could be doing this.* This is what she'd lived for since she was fourteen. A sigh escaped.

"Big sigh." Beside her, another cowgirl smoothed on a pair of gloves in preparation for her own ride.

Nettie started. "Sorry. I didn't realize I'd done that. You up next?"

"Almost. Couple riders ahead yet." The young woman extended a hand. "Vivian White."

Nettie introduced herself. Oh yes, now she remembered reading about Vivian in *Hoofs & Horns.* She'd won the women's bronc-riding competition here in 1937. Such an accomplishment for someone not yet thirty.

"Y'all riding?"

"No. Always hoped to. But I dislocated my shoulder a couple months ago and . . ." Nettie spread her palms in a gesture of futility.

"That's a shame." Vivian checked the fasteners on her buckskin chaps. "Where y'all from?"

Nettie grinned at the woman's accent. "Montana."

"Montana? Did you ride with Marie Gibson?"

"She was a dear friend."

"Great gal. Terrible thing."

Nettie's smile wavered and she changed the subject. "Where are you from? Didn't I see you trick riding yesterday?"

The other woman nodded. "Oklahoma. And yep, I'm a trick rider too. Gotta be a jack of all trades in this business. Been ridin' since I was fourteen. Figured I could do anything the boys could do."

Nettie raised her eyebrows. "Me too. But I guess my steer and bronc riding days are over. At my age, if I took a bad fall, well . . ."

"There's always that danger." Vivian adjusted her white hat. "But I ain't never been bucked off in the arena and I don't aim to start now." She peered into Nettie's face. "Nettie Moser, huh? Marie told me about that trail drive to Idaho in the thirties, how you set aside your dream and stuck by your husband and horse herd."

Nettie's head jerked back. "Really."

"Yeah. And ya know what? It takes the same amount of courage to do something like that. There's more than one way to win. I admire you for that." Vivian squeezed Nettie's arm. "Nice talkin' to ya. See y'all around."

Nettie stood in shocked silence. So like Marie to do that. Her friend's words echoed in her mind: "Never give up." Nettie watched Vivian climb up the chute and settle on the back of a big gray roan.

Nettie hadn't given up her dream. At long last, she was here, in Madison Square Garden. That was a big accomplishment, even if it were as a bystander. She strolled over to the arena fence to watch Vivian's ride.

When the gate swung open, the big gray leaped from the chute, front hooves pawing the sky. Vivian spurred and her body moved with the bronc. The horse sunfished, whirled, kicked his heels high, and then did it all over again. But Vivian never lost her smile or her white hat. She kept waving her left hand and spurring as if having the time of her life.

Nettie's heart raced and her legs tingled, feeling the rhythm of the dance right along with the young cowgirl.

The eight-second whistle blew, and the crowd came to its feet in a roar of approval. Vivian White had made a winning ride.

CHAPTER TWELVE

Nettie awoke in the inky predawn. Her heart fluttered like a moth trapped inside a lantern globe. She tried to inhale deeply, but the night breath of all the women in the sleeping room hung heavy over her. *Must have fresh air.* Nettie swung her legs over the side of the cot. She needed a nice, brisk early-morning ride on Tootsie. Regret sat like a weight on her chest. Tootsie was gone. Nettie was in New York City with no horse to ride.

She grabbed her clothes and crept out of the room to dress in the communal bathroom, then headed out the front door. At least she could take a walk. Streetlights illuminated the sidewalks and despite the early hour, automobiles and city buses whooshed by. Nettie headed toward the arena. How nice it would be to find a little spot of green amidst this hurried, noisy scramble of life. She could never live like this, with nothing but cement beneath her feet, and great towers of concrete, metal, and glass rising on all sides above. It was like the bottom of a canyon, but without the earth and rock. The city pressed against her, heavy on her shoulders. The early-morning air, instead of the Montana freshness Nettie longed for, was redolent with exhaust fumes.

Gosh, if she'd succeeded in rodeo, she would've spent more time in places like this. Maybe it was a blessing in disguise.

Nettie walked down Eighth Avenue, past the huge Garden arena edifice where lights blazed despite the early hour. She continued aimlessly, longing for a horse beneath her, Jake and Neil by her side, cattle lowing in the soft morning air. *I have to write to them tonight.* She longed to hear Jake's voice and wished they had a phone at the ranch. But she'd spent long winters without him when they were in Idaho. *I can handle this. It's only a couple of weeks.*

Today Ruthie and Lilly-Anne were scheduled to perform. Nettie's fingers itched with nervousness for the girls. Would they be able to hold their own against the McLaughlin Brothers?

After trudging along for another half hour, she stopped in mid-stride, her thoughts scattered to the breeze. Ahead in the pastel dawn, she saw what she'd been looking for: trees and grass. Nettie ran forward, past the sign announcing Madison Square Park. Her boots scrunched through the red and gold leaves covering the lawn. She fell to her knees, gathered up armfuls of the leaves, and tossed them into the air, laughing.

She kicked through the leaves, now imagining the buildings as tall buttes and the streets as deep coulees. Then she heard the clip-clop of hooves. A few minutes later, a mounted policeman rode up next to her. "You doin' all right, lady? Lost?"

Nettie laughed. "Not any more. I found trees and grass in New York City." She held her hand out to the horse. "May I?" At the policeman's nod, she stroked the horse's soft nose. "How do you manage to keep a horse in this huge city?"

He explained boarding stables and police training and confessed he was originally a farm boy from Nebraska. "This is the next best thing to being back home."

Nettie told him of the ranch in Montana and her love of horses. As he rode away, after the horse left a nice fresh pile of dung, she inhaled deeply. She picked up a huge, crimson maple leaf to press and take home to Jake. In the middle of New York City, Nettie had found a small slice of paradise.

◆～◆

A couple of hours later, Nettie walked into the arena to meet the girls at the underground corrals where their horses were kept. Lilly-Anne came running to meet her. "Mrs. Moser. Ruthie—" She gulped, her eyes red, face pale.

"What?" A chill ran up Nettie's spine. An accident? Marie's last ride flashed through her mind. "What's wrong with Ruthie?" The peace Nettie had found in the park shattered.

Tears flowed down Lilly-Anne's cheeks. "She won't get out of bed. She won't ride. She called me names." Sobs erupted. "She slapped me."

She gathered the girl in her arms, breathing a sigh of relief, then expelling the breath in annoyance. What now? That poor girl, giving in to fear. This was Ruthie's big chance, a chance Nettie would've killed for when she was that age.

Lilly-Anne tipped her head back. "Trixi's still there with her, trying to talk to her, but Ruthie just covers her head and won't move. Oh, Mrs. Moser, this is a disaster!" A fresh torrent of tears flowed.

"Okay, honey." Nettie patted Lilly-Anne's arm. "No more tears now. Let's go see what's happening."

They nearly ran back to the Y. Inside their sleeping quarters, a group of girls surrounded Ruthie's bed, patting and murmuring to the immobile lump beneath the thin blanket. Trixi stood from where she'd been kneeling. She shrugged. "It's no use."

The permeating odor of hopelessness overpowered Nettie, memories of her mother when little Essie died, the days she'd spent on needlework when all she wanted to do was ride, the grief that laid her low when Marie was killed. Why had she thought she could take care of these girls in such a foreign environment when she could barely function here herself?

She took a deep breath and shook off her own feelings. She was here to help Ruthie achieve her dreams, not give in to her own inadequacies.

"Everybody clear out," Nettie ordered. "Now."

Trixi led the girls out of the room, amid gasps and giggles and whispered questions. When the room grew quiet, Nettie knelt beside Ruthie, who lay curled in a fetal position, her thumb in her mouth.

"What's wrong, Ruthie?"

"I can't," came the small voice.

"You can. You are a Montana cowgirl."

A sniffle. "I'm scared."

"Montana cowgirls get scared. Then we do it anyway." Nettie stroked the girl's arm as if she were calming a skittish horse.

The thumb came out of the mouth. An eye peered up through disheveled hair. "I'm a Montana cowgirl."

"Yes, you are."

Ruthie turned her face fully from the pillow, both eyes on Nettie. "You think I can?"

Nettie smiled and brushed the hair back from Ruthie's face. "I know you can."

The girl shook her head, tears welling in her eyes. "I'm not a real cowgirl. I'm a fake. I'm not brave at all."

She continued stroking the tangled red hair. "Your mom told me about when you rode for miles to get someone to help when your baby brother came early. That was brave."

Ruthie wiped her eyes with the back of her hand, her eyes never leaving Nettie's.

"You are a brave Montana cowgirl."

Minutes passed in agonizing slowness while Ruthie sniffled and hiccupped. Finally she wiped her eyes with the back of her hand. "Okay." Her voice trembled.

"Okay, then." Nettie reached for Ruthie's new outfit, the green satin shirt with white piping, dark blue denims, and white chaps.

"C'mon, now. Let's get you dressed. We have a date with a horse. Lilly-Anne's waiting for you." She stuck her hand into her pocket and took out the silver disc from the bridle Jake had given her so many years ago. "Here's my lucky concho. Hold onto it when you feel scared."

At the underground corrals and stalls, where riders were coming and going, getting horses ready for events or currying them after a ride, the girls stood holding their sidestepping mounts' reins. Ruthie's body was stiff, her face stony. Lilly-Anne's pupils shone big in her blue eyes. Nettie put her hands on Ruthie's shoulders and squeezed gently. She looked into the girl's eyes. "You can do this. Now go out there and wow them."

Ruthie swallowed hard, then grinned. "Okay." She turned to Lilly-Anne. "Let's go show them McLaughlin Brothers how it's done."

With relief, Nettie gave both girls a quick hug. They mounted their horses and rode up the ramp into the arena. Nettie followed on foot, arriving in time to hear the announcer: "And now . . . ladies and gentlemen . . . we have two young girls a-a-l-l the way from Montana . . . with their debut ride. Let's welcome . . . Lilly-Anne Scott and Ruthie Miller!"

The crowd gave enthusiastic, welcoming applause as the girls entered the ring. Nettie perched on the fence beside Trixi to watch, hands clenched between her knees to keep them from trembling.

Her girls looked splendid in their matching green satin shirts, white hats, and chaps. Ruthie's red and Lilly-Anne's blonde braids flowed behind as their horses galloped around the arena. As if riding along with them, Nettie felt the saddle under her, the motion of the horse. She anticipated their first move.

In perfect synchronization, they stood atop their saddles, then slipped down to one side, standing in one stirrup perpendicular to their running horses. Nettie held her breath, feeling her own hand gripping the leather strap as Ruthie's weight shifted, her own feet reaching for a foothold as the girls touched lightly to the ground, leapt back up and across their horses' backs to touch the ground on the other side, and back up again.

The crowd cheered. Trixi hooted. "Way to go, girls!"

Nettie let her breath out, then held it again. *Here it comes. Oh, Lord, let them be safe.*

The horses galloped, their brown bodies sleek, muscles bunching and lengthening. Lilly-Anne nodded to Ruthie. Simultaneously the girls slipped headfirst down the horses' sides and under their bellies, their heads mere inches from the flying hooves.

Nettie leaned forward. *Ruthie, hold tight to the handhold. You can do this!* The girls hung there for agonizing seconds. *Now get your foot out of the stirrup. Don't get hung up!* The terrifying picture of Tad Lucas caught under her horse, being kicked with every step, made Nettie feel nauseated. *C'mon, girls, c'mon!*

Then the heads popped up on the other side, one red, one blonde, and the girls were back in the saddle again.

The roar of the crowd reverberated against Nettie's chest and echoed in her ears. "Yeehaw! They did it!" She and Trixi jumped to the ground, slapped each other on the back, hugged while jumping up and down. Then they dashed to the arena gate to meet Ruthie and Lilly-Anne. Nettie leaped into the air, her arm raised to the sky, waving her hat. The girls slid off their horses, matching wide grins lighting up their faces. They hugged each other, then Margaret and Thelma who came rushing from the stands, then Trixi and Nettie.

Ruthie gave Nettie an extra-hard squeeze. "We did it, Mrs. Moser! We did it!" Her green eyes were bright and shiny. "Thanks."

Nettie squeezed back. "You did it. It was all you." Her vision blurred with tears and she hugged both girls again. "You girls were fantastic. That under-belly move was smooth as silk. I'm so proud of you both."

After Margaret and Thelma had performed, adding a couple of simple rope tricks to their routine, Nettie and Trixi waited with the girls to get their scores. Lilly-Anne twirled her braids and chewed the ends, while Ruthie rocked back and forth on her boot heels, then paced in front of the chutes. "What if we don't win? We did good, didn't we?" She looked at Nettie with her big green eyes.

Nettie put an arm around Ruthie. "It doesn't matter if you win. You were brave, you rode, and you did the best you know how. That's what matters to us Montana cowgirls."

The microphone squealed, and the emcee announced the trick-riding results: The McLaughlin Brothers first, and Ruthie and Lilly-Anne second in the under-twenty category.

Nettie and Trixi herded the group of giggling, shrieking girls back to the underground corrals. Buck and Fritz Truan met them to help put the horses away.

"Well, congratulations, girls. You did real well, all of you." Buck hugged his daughter and Ruthie and shook hands with Trixi and her girls. "That was some show."

Fritz stood back and grinned. "How 'bout we take you young cowgirls out to celebrate tonight?"

"Yippee! Can we?" Ruthie grabbed Lilly-Anne and swung her around.

"Sounds great." Nettie caught Trixi's eye and they grinned at each other.

"We'll meet you at the Cowboy Café around the corner at six." Fritz touched his hat and strode off toward his own stall.

Trixi grinned. "Well, I wonder if they let cowgirls eat there."

Buck slapped his thigh and guffawed. "I guess they'd better, especially after today's ridin'." They all joined him in giddy laughter.

Nettie grabbed Ruthie's hand. "All right, girls, we have a little time to go back to our rooms and freshen up."

As the group left the arena, Vivian White met them. "Great trick riding today!"

The girls blushed and stood a little taller as they thanked her.

"I've done a little of that myself, so I know how hard it is." Vivian chuckled. "And you came in second to those McLaughlin Brothers. That is some accomplishment, especially for first-timers."

"I'm so proud of them I could just bust." Nettie patted the young cowgirls' shoulders. "Say, Vivian, we're all meeting at the Cowboy Café to celebrate. Why don't you join us?"

"I'd love it. See y'all there."

Nettie and the girls entered the long, narrow restaurant packed with Levi's- and boot-clad men and women. Autographed photos of cowboys and cowgirls adorned the walls, along with spurs, stirrups, and various styles of hats, even a wagon wheel "chandelier." It reminded her of the Range Riders Café in Miles City and she felt instantly at home. Buck, Fritz, and another man were already seated at a large, round table in the back of the restaurant, mugs of beer in front of them.

Buck was in the midst of a story: " . . . this cowpoke fell in love with a New York gal and came to live here. But he missed the west so much that after a time he started the Cowboy Café as a refuge for himself and his fellow westerners. I, for one, am eternally grateful." He turned to the women and stood. "Howdy, ladies. Please, have a seat."

Fritz introduced them to a young man with one arm bandaged and in a sling. "This here's my roommate, Wally McConnell, from Boise."

Nettie shook his hand. "Hello, neighbor. We're from Montana. Have you been to the Garden before?"

Wally shook his head. "Naw, this is my first time."

"Us too!" Ruthie giggled and glanced at Lilly-Anne who fluttered her eyelashes. Margaret and Thelma ducked their heads, grinning down at the table.

Nettie hid a smile. Young girls and good-looking cowboys . . .

The young man turned toward the girls. "I hear you done real good today."

Lilly-Anne and Ruthie blushed and tittered again. "Thanks."

"What did you win?" Wally asked.

All four girls dug into their purses and took out hand-tooled leather makeup cases. "We have to take them back and get our names on them," Ruthie explained.

Vivian joined them just then and asked to look at the cases. "Hmm, nice." She glanced at Nettie and Trixi. "I hear the McLaughlin Brothers got twenty dollars each."

Trixi nodded. "Yup. That's the way of the rodeo. The men get the cash, the women get the trinkets."

As proud as she was of the girls, disappointment washed over Nettie. Some cowgirls, like Tad Lucas, made a good living at riding, but most risked their bones and reputations for a few dollars and a cigarette case. "Doesn't seem right, does it?"

"Nope, it sure don't." Vivian picked up a menu. "And I think we need to do something about it."

"Yes, I believe we do." Nettie nodded. But how could they fight the male-dominated RAA and their rules? Women were already losing their ability to compete in many western rodeos. Fortunately, the east hadn't yet climbed on that bandwagon.

The waitress stopped at the table. Ruthie and Lilly-Anne sat up straight and politely gave their orders for steaks and pan-fried potatoes. "I'll have the same," Nettie added. The men ordered another round of beer.

"I'll have a beer too," Ruthie put in.

Nettie raised her eyebrows, but the waitress didn't bat an eye. "How about a root beer?"

Ruthie grinned and everyone at the table burst into laughter.

"Wally here just found out he drew Hell's Angel for tomorrow's final contest." Fritz gave a low whistle. "That's some ornery bronc. They save him for last. Ain't hardly nobody stays on him till the end."

"Wow. Really?" Ruthie stared wide-eyed at the men.

Wally shrugged and winced as he looked down at his arm. "I dunno. I'm so beat up from the nine rides I already done. As much as I'd like to give ol' Hell's Angel a run for his money, I don't think I'm in shape to do it."

"Aw, man. This is your big chance. I'd ride 'im again in a heartbeat." Fritz took a gulp of his beer. "He was good for me in thirty-nine."

The steaks arrived and conversation came to a halt while every-one attacked their meals with gusto. Nettie savored every tender bite, wishing Jake and Neil could be here with her to enjoy the food, the rodeo, and the friendly people.

Finally, Fritz mopped his plate with the last of his buttered roll, washed it down with a drink of beer, and leaned back in his chair. "You know what, Wally. If you don't feel up to ridin' ol' Hell's Angel, I think I might go find Dan Hines and see if I could give 'im a go."

Wally's face lit up. "Hey, that sounds like a good plan. I'd like to see you ride that ol' sonuvagun."

"All right, I'll do it." Fritz stood up, put on his hat, and touched his fingers to the brim. "Evenin', ladies. It's been a pleasure."

Nettie and her crew moved slowly with the crowd into the arena on the last night of the Madison Square Garden rodeo. The smell of popcorn wafted from the lobby. Lights blazed from the ceiling where streamers and red, white, and blue bunting hung around the perimeter. Speakers blared a Sousa march. Rodeo fans packed the seats to the rafters to see the final bronc-riding showdown and to hear Gene Autry sing again for the second year.

They found their seats halfway up the bleachers. Ruthie and Lilly-Anne clutched their paper bags of popcorn and swiveled their heads to take in the sights. Nettie watched the audience file in: women wearing smartly tailored dark knee-length suits and colored berets, others in flowered shirtwaist dresses, flat brimmed hats, and open-toed pumps. Nettie smoothed her own belted navy dress and adjusted the fox-fur stole around her shoulders. Thank goodness Jake had suggested she bring some "dress-up" clothes. She didn't feel too out of place.

The marching music stopped. Far below, Foghorn Clancy stepped up on the podium at the judges' stand and bellowed into the micro-phone, "Now, ladies and gentlemen, for your viewing pleasure, we have Gene Autry's Queen's Court."

Six young women rode out into the arena, decked out in white hats, bright-colored silk shirts with fringed leather hanging from the sleeves, and angora chaps. Silver conchos on their bridles and saddles sparkled in the lights.

Ruthie and Lilly-Anne gasped and oohed at the sight, watching the girls' every move.

Oh, yes, the rodeo queens. Nettie admired their stunning outfits, their perfectly coiffed hair, and their flawless skin. *I just wish there were more women competing.*

As Foghorn announced, "Miss Sun Valley, Mary Mercer . . ." introducing each, the girls paraded their horses around the ring, stopping to wave in each direction at the audience. Then they pushed their mounts into a canter around the arena, changing into a figure-eight pattern, waving long, bright scarves behind. Finally they reined the horses to a stop, splitting to form an opening in front of the gate.

"And now . . . the moment you've all been waiting for . . . please welcome . . . the 'singing cowboy,' G-e-n-e Autry!"

Ruthie and Lilly-Anne leaned forward in their seats as the performer burst between the rodeo queens' ranks and bounded up onto the floodlit stage, wearing a white hat and a green shirt with white stitching. His rich baritone voice launched into "Back in the Saddle Again."

One of Nettie's favorite songs. She scooted to the edge of her wooden seat to get a better look at the first big star she'd ever seen in person.

When he finished, the crowd erupted with applause and cheers. The girls screamed their adoration. "He's just so-o-o handsome!" Margaret gushed.

Thelma's face flushed. "Did you see him in *Rancho Grande* last year?"

"No, but now we gotta!" Ruthie shouted.

Nettie grinned.

Autry waved and smiled. "Good evening, ladies and gentlemen. I'm glad to be back at the Madison Square Garden." Then he began his new hit, "Blueberry Hill," to enthusiastic whistles and hoots. Nettie found herself singing along.

After Autry's concert, during intermission, Vivian came to sit with Nettie's group.

"Wasn't that keen?" Ruthie gushed. "He's so good lookin'!"

"Sings pretty good too." Nettie stood to stretch, the glow of the music still warming her. "I sure do like his songs."

"Me too," Vivian agreed. "He wowed the crowd last year, so the organizers decided to have him back again. I think it's helped bring in even more people this year."

The crowd ebbed and flowed as people got up to visit the concession stands and resettle for the bronc-riding finale. The rodeo queens returned to ride their patterns once again, bright and flashy. Nettie studied their posture to see if there was something she could relate to her girls, then turned to Vivian. "Those young women sit their horses pretty nice, but is that all they do?"

"Well," Vivian drawled. "They were hand-picked by Autry for their looks, and aren't necessarily rodeo riders, but most of 'em do have at least a ranch background. I've seen them put on steer-cutting exhibitions at the Boston Gardens."

Nettie pursed her lips. "This seems to be a trend. Ruthie was gung-ho to ride steers when I first met her. Will she and Lilly-Anne be limited to trick riding and beauty queen contests?"

Ruthie jumped in. "Well, that's not gonna happen to me!"

Foghorn Clancy's voice boomed over the loudspeaker, interrupting their conversation to introduce the first bronc rider. They watched several young men ride, some hitting the dust almost as soon as their horses bolted from the chute, some riding until the buzzer, but not putting on a spectacular show. The applause was warm, but subdued. Nettie shifted in her seat. *Boy, Jake could teach those cowboys a thing or two.*

Then Foghorn announced Buck Scott, Lilly-Anne's dad. The girls scooted to the edges of their seats. Nettie leaned forward. Buck had drawn Moonbeam, a silver stallion that burst from the chute, snorting and throwing his hind legs high, then pawing the air with his front hooves.

"Ride 'im, Dad!" Lilly-Anne yelled.

Nettie crossed her fingers.

Buck spurred high and waved his left arm, meeting every jump and twist. Then, as the bronc swung his head around to swap ends, Buck's spur caught in the head rigging.

The crowd gasped.

"No!" Lilly-Anne covered her mouth with both hands.

Nettie's heart stopped, watching as Buck's body rocked to the side. He struggled to keep his balance. The horse threw its head around to the other side and Buck flew out of the saddle. He hung off the horse, one hand clutching the saddle rigging. Two pickup men galloped to his side. One grabbed the bronc's halter. The other swooped down to grab Buck and untangle his spur, then set him down.

Buck limped over to retrieve his hat, swatting it against his leg to dust it off. He secured it on his head and gave a sheepish grin and a bow.

"Oh m'gosh, oh m'gosh, he could've been killed." Ruthie panted.

Seeing Lilly-Anne's ashen face, Nettie hugged her. "He's okay." She reached out to pat Ruthie's shoulder. "He's okay." She let out a long, slow breath. *Thank you, Lord.*

The crowd applauded. Then the girls jumped to their feet and cheered with relief.

Lilly-Anne leaned into Nettie's embrace as the next several rides allowed them to regain their breath and relax enough to enjoy the show once again.

Foghorn's raspy voice rose as he announced the last rider of the night. "And now . . . ladies and gentlemen . . . we've saved the best for last. . . . On Hell's Angel . . . voted the greatest bucking horse in America . . . is . . . last year's W-o-r-r-ld Champeen Cowboy . . . Fritz . . . Truan!"

The crowd's applause roared in Nettie's ears. She rose to her feet along with thousands around her as the big black bronc exploded from the chute and leapt for the sky.

Nettie saw a flash of daylight between cowboy and saddle. She gritted her teeth. Fritz regained his seat, spurred, and waved. Hell's Angel snorted. His great muscular body heaved. He twisted and turned, nearly kissed the ground with his head, and kicked his hind legs higher into the air than Nettie'd ever seen. She caught a glimpse of fiery eyes. *Like the devil himself.*

But Fritz settled into the rhythm of the dancing dervish as if he'd been glued to the saddle. A big grin on his face, he kept spurring and waving.

The buzzer blew. Nettie screamed with the crowd. Fritz slipped easily from the saddle and landed in a run. He raised both arms into the air. He'd done it! Fritz Truan had ridden the devil bronc!

CHAPTER THIRTEEN

Nettie hugged Vivian White goodbye on the train platform. Then the cowgirl scurried away to board her own train home to Oklahoma, calling back over her shoulder, "Let's keep in touch."

Nettie waved and blinked back a tear. She'd made a new friend.

"C'mon, Lilly-Anne, I'll race ya!" Ruthie grabbed her bag and rushed ahead to jump on the train. Lilly-Anne ran close behind.

"Girls! Slow down!" Nettie took a deep breath of the smoky air. "Wait for us." She turned to Trixi. "Are you ready for this?"

The other woman laughed. "We're goin' home. I'm just about as excited as they are."

"Don't worry. We'll go ride herd." Margaret trotted forward with Thelma.

Anticipation welled up in Nettie, warring with sadness at leaving the thrill of the rodeo events, the pomp of the parades and concerts, and the excitement of the crowd cheering around her. But this was not real. She was going home. Home. To Jake and Neil. Back to a normal life with the horses and cattle, chores and haying, yes, even cooking and cleaning. Oh, she had missed it all so much. She ached to feel Jake's arms around her. Taking a deep breath, she forced herself to board sedately and walked the length of the car to where the girls were already bouncing on the upholstery, vying for the seat closest to the window.

Thelma got up from her window seat facing them and pulled Ruthie into it. "There, now you both have a window."

Nettie eased into a vacant place across the aisle. Trixi sat beside her, and presently Buck joined them after having made arrangements for the horses. The whistle blew, smoke spewed past the windows, and the train began to move. Chug-chug, click-clack. The oily smell increased and Nettie covered her nose and mouth with her red bandanna.

Ruthie and Lilly-Anne kept up a running chatter as New York's tall buildings slid by. "Look at that one. It goes right up to heaven!" Their noses pressed against the glass. "No, look, that one's even bigger!"

After they could no longer see the city skyline, they took out their new leather makeup cases to admire their names hand-tooled on the front. Taking out their souvenirs—a brass coin from Madison Square Garden, necklaces, and postcards—the young girls reminisced with the older ones about their adventure in New York City.

Nettie pulled her footrest up and let her body sink into the upholstered seat. An adventure indeed, a dream come true. She didn't regret one moment of the trip, but she could hardly wait to see Jake and Neil and tell them all about it.

"Mrs. Moser!" Ruthie's voice startled Nettie out of a catnap.

She blinked. "Yes, Ruthie, what is it?"

The girl's freckled faced beamed above hers. "Mr. Scott says he's going to treat us to supper in the dining car!"

Nettie looked up to see Buck standing in the aisle. "Are you sure? There's seven of us."

He chuckled. "I'm sure. I won just enough in my rides to splurge on you ladies. You don't have to make do with homemade lunches this trip."

"All right." Nettie stood. "I guess I am a bit hungry."

Buck led the way and opened the door to the vestibule between cars. The roar of the wind and the clatter of the wheels on the tracks assaulted Nettie. She could see the railroad ties flashing beneath.

"Oh." Ruthie stopped and stared down at the moving metal plates that covered the couplings below.

"Just grab the handholds, here, and jump across when the plates overlap," Buck encouraged. "Like this." He stepped nimbly over to the other side.

Lilly-Anne copied his lead, and after a moment's hesitation, Ruthie leapt too. Nettie and the other women followed without mishap.

The dining car greeted them with low lighting, the savory smells of roasted meat, and the murmur of diners enjoying their meals. Buck led the way to where people lined up behind a tuxedoed maître d' at the end of the car.

Wide-eyed, Ruthie exclaimed, "Look at that man's suit. Just like on a wedding cake!"

Nettie put her finger to her lips as the waiting guests snickered and even the maître d' smiled. Ruthie's face matched her hair, but she still grinned.

The host seated them at a table covered in a white linen tablecloth with cloth napkins in pewter napkin rings. "Why do we need two forks?" With a puzzled look, Ruthie picked up the silverware that lay along the top of the plate. "And two spoons?"

Trixi smiled. "One fork for the salad and one for your meal. One spoon for soup and one for dessert."

"Wow." Ruthie gazed at her reflection in the silver spoon.

Nettie remembered her wedding trip to Great Falls when they'd eaten in the dining car and she'd been filled with wonder too, just like Ruthie. Everything was so fancy, so different from eating at home. It still seemed like a great luxury.

A Negro waiter brought a small loaf of warm bread and took their orders.

"Wait till Mama hears about this: a man with black skin and the fancy tables and all the silverware!" Ruthie's eyes were big and round.

Nettie covered a smile with her napkin, watching the young girl sit up regally and mimic the grown-ups, placing a slice of bread on a small plate and using the small knife to butter the bread. Ruthie and

Lilly-Anne watched to see which spoon Trixi chose to eat the vegetable soup, and stifled giggles when Thelma and Margaret dipped their fingers in a pewter bowl of water, then dried them on their napkins.

Nettie buttered her own bread. *Ruthie is trying to act more ladylike. Maybe she is growing up a little.*

The waiter brought a steak knife with Buck's T-bone, the girls tucked into their fried chicken, and Nettie and Trixi savored their breaded trout. Dessert was apple pie, served with a gray pottery crock of cheddar cheese.

"Mmm. This is the best meal I ever ate." Ruthie wiped her mouth with her napkin. "But don't tell Mama I said that!"

Smiling, Nettie pushed her plate away. "Buck, thank you for this wonderful treat."

"My pleasure, ladies." He leaned back and patted his stomach. "I think I'll retire to the bar car for a drink and a smoke."

Nettie led the girls back through the quiet dining car, then the noisy, lurching vestibule to their seats, and prepared for a night of sleeping upright. Lilly-Anne and Ruthie lifted their armrests up and stretched out together on the seats, giggling as they jostled for a tiny bit of room.

"I wish we could've had a sleeper car," Ruthie said.

"That would've taken a lot more money." Nettie leaned her head back against the linen-covered rest and closed her eyes. When she woke again she'd be that much closer to home.

The train slowed as it entered the outskirts of Miles City. Ruthie and Lilly-Anne knelt on their seats to look out. "We're almost there," Ruthie squealed.

Nettie peered out her window at the brown, windswept prairie. No skyscrapers here. You could see forever. No horns blaring from speeding automobiles or throngs of people rushing to nowhere. The cottonwood and willow trees lining the Yellowstone River welcomed her with jeweled fall leaves winking in the late afternoon light. She sighed happily. This was more like it. Home. Her personal cathedral.

The whistle blew, smoke billowed, and the train eased into the station. Passengers filled the aisles, laughing and chatting as they headed toward the exit. Nettie glimpsed two tall cowboys standing on the platform.

"Jake and Neil are here!" She hadn't expected them to meet her. Her heart fluttered like a leaf in the wind. Neil was as tall as his dad. *He's a man now.*

Buck stood. "Well, I see you have your own ride home."

Nettie grabbed her purse and overnight case and stood up. Across the aisle, the girls gathered their coats, lunch bags, and new leather makeup cases, checking newly applied lipstick in the mirrors one last time, blotting it with a handkerchief as Nettie had instructed.

"We're home! We're home!" Ruthie bounced on her toes. "Oh, I can't wait to tell Mama about the train ride and that huge arena and all the horses and cowboys and bulls and steers and how good we did and . . ." She ran out of breath.

Lilly-Anne grabbed Buck's sleeve. "Dad, can we come with you to get the horses when the freight comes in?"

"Sure." He nodded. "Mrs. Moser, it's been a pleasure. Maybe we'll do it again sometime."

"Thank you so much, Mr. Scott. I appreciate all you've done for me, and for Ruthie. It's been a wonderful experience." She turned to Trixi, still seated with her charges, waiting to travel on to Missoula. "Thank you, too. You were such an inspiration."

Trixi grinned. "I'm sure we'll be seeing you soon. Those two young 'uns will go far."

Nettie was as skittish as a colt, but she forced herself to move slowly and not elbow her way through the crowded, sweaty- and oily-smelling car. As the conductor took her arm to help her down the steps, she heard Neil shout, "There's Mom!"

She clasped her hands to her heart and turned. Big grins lit up the men's faces as they strode toward her. Nettie dropped her bags and ran to meet them, her arms held out wide.

Jake pushed ahead, enveloped her in his arms, and swung her around. "Welcome home, little gal."

Nettie kissed him long and hard, drinking in his warmth and the familiar sweet smell of horsehair and tobacco. Then she opened one arm to include Neil. "I've missed you guys so much."

"We missed you too, Mom. Especially your cooking." Neil grinned and stepped back.

Nettie laughed. "Well, I'm sure you did just fine. I'll be expecting my supper on the table every weekend night from now on."

Jake kept eyeing her. "You look different . . . sophisticated?"

"Me, sophisticated?" Nettie crossed her eyes and stuck out her tongue. "Naw. You know me better than that."

That evening Nettie regaled Jake and Neil with her adventures in the Big Apple. They ate the coconut macaroon cookies she had brought back from New York and drank countless cups of coffee. Complimenting them on the spotless kitchen, she presented Neil with a miniature statue of the Empire State Building and Jake a beaten-copper ashtray in the shape of New York, "Madison Square Garden" stamped on it.

Jake gazed into her face. "So has the travel bug got you now? You gonna be off to the next big doin's before we know it?"

Nettie covered his big calloused hands with hers. "This was an experience beyond my dreams. It was terrifying and overwhelming, but exciting and wonderful at the same time." She smiled. "But my home is here, with you and Neil." She looked over at her son. "There's no place I'd rather be."

Nettie thought she saw Jake's shoulders relax, and she launched into more tales from the trip. Neil rolled his eyes at Ruthie's antics, and Jake wanted all the details about the bronc-riding contests.

Nettie grinned at him. "I kept thinking you should've been there to teach them a thing or two."

He chuckled. "Yeah, sounds like I coulda. But I would like to have watched Truan ride Hell's Angel. That would be something to see."

She nodded. "Yes, it truly was."

It was long after midnight when Nettie snuggled next to Jake, her body thrilling to feel his next to her again. He took her in his arms. "Welcome home, little gal." He kissed her long and deep. She was truly home.

The next morning Nettie woke early. She blinked, expecting to hear the now-familiar noises of the communal bedroom at the YMCA. Peaceful quiet enveloped her; she heard a cow bawl from the pasture, and she reached for Jake, but he was already up. Nettie smiled. Home. Hearing Jake banging around in the kitchen, she rose and dressed. The smell of coffee and frying bacon made her mouth water. She wandered out of the bedroom through the living room, straightening a doily, touching the afghan her mother had crocheted, the pictures of Neil and Gary on the side table. Walking into the kitchen, she put an arm around Jake's waist.

"Mornin', little gal. Sleep well?"

Nettie stretched. "Oh, yes. There's nothing like your own bed." Little gal. How she'd missed that endearment. She tilted her head and kissed his cheek. "And your favorite husband beside you."

Jake paused with the ladle of pancake batter over the pan. "Oh, so you have more than one husband, huh?"

She cuffed him on the arm. "You know what I mean."

Neil came in from doing chores and set the milk bucket on the counter. "Dad drew the short straw, so he had to cook this morning." They all laughed, their easy camaraderie settling around Nettie like a warm quilt. Thank goodness, the guys seemed to have gotten along while she was gone.

After breakfast, Jake poured another cup of coffee and leaned back in his chair to roll a smoke, dropping stray bits of tobacco in the souvenir ashtray. Neil fidgeted in his chair, stacked the dishes, and took them to the sink. He sat again, his gaze moving from Jake to Nettie and back.

"What's got into you, honey?" Nettie reached over to ruffle his black hair. "You got ants in your pants?"

Neil looked down at the table. "No." Then to his dad, "Well, are we going to show Mom or not?"

Jake blew smoke from the upturned corner of his mouth. "In due time, son, in due time."

"All right. You guys have my curiosity up now." Excitement tickled her like a ten-year-old on her birthday. "What's going on?"

Neil jumped up. "C'mon, Mom." He took her hand and led her to the door. Jake followed, stopping in the yard to snuff out his cigarette butt with his boot.

When they reached the corral, Neil instructed her to wait and ran into the barn. Nettie glanced at Jake, but his face remained stoic. No clues there. The barn door opened, and Neil came out leading a gray roan mare.

Nettie took in a sharp breath. "Who's this?"

Jake grinned then. "This here's Pigeon. Your welcome-home present."

The horse held her head proudly, as if she had Arabian blood. Her light- and dark-gray dapples blended into an almost silver sheen. "Ohhh. She's a beauty." Nettie reached out toward the mare's nostrils, letting Pigeon snuffle her hand. Then she stroked the horse's face, moving down her neck and legs. "Good conformation." The regal head turned to follow Nettie's actions then rubbed against her shoulder. "She seems quite gentle."

"That she is," Jake agreed. "We took Windy in to auction and found her."

Nettie gasped. "You sold Windy? Why?" Her words came out halting, shaky.

Jake averted his gaze. "Yup. I never did trust that horse. Not a good ride for you."

"But . . . you sold him and didn't tell me?" Nettie put her fists on her hips and glared at her husband. They'd made changes while she was gone. What else had they done?

"Now, honey." Jake peered into her face. "I rode him every day for two weeks, thought I could dampen some of that skittishness. Neil did, too, every weekend. But it wasn't workin'."

Neil put a hand on her arm. "Mom, don't be mad at us. We just figured you'd be so much happier riding a horse that isn't going to throw you every time a sage hen rustles the brush."

Nettie's flare of anger melted under her son's wistful face and Jake's hopeful look. She'd loved Windy's thoroughbred spirit, but she had to admit he wasn't as enjoyable to ride as Tootsie had been. And she'd been on his back when she'd fallen and dislocated her shoulder. Finally, she smiled. "Okay, you two schemers. I know you're just trying to take care of this old girl. Thank you."

Relief flooded both men's faces. "We wanted to do it for you, Mom. We worried about you every time you went for a ride." Neil grinned.

Nettie grasped Pigeon's halter. "Go get my saddle for me. I'm going for a ride."

⌐⌐

The crisp late-October air enveloped Nettie as she nudged Pigeon forward, Jake and Neil following along on their horses. The mare's shoulder muscles rippled. "Good girl." Pigeon's ears flicked back as she eased into a lope across the sun-dried prairie. Nettie tightened her knees and leaned forward. Now a gallop. What a nice, smooth gait, like riding a cloud! The horse ran, never faltering, through the gullies and over the rolling hills, just like Tootsie had. Nettie shook her hair from its bun and let it blow free. Ah, this was the life she loved.

She reined Pigeon in at the top of a rise and waited for her men to catch up. "This horse is a dream to ride, just like Tootsie. Thank you."

Jake grinned back at her. "We figured you'd like her, little gal."

"Yeah, Mom, now I don't have to worry about you all week while I'm at school."

"Now, you guys just listen to me—you don't need to protect me. I'm a big girl. What will make me happy is you finishing school, young man." Nettie grinned gleefully. "Race ya!" She urged Pigeon forward, leaning low on the horse's neck. The three thundered over the prairie, whooping and laughing.

Nettie reined in Pigeon at the top of a rise overlooking the windmill and waited for her men to catch up. "You got me the bestest, fastest horse. Thanks!"

They rode down to where the cattle clustered around the well, taking turns drinking from the water tank. Jake dismounted, checked the pumping mechanism, and nodded his approval. "It's puttin' out water. That's what's important."

Nettie's heart felt as full as that well. Skirting the now-dry reservoir on their way home, she rode her dandy new horse over the familiar terrain, beside her men. Back at home, she glanced at Jake as she unsaddled and then threw her arms around him. "You know, there's no place I'd rather be than right here, right now. But New York was a fantastic experience and I do want to go with the girls to help them follow their dream."

His blue eyes lit up and he put an arm around her. "I'm proud of you, little gal. Just as long as you always come home to me."

She leaned into his strong, warm body, smiled, and closed her eyes.

CHAPTER FOURTEEN

November gusted in on heavy, cold snow clouds and by midmonth the ground was blanketed in white. Nettie and Jake loaded hay on the pickup every morning to take out to the cows and chopped ice out of the water tank, spending long hours out in the freezing cold. Neil came home for his birthday on the ninth, and again for Thanksgiving. They enjoyed a turkey dinner, then played gin rummy all afternoon, the new round-topped wood-grained Philco playing Christmas music in the background.

Contentment swaddled Nettie like a warm blanket. Her men seemed to be getting along so much better and here they were, all together. She sighed happily. Money in the bank, food on the table, a new horse, and Neil home. Life was good.

December brought even more snow, and Neil missed a weekend coming home from school because of a blizzard, but was able to come the next week.

Nettie heard Jake and Neil stomp the snow off their boots on the porch. It was nice to have Neil home to help feed the cows and horses. She turned the pieces of chicken frying in the cast iron skillet and stuck a fork into the boiling potatoes to test their doneness.

The door opened and an icy blast blew in with the men.

"Smells awful good in here." Jake shrugged out of his heavy sheepskin coat.

"Yeah. I'm starved." Neil sat in a kitchen chair to pull off his boots and bib overalls.

Nettie grabbed three plates from the cupboard and set them on the table. "Dinner's almost ready. Fried chicken. Sunday special."

Jake kissed her on the cheek, then held his hands close to the heat of the cook stove and rubbed them together. "It's nippy out there today. Hey, son, why don't you turn on the radio. Let's get some news."

Neil clicked the knob on the tabletop radio and turned the dial until they heard organ music and a choir singing the Doxology at the end of "The Lutheran Hour" broadcast. Suddenly the somber voice of a local newscaster broke in: "Hold on, folks . . . what is happening . . . ? Listen to this." Static. A pause. Then a national broadcaster's voice came on: "We repeat the devastating news—the Japanese have bombed Pearl Harbor in Honolulu, Hawaii . . ."

Nettie froze. Her spatula clattered to the floor. "What? What's he saying?"

All three of them huddled close to the radio. " . . . surprise attack by three hundred ninety aircraft of the Imperial Navy of Japan on the US Pacific Fleet and bases at Oahu, Hawaii, at just before eight o'clock this morning sank four US battleships . . ."

Neil's eyes were round behind his wire-rimmed glasses. "Oh my gosh."

Nettie put an arm around her son and held her breath.

The announcer continued. " . . . receiving reports . . . numbers of American dead are mounting . . . last report is in the hundreds, may reach a thousand . . ."

An icy chill shook Nettie. Americans. Dead. She looked into Jake's gray face. "We're going to war, aren't we?"

Rising from his chair like an old man, he walked to the window, staring out while he reached into his shirt pocket for his tobacco and cigarette papers.

"What if they bomb us next?" Neil's face shone with an eerie, expectant light. "We'd better get all our rifles cleaned and ready."

Nettie's stomach knotted. "Oh, honey, we're a long way from any-place they'd want to attack."

"Be more likely to happen out on the west coast." Jake's voice rumbled low from across the room.

The smell of burning chicken penetrated Nettie's fog and she jumped up to take the pan off the wood-burning stove. Tears splashed into the pan. Her whole body quivered. "I've ruined the chicken," she wailed.

Jake and Neil were by her side in an instant, encircling her with their arms. She sobbed. *What about Gary? And Neil? I can't even save the chicken.*

"There, there, little gal. A little burnt chicken isn't something to cry over." Jake rubbed her back, and she cried even harder. Finally wrung dry, Nettie got a dipperful of water and splashed it on her face over the dishpan.

Sunday dinner was forgotten as they huddled around the radio for the rest of the afternoon. Jake reached for her hand, and Neil got out the World Atlas to see where Peal Harbor was. At one point, Montana Senator Burton K. Wheeler broadcast a statement, changing his earlier anti-war stance. "We've got to lick them," he stated emphatically.

Jake and Neil jabbed fists in the air. "Yeah."

Finally, Nettie couldn't listen any more. While Jake and Neil stayed up late to hear more reports, Nettie lay in bed, tossed by worries. War. What an ugly word. How would it affect Montana? Her family? Neil. What if he got the idea to go too? She curled into a fetal position. He had just turned seventeen. At least he wouldn't be drafted until he was twenty-one, and he couldn't enlist until he was eighteen without her and Jake's permission.

The next day, Neil stayed home from school. After chores, they all gathered once again to listen to the staticky reports coming over the Philco from around the world.

" . . . and now, the president of the United States, Franklin Delano Roosevelt, as he addresses Congress . . ."

The familiar voice was forceful and penetrating. "Yesterday, December 7, 1941, a date which will live in infamy, the United States of America was suddenly and deliberately attacked . . ."

The president spoke for six minutes. Nettie's stomach turned sour. She covered her trembling lips with icy fingers and struggled to breathe.

Roosevelt concluded, "I ask that the Congress declare . . . a state of war . . ."

Nettie sat stone still for a moment. "This is it, then."

Jake put a big, calloused hand over hers and squeezed. His shoulders hunched.

Neil caught her gaze with bright eyes that seemed magnified behind his glasses.

The station returned to its regular broadcasting with the gentle notes of Beethoven's "Moonlight Sonata." Nettie stared out at the tranquil, snow-covered prairie. "Will things ever be the same?" she wondered. "What can we do?"

The news announcer broke into the music. "Congress has just declared war on Japan, with only one representative, Montana's own Jeannette Rankin, voting against the declaration."

Jake grunted in disapproval. "Leave it to a woman . . ."

Nettie faced him. "She has the courage of her convictions."

Jake pounded his fist on the table. "They attacked us, Nettie. We can't let 'em get away with that."

"Yeah, Dad's right." Neil leaned forward. "We can't just do nothing."

"Soldiers have to be at least eighteen." Heat coursed through her, melting away her numbness. Didn't Neil understand the danger? Didn't Jake realize he could lose his son? And Gary was already in the middle of it.

"I'm going out to feed the horses." She grabbed her coat off the hook by the door and strode outside toward the barn. The cold air prickled the hairs inside her nose, but she breathed deeply, trying to get a handle on the turmoil inside. As she walked into the barn, the horses greeted her with whickers and snorts. Nettie stood at the empty stall. *I wish you were here, Tootsie. I need my friend.*

She stopped and stroked each horse, breathed in their tangy scent, and finally buried her face in Pigeon's mane. Gradually her inner upheaval calmed.

After a short time, Jake came into the barn and rested his hip against the stall next to her.

Nettie grabbed his hand and looked into his eyes. "Neil."

Jake's lips squeezed into a tight line. "I know." He stroked her hair. "I know."

Nettie leaned into his warm tobacco smell, holding him for dear life.

~

The next Friday afternoon, Nettie and Jake drove to Forsyth to pick Neil up from school. More people than normal bustled through the streets with a buzz of unusual energy. A group of men gathered around a storefront window with a bright poster proclaiming, "The United States Army, Then, Now, and Forever" and another titled "Keep 'em Flying." Just yesterday the radio had announced that Japan's allies, Germany and Italy, had declared war on the US.

Nettie's breath caught in her throat. All those young men who'd already enlisted. Too young. How could their mothers bear it? How was Margie holding up, with Gary gone? She held both hands over her heart and closed her eyes in a silent prayer. *Keep them safe, Lord.*

Jake pulled up in front of the Stockman's Bar. "Since we're early, let's go in for a drink."

Old friends greeted them as they threaded their way through the crowd. The saloon hummed with war fever. Nettie caught threads of conversations all around her. "Might as well sign up. Can't make no money here." And, "Yeah, my cousin joined the army the day after the

Japs bombed us." Or, "Well, thank the good Lord I'm too old to go," all punctuated by fists slammed on the bar and colorful expletives about the "yellow menace."

Nettie rubbed her arms. How could they be so casual about this? Boys barely older than Neil would sacrifice . . . she shivered.

They sat at the long, wooden bar and Jake signaled for a whiskey. Next to him sat an older cowboy Nettie recognized but couldn't remember the name. "Howdy, folks. So what d'you think about all this hoopla over in the South Pacific?"

Jake shook his head as he reached for his drink. Nettie turned to the cowboy. "It's a terrible, terrible thing."

He nodded. "Yup. We all figured we'd just won the war to end all wars."

"You were there?" Jake signaled for another drink.

The old man nodded. He stared into his glass for a long time, muttering, as if retracing his war journey. Then he glanced up. "Your son going in?"

Nettie's mouth went dry at the mere suggestion.

Jake took a sip of his drink and thumped the glass on the bar. "If he's called, I s'pose he'll go. I hear Army pay's pretty good. Hell, I'd go if I was a few years younger."

Nettie's jaw dropped. Was Jake out of his mind? For a long moment she couldn't speak while Jake rambled on. She glared at him. "Neil is only seventeen."

Jake turned to her with raised eyebrows. "C'mon, little gal, he's a man now. You know we can't stop him if—"

A leather-faced woman leaned around from her perch at the bar. "Aw, honey, this ain't gonna get you anywhere. The men's got themselves war fever."

The pain made Nettie's heart feel as though it would burst from her chest. *Neil. My only child.* She grabbed Jake's arm and shook it. "Yes, we can stop him! We don't have to sign any papers. Promise me!"

The buzz of conversation around them died. Jake eyes widened and he leaned back. "All right, all right, little gal. Calm down. It's okay." He patted her shoulder.

Nettie pulled away, teeth clenched. As if she were just a child needing reassurance.

He tossed back his drink and stood. "Guess we better get going." He cradled her arm in his and led her to the door. Through her haze, Nettie heard someone say, "They all gotta go."

In the pickup, Jake peered at her. "Everyone has a duty to their country, little gal. Wars gotta be won."

Nettie released a breath past the lump in her throat. "Neil has six months to finish school and another year until he turns eighteen. I pray this war will be over before that."

Jake patted her hand. "I'm sure it will be."

A few minutes later, they pulled up to the dormitory to meet Neil, who ran out and threw his duffle bag into the bed of the pickup. He leaned into the window on the passenger side. "Mom, Dad. You'll never believe this—five guys from my class never showed up for school this week. They enlisted!"

Nettie's heart froze. "Oh, no." She looked at Jake, pleading with her eyes.

Jake opened his door, got out, and strode around the front of the vehicle. "Son." He put his hands on Neil's shoulders. "Finish school. Then we'll see."

Neil's hazel eyes blinked behind his glasses. "But, Dad—" He broke off and looked at Nettie.

"You've got to promise." She turned her face away, not wanting him to see the tear trickling down her cheek.

Neil let out a sharp breath and his shoulders slumped. "Can we at least talk about it?"

"No." Jake opened the pickup door. "Now, get in. We're going home."

Nettie scooted to the middle as Neil slumped into the seat.

Jake slammed the door shut.

He is too young yet. He is too young. Nettie repeated the phrase to herself over and over on the way home as if it would keep him from growing up and leaving her.

❦

The next morning, Neil came in from doing chores, shed his boots and coveralls, and slumped into a chair. Nettie put down her dishrag and sat next to him. "What's wrong, honey?"

He ran his hands through his thick, black hair. "Mom, Dad acts like he's mad at me or something. What did I do?"

Nettie chewed the inside of her cheek. How to answer. "Your dad's not angry at you. Why do you think that?"

"He won't talk to me. He just cusses and mumbles and stomps around."

Searching her son's face, Nettie delayed her answer. *Lord, give me the right words.* "That's just the way he is when he's frustrated."

Neil frowned. "What is he frustrated about?"

"This war. He's too old to enlist and . . ." Nettie took a breath, trying to still her heartbeat. *I can't tell him what to do; he might just do the opposite.*

"He can't go, but he doesn't want *me* to go. What does he want me to do?" He looked up at her, his hazel eyes blinking behind his glasses. "Maybe I'm the one who's frustrated! Dad doesn't like my music; he doesn't see any sense in going to college. I don't want to stay here and work for him the rest of my life." He got up and paced. "If you haven't noticed, we don't see eye to eye on ranching. Or anything, for that matter."

Dread pooled in Nettie's stomach. She was only too aware of that. But they had seemed to be getting along better lately. "Oh, honey. I know." She stood and reached up to put her hands on his shoulders.

"Listen, college is your dream. I don't know how we'll come up with the money, but I want you to go. I want you to follow your dream."

Neil straightened. "Well, the National Guard takes seventeen-year-olds. I could earn money to put toward college, and I probably wouldn't have to go overseas."

No. She had to sit, holding her arms tight over her stomach. Her voice came out quavery at first. "Neil, honey, I need you to promise me." Taking a deep breath, Nettie strengthened her tone. "Promise me you will not enlist in the National Guard. Promise me you will finish school and work with your dad at least a year. I will find a way to send you to college. I promise you that."

Neil went to the window and stared out, his shoulders slumped. Finally, he turned back to her. "I'll finish school." He let out a deep sigh.

Relief flooded Nettie as she hugged him.

Neil shrugged on his coveralls. "Guess I'd better get back out there and help with the feeding." He picked up his boots and stepped outside.

The door closed with a resolute thump.

CHAPTER FIFTEEN

January and February's snow and daily feedings turned into snowmelt runoff and gumbo mud that caked inches deep on Nettie's boots when she walked across the barnyard. A faint tinge of green painted the rolling prairie with a promise of spring.

In town, the talk in the grocery stores and the bars centered on the war. Farmers grumbled that rubber was being rationed. President Roosevelt called on citizens to help by contributing scrap rubber to be recycled: old tires, rubber raincoats and shoes, garden hose, bathing caps. Nettie heard remarks like "that traitor Jeannette Rankin" and "bomb them Japs (or Huns)." Everyone had a story about a relative or friend who had enlisted, even a new division of the army called the Women's Army Corps.

A letter from Gary gave the news that he was in Europe but did not disclose his exact location. Nettie worried about him, but Margie's last letter was filled with brave optimism.

Her blood curdled when she heard a woman proudly say, "My Howard is only fourteen and he ran away with the National Guard." Neil had promised to finish school, but he hadn't actually promised not to enlist. Besides, the new draft laws required that he would have to register when he turned eighteen in November. Even Jake would have to register until he turned forty-five next year. Jake remained optimistic the war would be over before that.

At home, an uneasy truce existed between Jake and his son. They worked together without much comment during the weekends, and as spring and graduation approached, Nettie tiptoed as if on broken glass to avoid any confrontation about school, music, or war.

"The Farmers' Co-op is having a meeting in Miles City tonight," Jake announced one morning. "There's talk of supplying beef and grain to the military. Wanna go?"

Nettie nodded. "Sure." She looked forward to getting away from the mud and chores of the ranch. And all the better, if this could help win the war before Neil was old enough to enlist.

They drove to town, did their grocery and supply shopping, and stopped for supper at the Rancher's Bar. Farmers and ranchers from the area filled the restaurant. Nettie saw Bob Askin, Chet Miller, and Buck Scott seated at one table. Chet waved at them as they passed by. "You goin' to the Co-op meeting?"

"Sure am," Jake replied.

"How are Ruthie and Lilly-Anne?" Nettie asked the men.

Chet laughed. "It's been a long winter. Ruthie is chompin' at the bit to get back out to practice."

Buck nodded. "Yeah, Lilly-Anne talks of nothing but that trip to New York. She's ready to go again—to New York, to Cheyenne, anywhere!"

"Wonderful. We'll look forward to that." Nettie smiled. "Good to see you guys. Tell Zelda and Mrs. Scott hello."

Jake found a table and they ordered. Nettie savored her fried steak, thinking of the steak she'd had in New York. This one was better. She paused. That trip just six months ago seemed half a lifetime ago, a magical memory, before the world was at war. Her attention snapped back to the hum of conversation in the room. Dread weighted her shoulders. Would life ever be the same? What would it take to win this war? How many would die before it was over?

At the meeting, Del Smith, operator of the grain elevator, spoke first. "We've received word that the federal government is interested in our Montana wheat to supply the military because it has such a high protein content."

Nettie exchanged a glance with Jake. That was good news for the farmers.

"Hear, hear," someone called from the back of the room to the accompaniment of murmurs and nodding heads.

Next, a representative of the Montana Stockgrowers' Association stood. "This war means the government is going to be the biggest food buyer in the country. And that means our beef, too."

Jake's chair creaked as he leaned forward, following every word, his eyes wide and head nodding. Nettie hadn't seen him look so eager in a long time.

When they got into the pickup, he slapped his hand on the steering wheel. "By golly, we might have a chance to help win the war, and even make some money this year."

Nettie smiled. Maybe Neil would be able to go to college after all. "That would be great, honey."

"We've got about a hundred head of cows. If we get a good calf crop, and we save twenty-five for replacements . . ." He drummed his fingers on the wheel.

"What is the market on calves?" Nettie asked.

"Last I heard it was about ten dollars a hundredweight."

Nettie did some quick arithmetic. "If they average five hundred pounds at market that could bring us about fifty dollars apiece."

"Yeah. And I figure if we plow up that pasture on the east side, we can get a wheat crop this year, too."

"Will that leave enough pasture grass?" A guilty twinge poked her. "It is right to make money off the war, Jake?"

"It's our patriotic duty to provide for our troops," he answered firmly. "We might have to rotate pastures more often." His left leg jiggled on the floorboard. "If we get decent rains, maybe we'll even get a second hay crop this year. We've already got the tractor and plow."

Nettie was silent.

"Everyone has to help if we're going to win the war." Jake opened his arm.

She nestled against him. "I know." Her tears wet his shirt.

Calving began in earnest, and Nettie rode the pasture every day, looking for newborns, making sure they looked healthy and were suckling. It was a joy to ride again, breathing in the soft spring air and looking for new grass and wildflowers. At night, she and Jake took turns getting up to check on the heifers calving for the first time. The young mothers often had trouble and Jake or Nettie would grab the calf-puller to help with the birthing process.

When Neil came home for the weekend, he took Nettie's turn. "I'll get up and check the heifers during the night, Mom."

"I sure appreciate that, honey," she told him. "I'm getting so I enjoy my sleep." She took a deep breath. If he left, it would be much harder to get all the work done.

Neil grinned. "Glad to help."

When the ground dried out enough, he and Jake broke sod to plant wheat. Nettie prayed there would be enough rain to let the grain sprout and develop luscious heads full of protein-rich wheat. It was always a gamble with farming, especially in this part of Montana. Her mind flashed back to the bare pastures of the '30s when they'd trailed their horses to Idaho to find grass. Their future rested on the whims of Mother Nature. On the price of beef and wheat. On the generals and the armies. If ever there was a time to pray, it was now.

Senior graduation was scheduled for Monday, May 11. Nettie dressed with care in her belted navy dress, fox-fur stole, and navy pumps, remembering the last time she'd worn the outfit, at the Autry concert in Madison Square Garden. She fussed with her hair, plucked a couple of gray ones, and pulled it back into a neat bun. Then she penciled in her eyebrows and applied a bright new shade of red lipstick. Would Neil think she was a classy-looking mom or an old fuddy-duddy? She just wanted to go and enjoy the ceremony, be a proud mama, and forget all about her fears and worry for one night.

With a deep breath, she smoothed her skirt and went to the living room where Jake waited, dressed in a natty dark western-cut suit and highly polished boots.

He gave a low whistle. "Ain't you one purty filly." He offered his arm. "Let's go to town."

Scarlet-and-white streamers had transformed the high-school gymnasium into a festive auditorium. The basketball hoops and bleacher seats had been pulled up against the wall and folding chairs filled the floor. People filed in, chattering and laughing. A high-school girl pinned a tea-rose corsage, the class flower, on Nettie's shoulder. Boys ushered parents into the rows behind the twenty-five chairs reserved for the seniors.

Nettie looked at the mimeographed program. "Class Motto: We have crossed the bay, the ocean lies before us." She caught her breath. Several boys who should have been here tonight had already crossed the ocean to fight in the war. How many more would follow?

Thankfully, the first strains of "Pomp and Circumstance" rose from the school band. The audience got to its feet as the graduates filed in to take their seats. Neil walked tall and proud in his blue robe, the tassel on his mortarboard bobbing. Nettie thought he was easily the most handsome kid in the group. He caught her eye and smiled, giving Jake a wink.

Nettie gripped Jake's hand to keep herself from rushing over to him. More than anything she wanted to gather him in her lap like she had when he was little, to sing to him and stroke his dark hair and keep him safe.

Nettie's heart was full as a new-dug well as the principal read the list of Neil's awards and achievements: first-place ribbons for grammar, physics, and economics from the Montana High School Scholastic Tests. And then Neil stood to give the valedictory address. He spoke of new beginnings and meeting them with strength and conviction. He mentioned his classmates who had already begun their adult lives, going off to war.

Nettie's shoulders tensed.

Then he paused and looked over the audience toward Nettie and Jake.

"I want to take this opportunity to thank my parents for their support, for teaching me right and wrong, how to work hard. And I want to especially thank my mom for her strength and courage and for teaching me to follow my dream."

Nettie gasped, fighting tears. The touch of Jake's hand on hers melted her resolve, and she let tears roll down her cheeks, brimming with pride.

"Our son," she whispered. She felt Jake squeeze her hand. He was proud too.

Mortarboards flew into the air as the principal pronounced, "I send you into the world to make your mark. Stay true and strong."

Nettie was composed and dry-eyed for Neil's sake when they searched for him in the hallway outside the gym. She saw him standing tall and handsome in the middle of a group of underclassmen, thrusting out their yearbooks for him to sign. When he was done, Nettie hugged him hard. "Great speech."

Jake touched two fingers to the brim of his hat. "Yeah, good one."

Neil beamed. "Well, let's go to the Cozy Café and celebrate."

They joined the throng of parents and graduates at the cafe, found a small table toward the back, and ordered, exchanging greetings with others.

After Jake finished a slice of apple pie, he leaned back and reached for his tobacco pouch and papers. "So, it's just your mom who taught you strength and courage, huh?"

Neil's bemused gaze met Jake's. "Aw, Dad. You're the strongest person I know." He planted his elbow on the table, forearm up. "Let's arm wrestle, see if you can still beat me."

Jake threw down his cigarette makings and took his son's challenge. They grunted and strained, while Nettie gave encouragement. Finally, Jake pushed Neil's arm to the table.

Neil cuffed his dad on the shoulder. "See, what'd I tell you?"

Jake's eyes glistened. He offered his hand to shake. "Proud of you, son."

When Neil winked at her, Nettie knew he'd let Jake win. She'd never loved him more.

Neil moved his clothes and books home from the dorm and settled into daily ranch chores. If he had thoughts of enlisting he kept them to himself, and Nettie slowly stopped walking on eggshells, expecting the worst. May's showers and warm sunshine brought lush, green pastures and a promise of a good hay crop. In mid-June, Jake and Nettie rode through their herd, admiring the calves' strong, muscular frames.

Jake counted. "Lots of big ones. Looks like time to think about branding." He and Neil spent the afternoon visiting the neighbors to schedule branding parties.

"They'll all be here Friday, then Monday we'll help the Millers, and Thursday the Scotts," Jake announced when they got home.

Nettie spent the next couple of days getting ready, putting beans to soak in a big kettle, bringing jars of shredded venison from the root cellar, and mixing up a tangy barbecue sauce. Neighbor women would bring salads and pies and cookies. The branding crew might have to work like dogs, but they'd eat like kings.

The morning dawned crisp and clear, the promise of a golden-peach sunrise painted across the eastern horizon. Buck and Chet arrived with Ruthie and Lilly-Anne in tow, their horses snorting and prancing in the early spring air.

Nettie waved. "Good morning, girls. Ready to ride?"

"Mornin', Mrs. Moser. We're ready!" Ruthie's red mane was tamed into a long braid. Lilly-Anne adjusted her hat and checked the lariat tied to her saddle.

Nettie saddled up Pigeon. The neighbor women would be along later to get the food organized. No way was Nettie missing out on the roundup.

Most of the herd had gathered around the reservoir. Their white faces turned toward the riders as they approached. Jake and Neil split up to ride in opposite directions around the perimeter of the pasture to gather any strays. Nettie and the girls rode around the back of the reservoir to take the rear of the herd as Chet and Buck got them moving toward the corrals.

The lead cow, old Betsy, headed off in a lope. She'd been through the process many times and knew her way home. The rest of the cattle followed along, mothers stopping occasionally to low softly to their calves. One young heifer decided she wanted none of whatever was happening and took off at a run for the hills, leaving her calf behind. Lilly-Anne spurred her horse after the fleeing cow. The calf, now without his mother, bawled in bewilderment, turned 'round and 'round, then headed in the opposite direction. Before Nettie could follow, Ruthie galloped after the little bull calf, now running as if for his life.

Nettie clucked the rest of the herd along and grinned as she watched the chase. It would be a challenge for Ruthie to catch up and turn that calf back. Those young calves could run like the wind. Just as it looked like a lost cause, Neil trotted over the rise, driving a cow and calf, in time to intercept the runaway. The calf finally gave up its escape plan and fell in beside the other cow and her baby.

As Neil and Ruthie approached the group again, Nettie heard her son say, "Good ridin', Ruthie."

Nettie turned to see the girl's face turn as bright as her hair and smiled to herself as Neil grinned.

Smoke from the branding fire spiraled into the turquoise sky when they neared the corrals. The Gibsons—Ed and Lucille, with their kids, Buck, Hoot, Bill, Kelly, Gail, and Sandy—had already arrived to start the fire and get the irons heating. The cowboys pushed the herd into the small pasture next to the corrals, then dismounted to separate the calves from their mothers and work them into the holding pen.

Nettie manned the gate while Ruthie and Lilly-Anne stood guard at the sides to make sure none escaped. How many times had she participated in this chore during her lifetime? She brushed flies away from her face. Would this be Neil's last?

Once that chore was done, and the cacophony of bawling mothers and babies amplified and echoed off the barn walls, the other women brought coffee and warm cinnamon rolls from the house.

"Thanks, gals, for taking care of the food." Nettie helped Lucille Gibson, Zelda Miller, and Lilly-Anne's grandmother serve the snack. Then she set up a tally sheet, Neil readied the vaccine guns, Chet sharpened his pocketknife, and the Gibson boys checked the branding irons.

Jake took one last swig of coffee and turned to the men. "Okay, I think we're ready."

Buck grabbed a burly white-faced calf and pinned it down while Ed sat on the ground, his boot holding one hind leg and his hands on the other.

Hoot Gibson brought the red-hot branding iron over and Jake applied the JM Bar symbol to the calf's side. The calf bawled as the smell of singed hair rose into the air. Ed yelled, "Bull," and Chet was there with his knife to castrate the animal. Neil gave it an injection to protect against deadly blackleg, Chet doused the wound with Blood-STOP, and Nettie ticked one mark in the "Steer" column. The men let the calf up and shooed it gently through the gate to find its mother.

Half a dozen worried-looking cows ran forward, each sniffing to see if it was hers. Finally, the mother found her baby and mooed softly, licking its head and leading it away from the chaos.

Meanwhile, Buck and Ed caught another. "Heifer," was the tally cry this time, and the day went on as the heat intensified, the dust swirling and mingling with the smell of burning hair and blood.

At noon they gratefully broke for dinner, the men heaping their plates with beans and venison, Jell-O, and potato salads, coming back for seconds and then dessert: several kinds of cookies and cakes. While the women cleaned up, the men found shady spots, leaned back with their hats pulled down over their eyes, and took a quick snooze.

After about twenty minutes, Jake rose and spoke to the group. "Let's get this bunch finished up." They all followed him toward the corral.

In the evening, after they'd trailed the herd back to the pasture and the neighbors had all gone home, Nettie sat at the kitchen table with Jake and Neil, tired and sore, but elated with the count.

Jake licked the end of his pencil as he pored over the tally sheet. "Fifty-eight steers and thirty-nine heifers. Not bad. Not bad at all." He grinned at Nettie. "Should fetch a purty good price come fall."

Neil's eyes lit up. "Do you think I could get a share, Dad? Maybe I'll use it to go to college."

Jake's eyes widened. "Oh. A share. Uh, hadn't thought about that." He got up, reaching for his tobacco pouch and headed out the door.

Nettie felt Neil's disappointment like a kick from a calf as he slumped in his chair. She patted his shoulder as she got up. "Don't worry, honey. He'll come around."

Later, as Nettie readied for bed, Jake came in, sat down, and pulled off his boots. Nettie took a deep breath. "We need to give Neil a share of the calves. It would help him decide to stay and help us on the ranch awhile longer. And if he uses the money to go to college, it would delay his enlistment that much longer."

Jake took off his socks and studied a blister on his heel. Finally, he exhaled between his teeth. "You're right." He shook his head. "Kid's all growed up. Happened so quick, I wasn't even thinkin' about it."

Nettie saw weariness etched in the lines of his face. Their hard life was beginning to catch up with him. She rubbed his shoulder gently. "I know."

Jake stood and went to the window, his head bowed. After a time, he turned. "Okay. Come shipping time this fall, we'll keep out some calves for him, get him set up in the ranchin' business."

Nettie embraced him. "Thank you, honey." Pride and respect for her man made her squeeze tighter.

CHAPTER SIXTEEN

One July Saturday, Nettie took a noon lunch out to the hayfield where Neil and Jake were raking and pitching hay onto a wagon. Jake wiped his sweaty brow. "Just in time, little gal. We were startin' to get a little peaked."

"Yeah, I was about ready to keel over." Neil grinned as he tucked into the fried chicken.

"How's the hay crop?" Nettie asked.

Jake surveyed the field. "Got a good one this year."

After Neil had eaten several pieces of chicken, he patted his stomach. "Good vittles, Mom. What's for dessert?"

Nettie swatted at his arm good-naturedly and handed him a dishtowel-wrapped plate with gingerbread cookies.

"Mmm. Thanks, Ma."

"Gimme those cookies, boy." Jake grabbed at the plate, but Neil pulled away in time, laughing.

Nettie joined the laughter. It was good to see them getting along. The offer of calves of his own had apparently pleased Neil. He was growing up.

Neil bit into a cookie, then offered the plate to them. "Mom, Dad, I'm going to Melstone to play for a dance tonight. Why don't you guys drive over?"

"Oh." Nettie brightened. "That sounds like fun. What do you think, Jake?"

To her surprise, he nodded. "Sure, why not? We've got a good handle on the hayin' and it don't look like rain. I think we can leave 'er for once."

———

Art, a friend of Neil's who played guitar, stopped to pick him up just as he was finishing supper. "C'mon, Neil. Let's go get set up."

Neil grinned. "Yeah, and practice a little." He ran upstairs and came back with his violin and trumpet cases in hand. "See you guys later. Don't claim the 'too old, too tired' excuse, now. You come, have some fun."

Nettie waved him off with a smile. She put the finishing touches on the potato salad she would take to share at the midnight supper and then went to get dressed. She looked through her closet and chose a navy shirtwaist with white polka dots and a white belt. White pumps completed the ensemble. Sweeping her auburn hair back into a bun, she grimaced at the strands of gray. She patted on face powder, added a spot of rouge, then clipped on dangly earrings.

Jake, dressed in black trousers, a white shirt, and a bolo tie, gave a low whistle. "You're gonna be the purtiest gal there!" He offered his arm, escorted her to the pickup, and, mindful of her skirt and high-heeled shoes, helped her up onto the seat.

When they arrived in the little town of Melstone, about twenty-five miles away, all activity centered around the community hall. A couple of newer Chevrolet two-doors were mixed in among battered pickups and old Fords. Joking men dressed in their cleanest Levi's gathered around the cars, some passing around bottles, spitting chewing tobacco, or smoking. Jake went to join that crowd, while Nettie went inside to set down her dish and help the women.

She recognized several of the players with Neil on the bandstand—Ole with his accordion, Hal on drums, and Sally on the piano—as they tuned their instruments and practiced song beginnings in various keys. About eight o'clock, they launched into an old

favorite, "When the Work's All Done This Fall." Art sang in a pleasant tenor voice:

A group of jolly cowboys
Discussing plans at ease
Said one, "I'll tell you something, boys
If you will listen, please . . ."

Nettie loved the song, and was impressed that it had been written as a poem by a Miles City cowboy. Several young couples swung
out onto the floor. Nettie tapped her foot as she listened, feeling the
familiar swell of pride for her talented son as the sweet, clear notes of
his fiddle soared above.

After several spirited pieces, the band switched to a slower rhythm
with "Are You Lonesome Tonight?" Just as Nettie turned to search for
Jake, he strode through the door and stopped in front of her with a
bow. "May I have this dance?"

She stepped into his arms and they waltzed around the dance floor.
The next number was "Zing! Went the Strings of My Heart," and Nettie's shoes barely touched the floor as Jake twirled her into a fast pace.

Laughing and out of breath when the music finally stopped, Nettie gratefully headed for a seat, while Jake went to get her some lemonade. The band announced a short break. Just as Neil came over to sit
with her, Nettie turned to see a group of new arrivals. A pretty young
girl with red curls flowing down the back of a bright flowered dress
entered, carrying a box wrapped in white paper and tied with a red
bow: a box lunch to be auctioned off to the highest bidder at midnight
supper. She was followed by another attractive blonde girl carrying a
blue-checkered cloth-covered basket. Buck Scott and Chet and Zelda
Miller walked in behind the girls.

Nettie gaped in astonishment. The pretty red-headed girl was
Ruthie Miller! The blonde was Lilly-Anne Scott. *All grown up*. She
waved and the group came over to greet her.

"Hi, Mrs. Moser. Hi, Neil." Ruthie smiled and ducked her head. A blush rose up from her neck and bloomed in her cheeks.

Neil paused a moment, surprise lighting up his face. "Hi, Ruthie," he said finally, his deep voice cracking just a little.

Nettie's mouth quirked as she watched him taking in the curls, the dress, the heels.

"Howdy, Buck, Chet." Jake came up, his hands full of lemonade glasses. He did a double-take when he recognized the girls. "Whooee. Aren't you two lookin' purty tonight."

Chet squeezed an arm around Zelda's waist. Buck put his arm around Lilly-Anne. "Aren't we the lucky men tonight, to be escorting such beauties."

Nettie hugged the girls and Zelda. "So good to see you. It's been too long."

"Yes, it has. I'm glad you're here tonight, so I have somebody to talk to." Zelda turned to the girls. "Girls, go take your boxes into the kitchen now."

With a sidelong glance at Neil, Ruthie turned and followed Lilly-Anne.

The band resumed with Neil taking up his trumpet for the "Beer Barrel Polka." Jake grabbed Nettie and Chet pulled Zelda onto the floor and they twirled and stomped. Nettie felt light and carefree, like a young girl. As they passed by the band, she caught a glimpse of Ruthie, standing near the raised platform, smiling and clapping to the beat, her eyes on one tall trumpet player.

"She likes him." Nettie grinned at Jake, nodding toward Ruthie appreciating Neil from the sidelines.

Jake followed her look. "But does he like her?" he teased.

Between dances, she and Zelda caught up on their busy lives while watching their offspring. Nettie shook her head. "I can't believe how grown up Ruthie looks tonight."

Zelda laughed. "Yes, it's the first time she's ever wanted to 'look like a girl.' She's still horse-crazy and wants to do nothing but practice trick riding, but I think maybe she's starting to mature a bit. She's been helping me more around the house without being asked."

"That's great." Nettie remembered how she hated doing housework at that age too. Still didn't "love" it, but knew it was a necessity of life. "Where are your little ones tonight?"

"Lilly-Anne's grandmother is taking care of them."

Zelda looked younger and more carefree than Nettie had seen her in the past. "I'm glad you came tonight."

At midnight, Ole stepped to the front of the bandstand. "And now, ladies and gentlemen, what you've all been waiting for: our box lunch auction. Tonight our collection will go toward the war bond effort, so all you guys out there, get out your wallets and let the bidding begin!"

A group of men carried a table from the kitchen, laden with brightly wrapped boxes and baskets. Ole picked one up and peered inside. "Mmm, smells mighty good. Looks like some good ol' beef stew, bread and butter, and a slice of Depression Pie. Who'll start the bid at fifty cents?"

Someone raised a hand, another voice chimed in with "Seventy-five," and another yelled, "A buck." Finally the bidding closed at two dollars and a young cowboy stepped forward to collect his lunch and see with whom he'd be dining. The young woman who had prepared it smiled shyly and they walked to the benches to eat.

One by one, the boxes were distributed amid good-natured shouts and spirited competition. Then Ole picked up a basket with a blue-and-white-checkered cloth. "Roast beef sandwiches and raisin cookies. Do I have an opening bid?"

Art raised his arm. "Fifty cents."

Neil stepped forward. "One dollar."

Art shot him a look as if he couldn't believe his friend was bidding against him. "A dollar and a quarter."

"Buck-fifty."

"Two dollars!" Art shouted.

"Two twenty-five," Neil responded.

Nettie watched the bidding with a half-smile. That looked like Lilly-Anne's basket. She glanced over at the girls standing in the kitchen doorway. Lilly-Anne's face was flushed and Ruthie's mouth turned down at the corners. Why was Neil bidding against Art for Lilly-Anne's basket? He'd surely seen what the two girls had brought.

"Three dollars!"

"Four!"

Art leapt onto the bandstand, flourishing a greenback. "Five dollars! Beat that!"

Neil grinned and shook his head in defeat. The crowd applauded. Art whooped and threw his hands up in victory, collected the basket, and stepped down to meet Lilly-Anne, who beamed up at him.

Nettie thought Neil looked a little surprised as he watched them go off to eat. *I'll bet he thought that was Ruthie's lunch.*

"And now, the last, but not the least." Ole picked up the box wrapped in white and tied with a red bow.

Nettie's heart lurched. That had to be Ruthie's. She hoped her little friend's lunch would bring a good bid. Zelda drew in a breath.

"Let's see what we got here." Ole took the lid off and inhaled deeply. "Oh, yes, fried chicken! Rye bread. And cinnamon rolls. Mmm. Maybe I'll just take this one for myself." He grinned as his wife shook a finger at him from across the room. "All right, let's start. Fifty cents, anybody?"

The room was silent for a long moment. Not many unattached cowboys left. An older cowboy with a scraggly gray beard and sun-wizened face doffed his hat. "Yup," he called out, showing a mouth missing several teeth.

Zelda grabbed Nettie's hand.

"Fifty cents, do I hear a dollar?" Ole scanned the room. Wives were taking their husbands' arms to lead them to the potluck in the kitchen. The group dwindled.

Nettie held her breath. Ruthie's face had turned scarlet and she hunched back into the doorway, her lips trembling.

"Fifty cents. I have fifty cents. . . . Do I hear seventy-five . . . ? Fifty . . . going once. . . . Fifty going twice . . ."

"Two dollars." Neil's voice broke into the chant.

"I got two dollah, do I hear two-fifty?"

Coot, the oldest bachelor in the county, nodded again. "Yup."

"Two-fifty, two-fifty, two-fifty. C'mon, gentlemen, do I hear three?"

The room was silent for a long heartbeat.

"We have two-fifty. Two-fifty going once. . . . Two-fifty going twice . . ."

"Four dollars!"

Nettie spun around to see Neil wave his money over his head. Ole looked at old Coot, who shook his head and walked off.

"Sold!" Ole held up the box. "To this handsome young man. The best lunch in the house!"

Ruthie straightened her shoulders and stepped forward, her eyes shining, her face radiant. Neil gave her a shy grin and they went to find a seat.

Jake stepped up beside Nettie and chuckled. "Well, looks like our boy got himself a supper partner. How'd you like to join me, Mrs. Moser?"

Pride and trepidation warred in Nettie's heart. Pride that Neil had stepped in and saved Ruthie from embarrassment. Trepidation because her son was a man now. He would be leaving her soon, whether to marry, to go to college, or off to war.

She smiled through the blur of tears as she clutched Jake's arm. "I'm with you, honey. Let's go eat."

❧

The next morning Nettie set a stack of pancakes in front of Neil and Jake and poured coffee all around.

She cut into her own stack. "So, son. Did you enjoy the box lunch last night? It looked good."

Neil glanced up at her, eyes wide behind his glasses. "Uh, yeah. It was good."

"I know fried chicken is one of your favorites."

He nodded, intent on the contents of his plate.

"Ruthie sure looked pretty." Nettie probed further, trying not to grin. What if the two became involved? For the first time she thought of a future daughter-in-law. Ruthie wasn't exactly the image she would've chosen. One night didn't transform the flibbertigibbet into a mature young woman.

Neil's ears reddened, then his face flushed, and he grunted something that sounded like "Uh-huh."

Jake smirked. "Yeah, she's sure filled out nice."

Nettie cuffed Jake's shoulder.

Neil swallowed. "Aw, we just had supper together. I didn't want her to feel left out. That's all." He stood and took his half-empty plate to the dishpan. "Going out to do chores."

The screen door thumped and his booted footsteps echoed across the porch. Jake chuckled. "Smitten."

Nettie objected. "Oh, I don't know." She got up and put the tea-kettle on the stove to heat water for the dishes. "He's too young for that." Was it true, or did she only wish it were true?

"Not for long," Jake said.

July and August brought grain-ripening heat in the nineties. Jake watched his new wheat fields turn to gold, listened to radio reports, and chortled. "Prices are heading for a buck a bushel."

His almost childish delight with this news warmed Nettie's heart. "You made a good decision to plant more this year."

"Yup. One good thing comin' outta this war. Just two years ago wheat was only bringing sixty-one cents."

"Yeah, Mom, and calf prices are up too." Neil seemed as pleased as his dad. "Last year they brought ten cents a pound, so we'll probably get at least that much."

Nettie smiled at her son. *He's counting the money he'll get at shipping time.*

The mail brought a letter from her sister, Margie. She said Glen was also ecstatic over the spring's good rains, good crops, and good prices. But her words reflected her worry about her son.

> *. . . I just don't know why Gary had to run away to Canada and enlist to go off to war even before the US got involved! I hear these terrible reports about all the bombing over there in Europe. Of course his letters are written to make me feel better, I'm sure, mostly going on about the castles and the nightlife and the British "lassies" . . .*

Nettie knew the frustration Margie must have felt. Gary's letters to her were much the same. He'd written to Neil a couple of times too, but Neil kept those to himself, except to say his cousin was doing just fine. But she worried about her favorite nephew. And her sister. Nettie was proud of Gary for being so patriotic, and yes, proud of Neil for feeling that way too. But if he did enlist or was drafted, would he be able to handle the demands of the Army, taking orders? He wasn't too receptive to that with Jake.

Nettie swatted at her prickly thoughts. *The war will be over before that anyway.* She walked out to the pasture and caught her horse. A good, fast ride over the sun-baked prairie always cleared her mind. She pulled the hairpins out of her bun and let her hair flow free, just like when she'd been a teenager, riding like the wind to get away from the chores at home. A lot like her little red-headed friend, Ruthie, who was growing up. Nettie wondered if her infatuation with Neil would be returned. He was normally so shy around girls and of course, playing for dances absolved him from having to ask anyone to dance. But if he did like Ruthie, maybe that would keep him close to home for awhile longer. Could she dare hope?

A large bunch of Herefords congregated around the reservoir, some standing in the water, tails flicking away flies, others lying in the shade of two cottonwood trees, chewing their cuds. A warm sense of satisfaction came over Nettie as she surveyed the group and admired the slick red calves with their bright white faces. They were raising some good stock. *Jake's right; we'll do well this year.*

She rode on to the top of a nearby flat-topped butte where she could look out over their land. Another small group of calves with a couple of "babysitter" cows rested in a gully at one end of the pasture. To the west Nettie could see the ranch buildings and the golden wheat fields, where Neil and Jake were harvesting.

Nettie took off her hat and fanned her face. Jake loved his farming almost as much as he'd loved rodeoing.

She sighed. The war was already changing everything. The local Fourth of July rodeos in Miles City and Forsyth had been cancelled. She'd been as disappointed as Ruthie and Lilly-Anne, who had been developing and practicing new tricks all spring. Nettie missed the dust and the heat and the manure and horse-sweat smell, and most of all the excitement of competition. And the cheers.

She closed her eyes, hearing the applause, basking in the warm pleasure the first time she'd ridden a steer at a neighborhood rodeo and stayed on him until he quit bucking. From that moment, she'd known she was meant to be a rodeo cowgirl.

But her chance didn't last long. She never got to London with Tex Austin. She lost Marie. Women were banned from riding—

Nettie let out a frustrated growl.

Pigeon blew and shifted beneath her as if to say, "Enough of this standing around, feeling sorry for yourself. Let's get going."

Nettie agreed, gratefully nudging the mare's flanks to head at an easy lope down the side of the butte and across the prairie.

The next day, Nettie rode over to the Scotts' to help Ruthie and Lilly-Anne practice their trick riding.

The girls were working with their horses in the corral. When they saw her coming, they waved and shouted their greetings. "Hi, Mrs. Moser! Guess what!" Ruthie's cinnamon pigtails bounced as she ran up to give Nettie a hug.

"Hi, girls. What?" Nettie asked, bemused, thinking of the young lady at the dance. Didn't take long for Ruthie to revert to her little-girl enthusiasm.

Lilly-Anne spoke up. "We have an invitation to do a trick-riding exhibition at the fair in Miles City in September."

Buck Scott ambled out of the barn to join them.

"Yeah, isn't that keen?" Ruthie twirled a braid in her fingers.

"Wonderful." Nettie felt a tingle of excitement race up her spine.

Buck shook Nettie's hand. "We're tryin' to get up a small rodeo for Miles City. Money's tight, young men gone to the war, all that stuff. But whoever can come to the fair should be able to enjoy a rodeo. You and Jake think you'll make it?"

"Absolutely. Maybe I can even talk Neil into team roping with his dad." Nettie saw Ruthie's eyes light up.

"Neato! I'll talk to him at the next dance too." Ruthie jigged from one foot to the other, obviously trying not to show her excitement.

Nettie smiled. "Well, in that case, maybe you'll have better luck at persuading him than I will." She turned to Buck. "Count us in, however we can help."

He touched his hat brim and turned to walk back to the barn.

"You gonna ride a steer, Mrs. Moser?" Ruthie looked at her, wide-eyed.

Nettie rolled her shoulders, testing the strength of the one she'd dislocated last year. It felt pretty good. "We'll see. Okay, girls, let's see what tricks you've got today."

Lilly-Anne and Ruthie ran back to their horses, galloped out into the corral and went through their paces. Nettie watched, pleased with their progress. "Stand a little straighter, turn that foot more to the right," she advised. "Point your fingers and toes when you pose. Get your horse back in rhythm. Good! Try that one again."

Nettie rode home that evening, humming "In the Mood," a Glenn Miller tune. She could hardly keep herself from bouncing like Ruthie when the men came in for supper. "There's going to be a rodeo at the Miles City Fair!"

Jake hung his hat on a peg by the door. "By jingo, that's great! 'Bout time."

Neil nodded. "Good, I guess." He headed for the washroom.

Nettie pursed her lips, wondering if she should bring up the subject of team roping or if she should let Ruthie do it.

Jake beat her to it. "Hey, son, wanna do some team ropin' with me?"

Neil came out, wiping his face on a towel. "I don't know. I'll probably see if some of the kids from school want to march in the parade. And if there's a dance, our band will want to be there."

Jake's face clouded, but Nettie shook her head at him. "Well, honey, you think about it. You'd probably have time to do all of those things." She motioned to the table. "Sit down, you guys, supper's ready."

CHAPTER SEVENTEEN

The next Saturday night, Neil headed off with his friend Art to play for a dance in Forsyth. Jake stubbed out his after-supper cigarette. "Let's go on in to the Oasis, play some cards."

Nettie had been looking forward to curling up and reading a Zane Grey novel, *Thirty Thousand on the Hoof*, but she shrugged. "Sure. We could do that."

They drove in silence the eight miles to Ingomar and parked in front of the saloon. Music from the player piano wafted through the open door into the cool September evening. The acrid smell of cigarette smoke and stale beer greeted Nettie as she followed Jake inside. He immediately found the poker table in the corner and joined the raucous group.

Nettie went to the big mahogany bar.

"Howdy, Mrs. Moser. What'll ya have?" Clyde the bartender wiped the counter in front of her.

"A whiskey for Jake and iced tea for me." Nettie peered past him into the little office behind the bar. "Hi, Alice," she called to Clyde's wife.

"Hi there." Alice pushed a pile of papers aside. She stretched, got up from the desk, and came out. "I sure was looking for a break. You ready for a game of hearts?"

Nettie nodded. "You bet. Let me take Jake his drink." She walked over to the poker table, set the whiskey down, and patted his left shoulder twice, their signal of good luck.

"Thanks." He grinned at her and fanned his cards.

Nettie joined Alice and two other women, Mary and Jean, at a table near the bar. Jean dealt the cards. "How are your kids, Alice?"

Alice shook her blond curls. "Doin' fine. Got two granddaughters from Wendy. Guess she's following in her mom's footsteps. Other daughter, Sharon, is starting Custer County Junior College this fall."

Nettie looked at her cards. College in Miles City. She wondered if Neil would go for that. He could still come home on weekends then.

While they played, the women each reported on their kids and grandkids. "I sure hate this rationing, especially sugar," Mary lamented. "My Bill has such a sweet tooth."

"Yeah, my guys do like their baked things too." Nettie reorganized the cards in her hand. "But at least we make our own butter, so we don't have to worry about that, like people in the cities."

"Have you heard they've started gas rationing in the east, like in New York?" Alice picked three cards and passed them facedown to her neighbor.

"Oh my gosh. I suppose that'll come here too." Jean adjusted the Peter Pan collar on her printed housedress. "How will we get around? We have such a long ways to get to anywhere."

"Rubber rationing's been bad enough for us farmers," Mary added, "and it's getting darn hard to get coffee anymore."

Alice frowned at her cards. "What about your son, Nettie, now that he's done with school? Will he enlist?"

Nettie's stomach lurched, but she forced herself to keep her face neutral. "Yes, the subject's come up a time or two, but he doesn't turn eighteen until November, and we've been trying to encourage him to stay on the ranch."

Jean chuckled, her double chin wobbling. "Good luck. We couldn't persuade Jimmy to stick around. He was all gung-ho to go as soon as Roosevelt said the word."

The poker table in the corner erupted in good-natured squabbling over a game. An old-timer, Joe, pounded the table. "I won fair and square!"

"You cheated. I saw you," someone else yelled, while the others hooted and shoved their dollar bills toward Joe.

Jake got up and ambled over to the bar. "Pour me another, Clyde. Gotta drown my sorrows and fortify me for the next round."

Nettie raised an eyebrow. He must have lost that game. She wondered how much he'd bet. Jake looked back at her, shrugged, and returned to the game.

By midnight, Nettie and the women had counted their toothpicks, declaring they were all winners, and gathered up the deck of cards and their snacks. Mary and Jean went to the poker table, whispering in their husbands' ears. Nettie couldn't stifle a yawn, more than ready to go home too. Finally the men counted out their cash and headed outside.

Jake glanced sheepishly at Nettie. "Ready to go, little gal? Might as well cut our losses."

"You mean *your* losses." She looked at him from beneath lowered brows.

He offered his arm and they went outside to the pickup.

Nettie caught a whiff of the whiskey on his breath. "Do you want me to drive, honey?"

"Naw, I'm fine. Just gotta keep it between the fences." He chuckled and helped her into her seat.

As they drove, Nettie kept watch for anyone else who might be on the road, but it was deserted that time of night. "How did you do tonight?"

Jake downshifted to head up a hill. "I've had better nights."

At home, Jake fell into bed and was snoring almost before his head hit the pillow. Nettie tossed and turned, listening for Neil to get home and mulling over the possibilities for his future.

Finally she heard the kitchen door open and Neil's stealthy ascent up the stairs to his room. The clock showed 2 a.m. Nettie turned over, her tense muscles relaxing. Her son was home safely. Now she could sleep.

It felt like she'd barely fallen asleep when she smelled coffee and heard noises in the kitchen. Opening one eye, she looked at the clock: 7 a.m. She rose up on one elbow. The early morning light slanted in through the curtains. Strange. Jake was still sleeping next to her. But it couldn't be Neil up already. Usually after playing at a dance, he slept late the next morning.

Nettie got up, slipped into her robe and slippers, and padded out of the bedroom. "Good morning, honey, what are you doing up so early?"

Neil turned from the oven. He was dressed in slacks and a white shirt and the menthol scent of Barbasol aftershave mingled with the smell of toasting bread. "Uh, well, the Millers invited me to, uh, go to church with them this morning."

Nettie raised her eyebrows. "Church?"

He grabbed the butter and jam and slathered two pieces of toast. "Yeah. In Forsyth."

"That's nice." Nettie cut a slice of bread for herself.

Neil poured them both a cup of coffee. "You don't mind?"

She pulled in a breath. "Of course not. I'm glad." Going to church regularly had never been an option, because they'd moved so many times while Neil was growing up and because the nearest churches were miles away and inaccessible in the winter snows. She'd always felt close to God, though, out on the prairie, riding her horse, witnessing the birth of new calves, and seeing the explosion of wildflowers in the spring.

She took a sip of her coffee. "How was the dance?"

"Good." Neil pulled at his buttoned-up collar. "Quite a few people came."

Jake shuffled out of the bedroom, scrubbed his hands through his hair, and yawned. "What's goin' on out here so early?"

"Neil is going to church with the Millers this morning." Nettie sipped her coffee.

Jake stopped short, uncomprehending. "Church? What brought this on?"

Neil shrugged and demolished the rest of his toast in one bite.

"Ruthie invited him." Nettie winked at her son.

"Aw, Mom." Neil stood and took his plate to the dishpan. "I just . . . I dunno."

A car horn beeped outside. Grabbing his coat off the wall, he rushed outside.

Jake stood, staring at the door, his brows furrowed, his mouth open slightly. He finally turned and met Nettie's gaze. "Well, I'll be durned. Church."

"You'll have to do the chores yourself," Nettie said with a grin.

Jake merely groaned and headed back to the bedroom to get dressed.

When Neil came back from church, he joined them for Sunday chicken dinner.

"How was it?" Nettie plopped a second helping of mashed potatoes on his plate.

He picked up the gravy boat. "Really good. Lots to think about." He turned to Jake. "Hey, if you still want to team rope at the fair, I'll enter with you."

Jake's face creased into a huge grin. "All right! Great!" He mopped the last of his gravy with a piece of bread. "Well, what are we waiting for? Let's go practice."

Nettie chuckled to herself as she cleared the dishes. Ruthie must have good persuasive powers.

The next day Nettie climbed to the top of the corral fence to watch Jake and Neil practice team roping. The sun shone warm on her back and she stretched like a cat after a nice nap. The cattle grazed in the pasture beyond, she had a rodeo coming up, and her men were not only getting along, but teaming up. What more could she ask for? She grimaced. Other than the end of the war.

As Nettie watched them practice, the dust and snorts and shouts took her back to her own rodeo rides. She closed her eyes and could feel the animal's muscles tighten beneath her, the moment of fear, and then the rhythm of the dance as she anticipated the steer's next move. For a moment she was a young cowgirl again and the cheers of the crowd bathed her in warm success.

The corral gate clanged and the steer's bellow brought her eyes open to watch Jake and Neil's next run. Gosh, she missed the competition, the feeling of adrenaline spurring her forward, the shouts of approval from the crowd. She'd had some good rides.

Nettie sighed and climbed down from the corral. Better ride over to the Scotts' to help Lilly-Anne and Ruthie with their trick riding.

The next couple of weeks continued much the same, with crisp September nights turning to warm summer-like days.

The day before the fair opening, while Nettie packed the food, Jake and Neil loaded their horses into the trailer, then threw their tent and bedrolls in the pickup bed. They all piled in for the two-hour drive to Miles City.

Seeing that Neil had brought his trumpet, Nettie asked, "Are you playing with your dance band in the parade?"

He shook his head. "No, the high-school band teacher asked us graduates to come back and play with them."

"Wow." She hugged him. "He's asked the best musicians. Quite an honor." Her heart shrank to feel him pull away.

"I guess." Neil shrugged. "Dad, how many team ropers you think will be there?"

"Hard to say. I think Buck and Chet will be for sure, but I haven't heard who else."

"We might have a chance?" Neil asked.

"Maybe even a good one," Jake said.

Nettie sat between her two men, glad for their connection, hating herself for feeling jealous over being left out.

As the truck rolled down the hill into the Yellowstone Valley that nestled Miles City, Nettie admired the turning foliage along the river. Cottonwood and willow leaves shimmered gold in the sun as the wind rustled through. It would be a good weekend for a rodeo.

The fairgrounds bustled with farmers and gardeners bringing their corn and pumpkins, housewives their jars of multi-hued canned goods and sewing projects, for judging. Horses milled in the pasture near the arena and canvas tents dotted the prairie like raisins in a fresh-baked cookie. Jake found an empty spot to park and set up camp. Nettie got out, stretching from the long ride in the crowded pickup cab.

Neil helped Jake unload, then grabbed his bedroll. "I'm gonna find Art and the gang," he called over his shoulder as he walked away.

"See you later, honey." Nettie watched her tall, handsome son stride away through the crowd.

Jake stepped forward, calling after Neil. "Hey—"

Nettie gently touched his arm and he relaxed.

"Howdy, Mosers. Good t' see ya," came the greeting from several rodeo friends.

Nettie waved at people she recognized. It was good to see a crowd gathering, although it was small compared to the fairs and rodeos of the 1920s and '30s. But now, many of the rodeo riders were men gone to war. Boys still, some of them.

Buck Scott shook Jake's hand. "Glad you folks could make it."

"We wouldn't have missed it for anything." Nettie smiled.

"Yeah, it's good to have something to celebrate," Buck said. "The girls are with the Millers. They should be along shortly."

"Are they excited for the exhibition?"

"Oh, you better believe it. The jitters and the giggles and the shrieks." Buck rolled his eyes. "I'm just glad they rode in with the Millers today."

Everyone laughed and then went on about pounding stakes and poles to set up their dark brown canvas tents.

⌁

That evening a bonfire attracted the camping cowboys. Nettie and Jake joined the growing group, who passed around tin cups and an enamel coffee pot. Conversations murmured around them, someone strummed a guitar, and a woman's clear alto voice sang, "Have you ever been lonely? . . . Have you ever been blue?"

Nettie leaned against Jake's shoulder and stared into the fire. How many such campfires had they sat around in their life together? Every night for three months in the early 1930s when they trailed their horse herd from Cut Bank to Salmon, Idaho, in search of grass. Every night during the summers they'd lived in their canvas tent, moving from one abandoned homestead to another. Images of broncs and steers danced in the flames: those steers and broncs she had ridden. The crackling became the sound of applause, as Nettie closed her eyes, reliving those glory days.

"Hey there, Jake, Nettie." A voice startled Nettie back to the present. Good ol' Bob Askin. The man who had told her riding was like dancing: *Get into the rhythm and the rest comes naturally.*

Jake stood and shook the cowboy's hand. "Pull up the ground and have a seat."

"Don't mind if I do." Bob chuckled and settled next to them with a young girl. "You remember my daughter, Birdie."

Nettie smiled at her. She must be about twelve now. "Of course. Hi, Birdie. Are you in the trick-riding exhibition tomorrow?"

She bobbed her dark braids. "Yes, ma'am, I am."

"And Nettie, how about you?" Bob asked. "Is there a buckin' steer waitin' in the chute for you?"

Nettie drew in a breath to hide a sudden spark of excitement. "Oh, I don't think so. I'm getting a little old for that sort of thing."

Bob spat tobacco into the fire. Sparks flew and the juice sizzled as it hit the logs. "Naw, that ain't so. Never too old, I say. I'm gonna whup up on some ol' bronc, by golly. Just see who gets the best of who."

Nettie laughed. "Well, that I'll be watching for sure."

Someone passed around a whiskey bottle and the men added a generous dollop to their coffee. The guitar player launched into the Sons of the Pioneers' song "One More Ride." A yearning came over Nettie as she hummed along. If only she could ride one more time. But she was doing the right thing at the right time, and she was still involved in rodeo, helping her girls.

Nettie awoke early the next morning to the sounds of tent flaps rustling, horses whinnying, and men's voices greeting each other. Smelling wood smoke and coffee, she crawled out of her bedroll, stretching her aching shoulder. She slipped into her denim pants and her red satin shirt. Outside, Jake had a fire going, the coffee pot on, and bacon in the sizzling cast-iron skillet.

"Mmm, that smells good." She held out her cup for coffee and sat on a stump. "Have you seen Neil this morning?"

"He came by to pick up his trumpet. Stayed with Art last night." Jake scooped the bacon out of the pan and added generous spoonfuls of flapjack batter to the popping grease.

"They're probably practicing for the parade." Nettie yawned and stretched. "Are we going to ride in it this year?"

"Sure, why not?" Jake dished up a plate and handed it to her. "Ain't as many people around to be in it this year."

Nettie spread homemade purple chokecherry jam on her pancakes. "I know. It sure isn't the same. But they'll be back soon. And we are stepping in to take up the slack." She took another bite, savoring the sweet-tart flavor of the sun-ripened berry jam. She used to help Mama pick the berries every summer.

"You spoil me, Jake Moser. Thanks."

He winked and sat down beside her to eat.

Later, after Nettie had washed up their plates, she and Jake saddled up, rode to where the parade was to start, and waited for their turn to join. A group of grade-school kids assembled, all wearing red, white, and blue, and carrying miniature flags. A drum major lined them up and barked out last-minute instructions.

Neil had been invited to join the high school band, and he arrived with them, stepping tall and confident in the blue-and-white uniform. Nettie couldn't help beaming with pride at Jake, who grinned and nodded. The band launched into "Stars and Stripes Forever" and led off the parade. The kids, waving their flags, followed.

Ruthie, Lilly-Anne, and Birdie, each dressed in her own version of red, white, and blue, rode by, waving at Nettie. Another group of kids, wearing red-and-white-striped top hats, marched behind, holding signs reading BUY WAR BONDS and SUPPORT OUR MEN IN UNIFORM, to the crowd's enthusiastic cheers and applause.

The music, colorful costumes, and patriotic displays gave Nettie a feeling of happy pride. Then her brave heart broke to watch a woman ride by on a white stallion with a red-bordered flag adorned with a single gold star. *She's lost her son.* A chill crept up Nettie's ribcage.

She and Jake fell in behind another group of horse-mounted cowboys and joined the parade, waving to the people lining the streets. Nettie shook off her chill. Today was like old times, and she wouldn't squander it. She smiled and waved as Pigeon pranced down the street.

─◦◦─

When they arrived at the rodeo grounds, the stands held only a sparse crowd, many waving flags and war-bond signs. The emcee announced the first event, the trick-riding exhibition. Birdie galloped her pinto into the arena while standing upright in the saddle. The crowd cheered as she converted to a handstand and then dropped to the ground for just a second, back across the saddle, down to the other side, and back again.

Nettie, watching from her perch atop the corral fence, applauded. Birdie made the difficult moves look so smooth and easy, but Nettie knew how many hours of practice it must have taken. Very impressive. That Birdie was going to be somebody someday.

Then Ruthie and Lilly-Anne made their grand entrance, simultaneously hanging by one foot from the saddle, one arm reaching toward the ground and the other arm and leg extended upward in a near-split. The crowd roared. Nettie bounced on the corral rail as she cheered. Her girls had come a long way since she first began working with them. She watched every move, every foot position, every pointed hand, with a critical eye. Great! They continued to draw applause as they worked in tandem, executing their tricks with grace and beauty. Her girls made it look easy, but oh, the hours they'd spent, doing each trick over and over, the spills they took, the frustration!

She met them in the holding pen and gave them all a big hug. "You three are the tops!"

Ruthie pranced on booted tiptoes. "Yeah, I wanna go back to Madison Square Garden!"

Lilly-Anne grinned widely. Birdie looked down at her boots, shyly saying, "Thank you, Mrs. Moser."

"Come on, let's get your horses taken care of, and we'll go look at the fair exhibits before the men's events." Nettie helped the girls unsaddle and brush down their mounts. Then they ambled to the buildings that showcased the farm women's prized garden fare, the colorful canned goods, and a poster displaying ideas for preserving Victory Garden produce.

Ruthie snorted at the carefully stitched needlepoint and sewing projects. "I tried to make something to enter one year. That was a disaster."

Nettie grinned, remembering her trials as a young girl, trying her best to please her mother with stitchery, when all she wanted was to get outside and ride her horse. "I was terrible at needlework, too. Once

I tried to get out of darning socks by doing a terrible job. Mama cut it all out and made me do it over."

Ruthie and Lilly-Anne dissolved into hoots of laughter.

Nettie joined in their laughter, then felt a stab of guilt, missing her mother. *I've got to get a letter off to Mama.* It had been so long since she'd been to see her family. Not since they'd moved from Cut Bank to Ingomar. Her parents were approaching their seventies now. Thank goodness her sisters, Margie and Lola, still lived close by.

The megaphone squealed from the rodeo arena and the announcer's voice echoed over the fairgrounds. "And now, ladies and gentlemen, the event you've all been waiting for—saddle-bronc riding!"

Birdie sobered. "Can I go back and watch my dad ride?"

Nettie took her arm. "Of course. Let's all go cheer him on."

Back at the grandstand, they watched a series of cowboys bite the dust. Finally, Bob Askin's pawing, snorting horse burst from the chute. Birdie and the girls burst out with wild cheering.

"He's dancing," Nettie yelled to the girls as Bob stuck with the animal's every move, waving his left arm high. The whistle blew. The older rider had bested his bronc. The girls screamed their approval and pounded their booted feet on the bleacher boards.

They headed for the chutes to congratulate Bob. Birdie flung her arms around her dad. "Good ride, Dad!"

Jake was already there with Bob. "Good ride, for an old timer."

Bob chuckled. "Age and treachery will outdo youth and skill every time."

Nettie followed the girls as they climbed the corral fence to watch the team roping. She saw Neil gallop up on Blue to join his dad behind the chutes and breathed a sigh of relief. He wasn't going to let his dad down. Beside her, Ruthie sat up a little straighter.

The emcee announced the Moser team. Ruthie held up crossed fingers.

"They're so good together. They'll do great." But Nettie still held her breath.

The gate opened and the red-and-white steer dashed out, Jake and Neil close behind, both with lips pursed in intent focus. As if in slow motion, Nettie noted the way Neil leaned into his horse, just like his dad. Jake twirled his lasso and flipped his wrist. The loop settled over the steer's horns with ease. Neil's wrist mimicked Jake's, his loop caught the hind legs, and the animal was down. They exchanged satisfied grins.

"Yahoo!" Nettie whooped with pride, waving her arms high. "Flawless," she bragged to Ruthie. If only her men could always work together so well.

Ruthie bounded down from the fence and was the first to meet the men as they rode out of the arena. Neil slowed to a stop, then swung his long legs down from his horse to join her.

"Congratulations, Mr. Moser, Neil. That was great," Ruthie gushed.

Neil ducked his head. "Thanks."

Nettie caught him and Jake in a hug. "A fast time. I think you may have won it."

Jake grinned. "Not bad, huh?" He turned to Neil. "Good ropin', son, thanks."

Nettie's heart felt like it would burst, seeing Neil's face light up at his father's praise. She didn't even mind losing him as the other girls joined Ruthie and they talked him into going with them to find a cold drink.

"I gotta go talk to Chet about that bull. Catch up with ya later." Jake gave her a peck on the cheek and took off in the other direction.

Nettie stood by the holding pens, watching the cowhands working the steers. One bowlegged, leathery-faced cowboy looked over at her. "Howdy, Mrs. Moser. You want to ride one of these guys? We don't have any women signed up today. I'll get you registered while you get ready."

The breath caught in her throat. "Oh, gosh. I don't know." It had been so long since she'd ridden a steer. Her palms itched. How she longed to feel that familiar clench and release of muscles beneath her. Why not? They were still letting women ride here. She surely hadn't forgotten how, had she? She'd been riding her horse a lot, was in good shape.

Nettie swallowed. "Yes." She stepped forward. "By golly, I think I will."

The cowboy shuffled back a step. Then he grinned. "Great! You want me to cut out a small one for you?"

"No." Nettie let her gaze roam over the bunch of steers in the holding pen. She eyed a big, mottled descendant of the Texas longhorns. The steer rose up on its hind legs, pawing at the fence in an attempt to climb over. It snorted and butted the rails with its horns. Nettie pointed. "That one."

"You sure?" The cowboy raised his eyebrows. "He looks a little tough."

Nettie stood tall. "I'm sure."

"You got 'im." The cowhands jumped into the mix and herded the steer kicking and snorting into the chute, where they struggled to fasten a surcingle around its withers. Nettie climbed to the top rail, and before she was able to change her mind, plopped down on the animal's back. She seated her hat more firmly and slid her gloved right hand under the rope, feeling the familiar tightness. Then as an afterthought, she grabbed hold with her left as well. *I'm out of practice. Better hold on with both hands.* A deep breath and a nod, and the gate flung open.

With a lusty bawl worthy of a Brahma bull, the steer lunged through the opening, kicked its hind legs toward the sky, and landed with a twist. Nettie clenched her knees against its sides and fought to feel the rhythm. Up and down, back and forth, the steer bucked and twisted and twirled.

Nettie's body flung forward and whipped backward. Her legs quivered. Her arm muscles strained with the effort to hang on. She struggled to find that old connection, that dance rhythm she had so enjoyed in the past.

With a grunted snort, the steer sunfished, and Nettie felt her grip loosen. She slipped sideways. Her knees dug into the heaving sides and she pulled herself upright. Rhythm. Rhythm. Now, it started to feel good again. Finally, as though from far away, the whistle blew. She'd made it!

Nettie loosened her grip to slide off the steer. As the steer jerked away, her glove caught in the rope. She felt a sickening pop in her left shoulder, but she landed on her feet to wild cheering. She saw Neil and the girls running toward her, and tried to raise both arms in victory. *Oh, darn!* She staggered as her vision blurred with pain.

CHAPTER EIGHTEEN

Nettie gasped in a breath and held it until the dizziness passed. She clenched her left arm tight to her side, forced a big smile, and lifted her right arm to wave her hat at the cheering crowd.

"Mom! What happened?" Neil peered into her face.

"You did it!" Lilly-Anne and Birdie chorused.

"Mrs. Moser, what a dandy ride!" Ruthie fairly danced beside her, then her face changed to a frown. "But you're hurt."

"I'm fine." Nettie grinned. "I did do it, didn't I?"

She walked out of the arena, still waving, gritting her teeth against the pain. Once out of sight of the crowd, nausea washed over her and the earth tilted. She leaned against Neil. "I'm going to the first-aid tent." She tried to speak matter-of-factly.

The kids walked her to the tent, where she told the medic, "I've dislocated my shoulder . . . again. I need you to pull it back into place, and if you have a shot of pain killer, that'd be great."

The doctor raised his eyebrows. "I'm surprised you're still on your feet." He pulled a folding chair forward. "Here, sit down. I'll get that needle."

Ruthie's freckled face paled as he brought the syringe and plunged it into Nettie's arm. The girl hurried out, bending double just outside the tent opening. Lilly-Anne followed to comfort her.

After a few minutes the doctor said, "Okay, let's give it the ol' heave-ho. Get that shoulder back in the socket. You know the drill."

Neil held her right hand as the doctor applied the maneuver. Even with pain medication, Nettie felt the shock and grind of bone on bone and heard the pop as the shoulder went back in place. The lights swirled above her and for a moment everything went black.

When Nettie opened her eyes, Neil was kneeling by her side. He squeezed her hand. "That took sheer will to find the rhythm on that steer, Mom. I'll never forget that ride."

"Thank you, honey." Nettie stood and walked back out to the chutes, her shoulder bound and arm in a sling.

Jake was there, talking to Chet and Bob. When he saw her, his face blanched. "What happened?"

"Oh, just another little shoulder dislocation. It's nothing." Nettie waved off his concerns.

Jake shook his head. "You're bound and determined to scare the life outta me, aren't you?"

"Hey, how many times have you men been thrown, gotten hurt, huh? 'No big deal,' you all say. Well . . ." Nettie gave him a lopsided grin.

Jake brushed the hair off her forehead and kissed her brow. "My little gal. Once a cowgirl, always a cowgirl."

The next day Neil and Jake stumbled over each other, plumping up pillows in her rocking chair, bringing her tea or coffee, and attempting simple household chores. Nettie seethed at not being able to do anything. "Stop fussing over me! I'm not an invalid."

"Aw, Mom, just relax. Enjoy us taking care of you for awhile," Neil told her, his eyes twinkling behind his glasses. He went back to the kitchen to help Jake fix supper.

"Flapjacks and bacon again? Did you guys forget how to cook?" Nettie teased after the third such meal.

"How about bacon with flapjacks tonight?" Neil joked back.

"There's some canned venison for a stew, or—"

"You just go sit down and let us handle it." Jake led her back to her chair. "Cowboys can cook anything."

Late that afternoon, Nettie heard the two men in the kitchen, whispering and laughing. She padded to the doorway and peeked in. Jake was poring over one of her cookbooks and giving directions. "Separate two eggs."

Neil set one egg on the stove and walked across to the table. "How far apart?" They both broke into laughter again. Jake slapped his leg and cuffed his son on the shoulder.

Nettie stayed in her rocking chair and let them have their fun.

"Mighty tasty," she assured them as she ate their supper. "What is it?"

Their laughter was her best medicine.

Over the next couple of weeks, Nettie gradually eased them out of the kitchen and was able to manage one-handed. Ruthie and Lilly-Anne rode over occasionally and spent one afternoon baking bread and molasses cookies. Neil and Art took the girls to dances on Saturday nights, and Neil continued to attend church with the Millers every Sunday.

Nettie's shoulder healed slowly as September's Indian summer days turned to October's crisp nights. She daydreamed about the next rodeo and what the girls might work on, while the men winterized the haying and harvesting machinery.

One late October night before shipping their calves, Nettie pulled the curtains closed against the wind and joined Jake and Neil at the kitchen table. Each was scribbling figures on the back of an envelope with a stubby pencil.

"What did you hear about prices on the radio today, Dad?" Neil licked the point of his pencil, just like Jake.

Nettie held her breath, hoping for good news.

"Said they're bringin' about twelve, twelve and a half a hundred."

"So, if a calf weighs five hundred pounds . . ." Neil quickly did the math in his head. "At twelve dollars, that'd be sixty dollars. Not bad."

Jake nodded. "It's good. Two dollars a hundred more than last year." He turned to Nettie. "Remember in the early thirties when it was under four dollars? 'Course, we were raisin' horses then, and nobody wanted to buy horses at any price."

Neil looked up. "I remember our trail drive to Salmon when I was six."

How well Nettie remembered that long, frightening trip, driving their fifty horses four hundred miles over steep mountain passes into Idaho to find grass. That had been the low point of their lives.

Neil hunched over his figures. "You said you'd hold five calves for me, so if I sell all of them, that would bring me three hundred dollars." He raised his eyebrows, eyes bright behind his glasses. "That's half what I'll need for the university in Bozeman."

Jake pursed his lips. "Well, son, it doesn't work quite that way."

Nettie watched Neil's expression darken into suspicion.

"How does it work, then?"

The silence was awful.

Jake got up and poured himself a cup of coffee. "I figured to get you started on a herd of your own with five heifers. Breed 'em next year and then sell any steers the year after."

"You want me to wait to sell them in three years?" Neil was incredulous.

"That would be the smart thing to do," Jake said.

Nettie interrupted to try and stop the inevitable fight. "Why don't we give him three heifers and three steers this year?" she suggested. "That way, he could start his herd and save some money for tuition."

"Phff," Jake snorted. "What's the sense in spending that kind of money when you're going to be a rancher and partner with me?"

Nettie watched Neil face Jake, unblinking. "I want to be a teacher, not a rancher."

Jake stared back, silent as a stone.

Jake reached for his cigarette makings. Nettie and Neil watched as he rolled the thin paper around the tobacco, lit it, and inhaled deeply, letting the smoke hiss between his teeth. He stood and turned his back on them, staring out the window as he smoked.

"I'll give you three heifers to start a herd," Jake finally said.

Neil looked to Nettie, who silently pleaded for him to let Jake finish.

Jake turned to Neil. "And you can have two steers. You're on your own for this college idea." He walked out to finish his cigarette on the porch.

Neil leaned back in his chair and took off his glasses to polish with his shirttail. "You'd think he'd be glad to get rid of me."

Tears sprang to Nettie's eyes. "Oh, honey, he wants you here. We both do."

"Yeah, and we'd probably end up killing each other." Neil gave a dry, humorless chuckle as he put his glasses back on. "I can't go anywhere on a hundred twenty dollars this year." He tossed his pencil on the table. "I might as well enlist."

Nettie's hands shook as she picked up her coffee cup. "Billings has that normal school for teachers. That might be less expensive. And, it's closer to home."

"Yeah, I could look into that, I suppose." Neil neatened the stack of papers.

"Oh, you know what? I just remembered talking to Alice Easterday about her daughter going to Custer County Junior College in Miles City." She chewed on her lower lip. If only Neil would stay close to home. If only he and his dad would continue to work together. If only he wouldn't be drafted. If only . . . "Let's find out about the college in Miles and go over the numbers again. We don't have to decide right now. Promise me."

"Okay, Mom." Neil grudgingly promised to wait until he was eighteen.

Nettie counted the days with equal measures of motherly pride and dread. She invited the Millers and Scotts and Neil's friend Art to celebrate his eighteenth birthday. November 9 dawned sunny and unseasonably warm, reaching a high of fifty-eight degrees. Nettie baked a spice cake, sweetened with molasses in place of now-scarce sugar. Conversation flowed over the meal of fried chicken, mashed potatoes and gravy, and canned peas. Buck, Jake, and Chet discussed cattle prices and their hopes for good grain crops next year. Neil and Art took second helpings and talked with Ruthie and Lilly-Anne about music and dances and school.

Nettie felt the comfort of camaraderie with friends. It was good to see Zelda again. She was looking less frazzled than when Nettie had first met her. The baby was now a toddler and the toddler a four-year-old and they kept each other entertained. Nettie poured her friend a cup of coffee. "You're looking relaxed and happy."

"Ruthie has been a big help to me this past year, and Lilly-Anne comes over often too. Thank you for taking them under your wing and being a good example as a cowgirl."

Nettie smiled in surprise. She hadn't really thought of what she was doing in that way. "I'm glad. It's been my pleasure to work with them. They have a good chance of being top trick riders." She sighed. "If we have any more rodeos."

"The war sure has changed our world, hasn't it?" Zelda shook her head. "I suppose Neil will have to register for the draft now."

Silence hung between them. Finally Nettie found her voice. "Not today, Zelda."

"I'm so sorry. I—"

"Neil," Nettie called, determined to have a happy day with her son. "Play something for us."

Glad to oblige, Art went out to his car for his guitar and Neil brought out his fiddle, and soon everyone was tapping toes and singing along to "Can the Circle Be Unbroken," and "Tumbling Tumbleweeds."

Nettie went to bed that night with the warm glow of music, friend-ship, and memories of Neil's past birthdays.

Jake kissed her goodnight and turned out the light. "That was a fun evening, wasn't it?"

Nettie squeezed his hand. "Oh, yes, it was a special day." But as sleep was about to claim her, she had the nagging thought that this could be the last time.

The next week, Neil went to town to register for the draft. Nettie couldn't object, even though she wanted to. It was the law. Neil seemed nonchalant when he came home, as if it were no big thing. "Don't worry, Mom. Farmers are being deferred all the time."

Through the days of November and December Nettie held her breath every time one of the men brought home the mail. But it never included Neil's deferment.

CHAPTER NINETEEN

One late morning in mid-January, Nettie shed her work clothes after she came back from feeding cows and fired up the stove to start dinner. She shivered and tucked a shawl around her shoulders. From a warm forty degrees a few days earlier, the temperature now hovered just above zero, with several inches of snow on the ground and a forecast of colder weather to come.

She heard a vehicle drive up to the house and scratched at the frost on the window to see out. A tall, lanky figure emerged from his pickup and strode toward the door. He was bundled up so Nettie couldn't recognize him. "Neil, would you see who is here?"

Neil got up from the kitchen table and opened the door. "Hello, Mr. Beam, come on in."

Horace Beam, the telegraph operator at the Ingomar freight station, unbuckled his rubber overshoes, kicked them off, and stepped in.

Jake came to greet him and stretched out a hand. "Horace, what brings you out this way?"

Nettie braced herself, barely breathing. Maybe it wasn't bad news. Maybe draft deferments came by telegram now.

Horace reached into his coat pocket and retrieved the yellow paper with bold black printing. He stepped forward and held it out to Nettie. "I'm sorry, ma'am. Thought you might want this right away."

Nettie's knees weakened and a moan rose in her throat. Neil and Jake both came to save her, but she took the telegram and opened it with her own shaking hands.

MAMA ILL PNEUMONIA STOP COME SOON STOP MARGIE STOP

"Mama," she told them, helplessly. The telegram fluttered to the floor. Nettie covered her mouth with her hands. Cold dread took hold of her muscles and organs, and she shivered as though with the ague.

Jake and Neil caught her arms. "You need to sit down, Mom." They guided her to a chair.

Jake read from the telegram. "Pneumonia."

Nettie stood up, going to the stove, numb. "I'm sorry, Horace. I'm not very hospitable. Do you want some coffee?"

"Oh, no, ma'am. I have to be goin'. I'm real sorry about your mother." Horace awkwardly backed out the door.

Nettie picked up a spoon, turned and looked at Jake and Neil, then back to the stove. "I . . . dinner . . ."

Jake took the spoon from her. "Go pack. I'll take you into Miles for the three o'clock train." He gave her a quick hug. "The pickup's still warmed up and the roads are clear enough."

Nettie kissed his cheek in gratitude before hurrying to her bedroom. Heart thudding against her ribs, she mindlessly grabbed long underwear and sweaters from her bureau and stuffed them into her scuffed suitcase. Seeing the doily her mother had crocheted, she grabbed it off the dresser and tucked it into her pocket. She was back in the kitchen in ten minutes, ready to leave.

Neil handed her a brown paper bag. "Lunch for the train."

Nettie hugged her son and blinked back sudden tears. "The last time I saw her, you weren't even in high school yet."

"I know, Mom. We'll be okay." He gazed into her eyes. "I'll pray for Grandma."

She kissed him on the cheek again, then hurried out the door that Jake held open for her.

The ride to Miles City was silent except for the swish of tires on pavement and the change in engine roar as Jake shifted to go up and down hills. Nettie sat staring straight ahead, numbness turning her to stone. She hardly dared to breathe. If she didn't think about it, maybe she would wake up from this horrible dream.

At the Northern Pacific depot, Jake carried her suitcase to the porter and gathered her in a bear hug. Nettie clung to him for a long minute. "I'm sorry to be leaving you and Neil." Her breath floated wispy on the frigid air.

"We'll be just fine, sweetheart. Give your mom a hug from ol' Jake, okay?" He helped her climb the steps. "I'll send Margie a telegram to let her know you're coming."

Nettie found a seat and watched Jake's waving figure diminish as the train chugged westward. She wrapped her arms tight across her heart and tried to swallow the thickness in her throat. Dusk shrouded the snow-clad prairie in lavender and navy shadows and it was dark by the time they reached Billings. She descended from her car and as if sleepwalking, headed toward the depot. She nearly tripped over the luggage being unloaded, found her own, and went inside to wait for the Great Northern to take her to Cut Bank.

Nettie sat on the hard wooden bench, staring at the people milling around but not really seeing them. Her stomach growled, reminding her of Neil's lunch. She took a bite of the sandwich, but her mouth was dry as dust and she could hardly swallow, so she rewrapped it and put it back in her bag. Her eyes stung. Her mother would be sixty-eight this year. Last time Nettie had seen her, her hair had turned gray and her back was stooped. She couldn't lose her mama.

It was nearly midnight before Nettie boarded the train for Cut Bank. She covered herself with a blanket, huddled in the seat, and tried to sleep. The train's clickety-clack rhythm sounded just like Mama's knitting needles. Mama was always knitting or hand stitching something, and had given Nettie so much trouble when she was fourteen for sneaking off to ride in a neighborhood rodeo instead of staying home to darn socks. Mama's face had turned red and angry. "Wearing pants in public!" she'd fumed. "Riding in a rodeo!" Nettie's defiance had caused Mama so much grief.

Nettie felt anew the pain of her pinpricked, bleeding fingers as she finished the darning she'd abandoned. And later, the summer she'd spent sewing and embroidering her wedding trousseau, long days imprisoned inside the house without riding her horse. And then she and Jake had eloped. A tear trailed down her cheek. Mama had nearly disowned her then.

When she became a mother, she finally understood Mama's fierce protectiveness and determination to keep her child from trouble and harm. And watching Neil grow up and become his own person, she'd finally been able to forgive herself her own troublemaking and defiance. Why had she waited so long to tell Mama how much she loved her, that all was forgiven?

Nettie snuggled into the blanket. The rhythm of Mama's knitting needles at last soothed Nettie to sleep.

The train whistle startled Nettie awake. She rubbed her stiff neck and peered out the window. Cut Bank glistened under a blanket of snow in the early morning sunrise as the train screeched to a stop at the depot. The familiar US flag drooped from the pole out front, but now war-bond and UNCLE SAM WANTS YOU posters adorned the windows.

She smoothed the escaped wisps of hair back into her bun and put on her coat. Would she be too late? *Mama, please be all right.* She threaded her way to the exit and stepped out into the crisp, cold air. Several cars sat near the tracks, exhaust rising in steamy plumes. The door of a blue Buick opened and Margie's husband Glen stepped out.

"Good to see you, Nettie." He enveloped her in a hug.

Nettie drew a sharp breath. "Is Mama . . . ?"

"She's resting comfortably for now. Doc Campbell will be out later to check on her." He turned to where the porter unloaded luggage. "Let me grab your suitcase and we'll get going."

She waited while he loaded the bag into the trunk, then helped her into the car. They drove through the tiny town and started on the last interminable twenty miles of her trip to the ranch. To Mama.

"How did she get so sick?" Nettie asked.

"Well," Glen told her, "your mother had the influenza before Christmas, and we thought she was getting better. But then a few days ago she developed pneumonia." Glen steered expertly around a drift in the road. "We've got her in a steam tent, and that helps her breathe better, but she's very weak. She's been asking to see you."

Guilt made her shiver. "What does Doc say?" She rubbed her arms.

Glen shrugged. "Not much. Maybe we'll know more when he comes out today."

"And Papa. How is he?" She couldn't bear it if Papa wasn't his usual strong self.

"He's doing pretty well for a seventy-one-year-old. The arthritis got him pretty bad and he can't get around so good anymore."

An icy lump formed in Nettie's throat. Why hadn't she taken the time to visit her parents? An occasional letter just didn't cut the mustard in keeping up with family. But regrets weren't going to do much for her mother or father, either one. Life and times just hadn't allowed for much travel these past four years. She squared her shoulders. She was here now.

Finally, Glen pulled into the familiar driveway. The ranch was a sight for sore eyes. Smoke drifted from the chimney. Horses whinnied from the barnyard. And a collie rose from a nest of old clothes on the porch, stretched, and watched them.

Nettie hurried out of the car. "Shep," she called, and the gray-muzzled dog's tail wagged as he walked slowly down the porch steps to greet her. "Hi there, boy." When she'd left, his coat had been golden and glossy and he'd been cavorting around with the grandkids.

She stepped onto the porch. The door opened and Margie stepped out with her arms wide. "Oh, Nettie. I'm so glad to see you."

Nettie buried her face in her sister's hair, hot tears coming now.

"Well, if it isn't the prodigal daughter." Lola's voice pierced Nettie's heart. But when she turned, ready to defend herself, she found herself in another warm hug.

"I'm so sorry." Nettie's voice cracked.

"Hey, you're here now. That's what counts." Margie tugged on her arm. "Come in out of this cold. I've got coffee on the stove."

Nettie's gaze swept the familiar kitchen. Everything was still put away neatly, although the blue flower-print curtains were faded to a pale hue and cobwebs hung in the corners. The old speckled enamel coffee pot perked on the stove. Everything seemed the same, but everything was changing.

Margie took a cup from the shelf. "Let me pour you some coffee. I have to warn you—"

Nettie strode toward her parents' bedroom. "Mama?" Her stomach knotted as she turned the doorknob.

The moist, warm air engulfed her as she opened the door. Drops of condensation trickled down the windowpanes. Papa sat in a rocking chair by the bed, where a tent had been rigged from a sheet. When he saw Nettie a big smile warmed his creased face. He put his hands on the chair arms and slowly pushed himself to stand.

"Papa." Nettie wrapped her arms around her father, breathing in his familiar scent of pipe tobacco and leather. Suddenly she was a little girl again, finding refuge in his loving arms. They stood like that for a long time, until a hoarse cough came from the bed.

Nettie lifted the corner of the sheet. A pale, skeletal figure lay against raised pillows, gasping for breath. "Nettie?"

This couldn't be Mama. She steadied herself with a hand on the bedpost and summoned all her courage. "I'm here, Mama." She took her mother's wizened hand. "I'm here now."

Her mother's fingers tightened around hers and Mama's lips turned up slightly at the corners. "Glad." That one word seemed to exhaust her and she closed her eyes again, disappearing into the pillows.

Nettie's knees wouldn't hold her any longer. She sank onto the side of the bed, let the sheet tent fall back over Mama and sat holding her hand.

"I'm afraid she's not doing too well." Papa was in his chair again. His eyes were wet.

Nettie reached out her other hand and took his. They sat in silence for a long time, listening to Mama's rattling breaths and the gusts of wind that played around the corners of the house. Nettie's thoughts swirled too. *Why didn't they tell me? Why am I always the last to know?* Irritation prickled her eyelids.

Finally, Margie came in with a steaming kettle of water to put under the tent, and Lola followed with coffee for Nettie and Papa. "Would you like something to eat?" Lola asked.

Nettie shook her head. "I'm not very hungry." She cradled the warm cup in her palms and took a sip. The hot liquid trickled down her throat and warmed her frozen core. Inside, she felt all loose and splashy as if she might melt away. She met Margie's eyes through a watery haze.

A loud engine sputtered to a stop outside. Shep barked once. Lola stood. "That'll be Doc." The three sisters went into the kitchen and Margie opened the door.

"Hello, hello, and how are we today?" Dr. Campbell stomped the snow off his boots and ducked under the doorframe into the kitchen. Anger swelled through Nettie and heat came roaring up from her depths. How could he be so cheerful in the face of Mama's illness?

"*We* are not doing very well at all." She stretched herself to the limits of her height, looking up at the doctor. "How could you let her get so sick?"

Doc raised his eyebrows above his wire-framed glasses and held out a hand. "You must be the younger sister."

"Nettie Moser." She ignored his hand. "Why isn't she in the hospital?"

"Nettie," Margie interrupted.

Nettie turned on her sisters. "As usual, I'm the last to know! Why didn't you write me sooner?"

The doctor quietly excused himself and left the kitchen to tend his patient.

"Oh, sweetie," Margie said. "I should have. But we didn't want to worry you. After she had the influenza, she seemed to bounce back in her usual Mama style. 'Nobody's gonna take care of me.'" Margie imitated Mama's former strong stance. "But then things suddenly got worse again." Her face crumbled. "I'm sorry."

"We should have told you sooner," Lola agreed.

"Yes, you should have." Nettie pinched her lips together.

"But you hurt your shoulder," Lola said, "and it's winter, and it's an expensive trip."

"But how did she lose so much weight so fast with just the flu?"

Lola looked down at the floor. "She always gets thin in the summer and fall. She always worked from can to can't. But she didn't put it back on this winter."

"What's he going to do to get her well?" Nettie started for the bedroom door, but Margie put a hand on her arm. "Just let him do his exam. It gets too crowded in there with all of us."

Sure, she can say that. They've been with Mama all along. Nettie drew in a long breath and let it out slowly, forcing herself to speak calmly. "No. I'm going in." She marched into the room.

Doc Campbell had the tent sheet pulled back and leaned over Mama, smoothing a hand over her brow.

The doctor's tenderness stopped Nettie still, her heart going soft and her knees unpredictable.

He murmured something and Mama's lips parted. "Nettie."

"Yes, she's here." Doc turned to Nettie with a smile. He slipped a thermometer under Mama's tongue and felt for her wrist pulse, then took out his stethoscope to listen to her heart. After his exam, he stepped over and shook Papa's hand.

"Is it . . . ?" Papa rasped.

The doctor motioned for Nettie to come closer, out of Mama's hearing. "I took a culture a few days ago and ran a test. It's a bacterial infection."

Papa shook his head, looking resigned. His mouth trembled and his arms shook as Nettie took his hand and gave it a squeeze. So frail.

"What does that mean?" she asked the doctor.

"Let's go out and talk to your sisters." Doc patted Papa's shoulder. "I'll come back in and check on you again before I leave."

Nettie followed him out of the bedroom and sat at the table with her sisters. "Tell us what a bacterial infection means, Doctor."

He shook his head. "Ladies, I'm afraid it's not good news. I don't have any more sulfa drugs. When I get back to Cut Bank, I will telephone the hospital in Great Falls to see if they might have some they could spare. But I can't promise I'll find anything in time."

Nettie's chest felt full of shattered ice. "Why not?" she demanded.

"There's a war on," Lola said into the silence.

"I'm sorry," Doc Campbell said, "but I think your mother has only a day or two. It's time to say your good-byes."

Nettie couldn't breathe. "No." She felt kicked and trampled. "No."

Margie and Lola grasped each other's hands. "There's nothing you can do?" Margie asked.

Doc shook his head.

"Why didn't you put her in the hospital and start looking for the drugs when she first got sick?" Nettie pressed shaking hands to her stomach, afraid she might lose the coffee she'd drunk earlier.

"I thought it was a virus at first." The doctor rubbed a weary hand over his face.

"And Mama refused to go to the hospital. She's never been in one and said she wouldn't start now." Lola reached for Nettie's hand. "You know how stubborn she can be."

Nettie nodded. "But . . . there must be something we can do?"

Lola squeezed her hand. Margie put an arm around Nettie's shoulders. "We can pray."

Nettie padded back into her parents' bedroom, the prayer still on her mind. "Thy will be done," the perfect prayer, Margie said. But why did God's will have to take Mama away? Nettie wasn't ready. She squatted by Papa's chair and took his hands in hers.

"We'll see her again one day, honey." He smiled at her through watery eyes.

"I feel bad I haven't been home in so long, Papa. Forgive me."

"Mama understood. You have your own family."

"You're my family too." She stood, walked over to the bed, lifted the curtain, and lay down beside her mother. "It's Nettie, Mama. I love you."

Mama's eyes fluttered and her lips formed the word "love" before she drifted off.

Nettie molded her body close to her mother's frail form and held her, not wanting to let go. She inhaled the medicinal smell of camphor, listening to Mama's wheezy breaths.

Nettie never wanted to forget the memory of her mother as a younger woman—before the creases in her brow and when her hair was still dark—in the garden, filling her apron with fresh-picked peas or in the kitchen lifting heavy kettles full of canning jars. She smiled at the image of Mama playing the piano and trying to teach Nettie a few basic notes. Singing Christmas carols around the tree. After Nettie's marriage, sitting at the kitchen table, sharing the warmth of a cup of tea and women's secrets. That's when she knew she'd been forgiven for eloping with Jake.

Nettie awoke to a strange silence. For a moment she couldn't remember where she was. Her eyes took in the tented sheet above her, the warm, damp air. Nothing stirred, not even the wind. She turned her head toward Mama, so still and quiet. She saw Papa's hand clutching her mother's on the other side of the bed. Nettie's breath caught in her chest.

She lifted up the sheet and gazed into Papa's eyes. They both turned to look at Mama and then back again at each other. He nodded. She swallowed.

An odd serenity filled all the hollow corners inside Nettie. She smiled at Papa, lifted his leathery hand and kissed it. As if borne by a cloud, she walked quietly out to the kitchen where Margie and Lola sat at the table, staring into cups of coffee growing cold in front of them. They simultaneously lifted their eyes to Nettie.

She nodded and they rose to hug her. Arms intertwined, the sisters glided into the bedroom and knelt on the floor beside Papa.

His voice was strong and true. "Our father, who art in heaven . . ."

CHAPTER TWENTY

Nettie pulled up a straight-backed chair next to Papa. Margie and Lola sat on the bed next to them, all silently holding hands.

Finally Lola spoke in a quavery voice. "She was a good mama. She loved us."

Papa nodded. "Yes, she did. I know you kids thought she was being mean sometimes, but it was because she cared so much."

Nettie gazed at Mama's face, so peaceful now. "I'm sorry I was so much trouble."

"We loved you all," Papa said.

"We've got to tell the boys and Joe," Lola reminded them.

Nettie knew their brothers would be devastated.

"Floyd can drive out and tell them tonight." Lola massaged the back of her hand with a thumb.

Margie's lip quivered. "This happened too fast. I have to call Glen."

Nettie had to call Jake and Neil, but not right now.

"We have to plan the service," Margie said.

"Not yet," Papa said.

Nettie waited for her older sister to stand up and take charge, but she didn't. Tears trickled down Margie's cheek, her hands trembling as she clutched her mother's lifeless, thin hand. "We need to wash her, but . . . I can't do it." She doubled over, sobs wracking her body.

Nettie and Lola held Margie and let her cry. Margie was the oldest, the strong one, and had carried the burden of Mama's illness. Nettie wiped her face with a handkerchief. Her sisters had already done so much. It was her turn to do what was necessary, for the family. "Lola,

I need you to heat some water. Margie, I want you to pick out her favorite dress. Can you do that?" Both of her sisters nodded, numb but grateful. "It's what Mama needs from us now. Be strong." She kissed each tear-wet cheek, then watched them help each other out the door.

Glen arrived and paid his respects to Mama from the doorway. Nettie asked him to help Papa to another bedroom to take a nap. Lola returned with a basin of warm water and some towels, then left the room.

Nettie was alone with Mama for the last time. She dipped a washcloth into the basin. She gently daubed at her mother's face, smoothing back the thin wisps of gray hair from her forehead. Her aching heart filled with a tender, precious love, much like she'd felt when Neil was born. The clock on the wall ticked off the minutes, but time held no meaning as she cried freely and bathed the body of her mother who was at last free of suffering.

When the setting sun slanted through the window, Lola came into the room with a towel she'd warmed at the stove and used it to dry where Nettie had washed.

Then Margie tiptoed in holding a navy dress with white piping. "This was her favorite Sunday dress."

Together, the sisters put the dress on their mother, but it was much too big on her wasted frame.

"She wouldn't like for people to see her like this," Margie said, tears streaming.

"She wouldn't want us to buy her a new dress," Lola said, and they all agreed Mama would consider it a waste of good money.

"Where's her sewing basket?" Nettie asked. "We can make it fit."

They gently turned their mother on her side, propped against soft pillows, and basted her dress down the back. Then they combed and pinned her hair.

When they had finished, Mama lay on her back looking peaceful at last. They folded her hard-worn hands on her chest. Each daughter gave her a final kiss on the forehead.

Lola brought in candles and lit them. Papa shuffled back in and smiled to see his wife. "So beautiful. My beautiful bride." He eased himself into his rocker. "I'll sit with her tonight."

"But you need your rest, Papa." Nettie caressed his shoulder.

"I just had a nice long nap. I'll be fine."

Nettie sat. "I'll stay with you."

Concern etched Margie's weary face. "But you haven't had any rest either, Nettie. You sleep. I'll stay."

"No, no. I'd like to stay. We can take turns. You and Lola go rest awhile."

After her sisters left, she watched the candlelight flicker and soon heard Papa's soft snores. *Is Mama in heaven already? Has she forgiven me for living so far away? Is she watching over us now, our guardian? Can Mama help Papa find the strength to live without her?*

The next morning Glen and Floyd headed into town to telegraph Jake with the news, contact the doctor, see the minister, and pick up a pine coffin.

Nettie helped Papa move his rocker out to the living room, settled him by the stove, and wrapped him in an afghan Mama had knitted. Her fingers lingered on the soft wool as she tucked it around his thin shoulders. He smiled up at her. "Thank you for being here, dear daughter."

She kissed his mottled forehead, brought him a cup of tea, and sat with him until he fell asleep. "I love you, Papa," she whispered. Would this gray veil of sadness that enveloped her ever lift?

In the kitchen, she found that Margie and Lola had tied scarves around their hair and were bustling about, heating water, and scrubbing countertops and windowsills.

"What are you two doing?"

Margie blinked at her with red-rimmed eyes. "We need to get ready for everyone to come for the funeral."

Nettie grabbed a broom and began to sweep. Funeral. It had been winter when Essie died, too. There would be another mound on the hill now. Mama would join her baby girl dead from influenza.

Nettie swept the same spot, digging the bristles harder at the worn linoleum as if she could sweep away the sadness.

"You sure are giving that floor the what-for." Lola climbed onto a chair to remove the blue-and-white-checked curtains.

Nettie bit her tongue to keep from giving Lola what-for. She wanted to find the peace. "What was the most trouble to her, do you think?" Nettie asked. "My defying everything ladylike or you, Lola, criticizing everything for its own improvement or you, Margie, for being so darn perfect?"

"I was not." Margie flicked a towel at Nettie's derriere and found her mark.

"Ow! Were too," Nettie objected.

She picked up the dustpan. "Remember the time we were making pies for the threshing crew, I was trying to roll out crusts with my broken wrist, and we got into a food fight?"

"Like this?" Lola threw her wet rag at Nettie.

Nettie deftly caught it and served it right back into her sister's face.

"Oh no, you don't." Lola picked up a dishpan full of water, but as she started to slosh it toward Nettie, she slipped on a wet spot and landed on the floor, water flying everywhere.

Nettie shrieked with laughter, doubled over, and then sank to the floor beside Lola. Margie stood, arms akimbo. "Well, I never!" Then a chuckle erupted that she could not suppress and she fell into the puddle with her sisters.

"We're terrible," Lola said with a laugh.

"She'd never approve of this behavior," Margie agreed.

And, through laughter and tears, they all agreed what terrible daughters they'd been to the best mother in the world.

One morning a week later, Nettie came out of her bedroom to find Margie kneading bread dough. The warm, yeasty aroma tickled Nettie's taste buds. She took in the countertops, laden with pies, plates of cookies, and rolls. The sisters had already been baking all week, and the neighbors had been stopping by with condolences, bringing casseroles and desserts.

Just like when Essie died. The neighbors had been so kind and so generous after her little sister's death.

"All this plunder, and you're still baking?" Nettie poured herself coffee.

Margie gave a rueful smile. "I need to be doing. None of it will go to waste with all the people coming after the funeral, and our houseful of hungry men."

Nettie knew Margie was right, since their married brother Joe drove over from his ranch every day, and the "boys," the three eternal bachelors, Ben, Eddie, and Chuck, had all arrived, shuffling and mumbling in their broken-hearted, embarrassed grief.

Nettie selected a lush cinnamon roll and slathered it with fresh-churned butter. "And we've been polishing the whole house shinier than a new penny. Mama would be so proud of us."

Margie stared out the kitchen window where the silent snowdrifts glistened in the sun. "I keep expecting her to come into the kitchen and give me advice."

Nettie took a bite of her roll but couldn't swallow past the lump in her throat. She blinked a few times and then got up to put her plate and cup in the dishpan. "The guys out feeding?"

Margie nodded. "I've got a stew simmering. They'll be starving when they come in."

"Anything I can do before Lola gets here?"

"Go check on Papa. See if he's awake and ready to come out for a bite."

Nettie walked through the living room, where the wood floors gleamed and not a speck of dust showed in the weak winter sunlight streaming through the window. She knocked at the door of her parents' bedroom, remembering how she had sneaked past it that night nearly twenty years ago to escape and elope with Jake. What a lovestruck child she had been.

Papa didn't answer, so she knocked again and turned the cold metal knob. He lay in bed, his arms wrapped around Mama's pillow. What a sweet image. Even after forty-five years of marriage their love had still burned bright. She should just let him sleep. He looked so peaceful, the lines in his face relaxed. Tiptoeing across the floor, she leaned over to kiss his forehead. Her lips touched cold skin.

She recoiled.

"Papa?" Nettie shook his shoulder. "Papa, wake up." He didn't move. Her hands trembled as she felt for his pulse. Nothing.

No, this couldn't be. Not Papa too.

Nettie sobbed.

"What is it?" Margie rushed into the room. "Nettie?"

"Papa's gone too," Nettie choked out.

Margie screamed. Lola raced into the room and stared, understanding with a moan. "He said he couldn't live without her."

The next morning dawned bright and sunny, although the temperature was near zero. With a leaden heart, Nettie pulled on one of Lola's dresses, a dark-brown shirtwaist with ivory buttons. She automatically applied powder and lipstick and smoothed her hair back into her usual bun, wishing Jake and Neil could be here with her today. But she knew they couldn't leave the stock in the winter. Even with her large family around her, she'd never felt more alone.

When the men came in from doing chores, they changed clothes, and everyone piled into their cars for the solemn drive to the country schoolhouse, where church services and funerals were conducted. Reverend Johnson greeted them and escorted them inside.

The schoolhouse was filled with friends and neighbors, whose soft murmuring hushed as the family entered. At the front of the room, instead of the teacher's desk, two open pine coffins rested on benches, surrounded by flowers. Nettie gripped her sisters' hands and failed to keep her tears at bay. The family sat in the front row of chairs, silent, tentative, unbelieving. The men shuffled their boots on the worn wood floor. The women clutched their handkerchiefs to hold onto their calm.

The pastor opened his Bible and read from the Gospel of John, "My Father's house has many rooms. . . . I go to prepare a place for you . . ." When he finished the passage, he looked out at the congregation. "And now Ada and Charles Brady have taken up residence together in one of those heavenly rooms . . ."

Mama would never again work in her garden. Papa would never again oil tack in the barn. Nettie's world was forever changed. She pictured Mama bustling about one of those heavenly, sunlit rooms. She'd quickly find something to dust or rearrange. Papa would smoke his pipe, watch his hard-working wife, and love her.

Nettie's tears eased as the emptiness in her heart filled with her faith in her parents' heavenly reunion.

After the service, the family went forward to the open caskets to say their goodbyes. Nettie reached into her pocket and took out the lace doily she'd brought from home—one her mother had crocheted for Nettie's wedding—and placed it over Mama's folded hands. At Papa's coffin, she leaned over and kissed his forehead one last time.

The sounds of sniffs and quiet hiccupped sobs and shuffling feet filled the small room as the rest of the crowd filed past the pine boxes. The women paused, some smiling, some wiping away a tear. The men held their hats over their hearts and gave a small nod.

Then they all silently followed the pallbearers out to the community cemetery for the burial, clutching their coats tightly closed against the heartless winter air.

———

Back at the house, Nettie poured coffee and delivered trays laden with food to the parlor full of black-clad neighbors, their shoulders hunched like crows. Old Mr. Jenkins fished a whiskey bottle from his coat pocket and poured a generous dollop into his coffee, then passed it to the next man.

Snippets of conversation played around Nettie, lifting her heavy heart. "Wonderful woman . . . always had food or a remedy. . . . Charles . . . hard-working . . . heart of gold . . ."

Nettie pressed her hands to her chest. Mama and Papa were beloved by their neighbors. Just like her parents, these friends and neighbors were always available to help each other when needed, willing to drop their own critical planting or harvesting to come to someone else's aid.

───

Nettie's train ride home stretched with the endless miles through frigid snow-covered fields and pastures. She laid her head back on the headrest and watched the dusk deepen the sky to indigo. She let out a long, deep sigh, trying to release the tension and chaos of these past two weeks, to find an end to the fear and sorrow, the tears. At last, she slept.

Nettie awoke when her head bumped the window, the train screeching to a stop in Miles City. She quickly dug a mirror out of her purse, checked her hair, and applied fresh lipstick. After putting on her coat, hat, and gloves, she picked up her valise and stood, ready to escape the train as soon as the doors opened. Her heavy heart flip-flopped when she saw Jake and Neil standing on the platform.

Jake grabbed her in a bear hug, whispering, "I'm sorry, honey, I'm so sorry I couldn't be there with you."

Neil came up behind and wrapped his long arms around them both. "Welcome home, Mom." His voice was husky. "We sure missed you."

Nettie smiled through surprising new tears, drinking in the welcome and love of her men. "Me too." She buried her face in Jake's strong, solid chest, breathing in the familiar aromas of horsehair, tobacco, and smoke.

Home. She was home at last.

CHAPTER TWENTY-ONE

Nettie plunged back into chores with a fervor that kept her from dwelling on her sadness. She went out feeding with the guys every morning, mucked out stalls, and brushed the saddle horses. She even tackled an early "spring cleaning" in the house, beating rugs and washing walls. Nettie thought she was managing her grief very well—until she sorted out a closet and found her well-worn cowboy boots with the green stitching. She had coveted those expensive, perfect boots for a long time, before she defied her parents and eloped with Jake. Sitting in the closet of the home she'd made with Jake, her mother buried, she held the boots to her heart and wept in gratitude for her mother's long-ago gift of the boots—and forgiveness.

Gradually, as the snow receded and a tinge of green began to blanket the rolling landscape, a sense of peace slowly took the place of Nettie's emptiness and sorrow. She woke up eager for the day again. She rode out to check on calving. Being on Pigeon's back, feeling the sun warm on her face and the wind in her hair, made her feel hopeful, weightless.

Nettie checked fence lines, stopping to pound in a staple where the snow had pulled the barbed wire loose. She smiled to watch the sleek red calves gamboling in the pasture, their pristine white faces gleaming in the sun.

Neil and Jake continued to work together—with an occasional loud argument—getting the machinery ready for planting and haying. In the evening, Neil pored over papers extolling the virtues of various colleges, and Saturday nights he and Art often went to play for a dance nearby. Jake still grumbled when he and Nettie heard their son getting up extra-early on Sunday mornings to go to church with Ruthie. "Must be love to do that," he muttered.

Nettie just smiled, hoping that this budding relationship might keep him home—if he wasn't drafted. If the war didn't end soon.

Summer brought the heat and dust. While Jake and Neil worked in the fields, Nettie rode over to the Millers or the Scotts to work with the girls on their trick riding. One afternoon, she arrived to find Ruthie spinning a rope.

"Hi, girls. You're already adding rope tricks? I thought we were going to wait until Trixi came to teach us."

Ruthie tossed the still-twirling loop over Nettie's head, spun it down the length of her body, back up, and over her head.

"Hey, that's great." Nettie applauded as Ruthie danced in and out of the spinning loop. That giddy little girl seemed to be growing up. "Where did you learn that?"

Ruthie flushed bright. "Uh, Neil showed me how to keep the loop going."

Lilly-Anne laughed. "She's been twirling that rope nonstop for days."

"Next step is doing this on horseback." Ruthie smiled proudly. "If Trixi can do it, I figure I can too."

Nettie nodded. "It would be a great addition to your show. Are you practicing twirling too, Lilly-Anne?"

The younger girl shook her head. "No, I never was good at roping. I'll leave that to this cowgirl."

Nettie mounted Pigeon again and joined the girls in the corral. "Okay, let's go through your routine again. I want to see you work on that 'around the world' move together." She rode alongside the girls as they circled the corral, grasped their saddle horns, and swung their bodies to one side of their horses. Then their feet went up in the air and they turned a complete circle with their bodies, landing back in the saddle.

"Okay, that was pretty good," Nettie called out. "You were a little out of sync with each other. Do it again to my count. One . . . two . . . three . . ."

After they'd gone through the move several times, Buck Scott ambled over to stand beside her. "What d'ya think? Are they makin' progress?"

"You bet they are. Their synchronization is excellent. Lilly-Anne is getting really good at the under-the-belly pass. And have you seen Ruthie twirling that rope?"

"Yeah. They're really coming along, thanks to your coaching." Buck pushed his hat back and chuckled. "And you said you weren't a trick rider."

Nettie grinned back at him. "Well, I'm learning, right along with them. I can't do the moves, but I can see what they need to do. We're going to put on one heckuva good exhibition at the fair in Miles City this year."

<hr/>

As she rode home over the sun-ripening hills, Nettie thought of the parallels and obstacles of her rodeo career and the girls'. It was never easy for women who had that competitive urge, but the heyday of women's contests seemed to be over. "I hate seeing Ruthie and Lilly-Anne working so hard with nowhere to test their skills," she muttered to Pigeon. The horse flicked her ears back and bobbed her head in sympathy.

When Nettie got home, she thumbed through the mail. A head-line, FAIR CANCELED, in the *Miles City Star* caught her eye. Because so many young men were gone, the lack of participation by the usual sponsors, and gas and tire rationing, the fair and rodeo would be canceled for the first time in fifty years.

Hoofs & Horns magazine confirmed that rodeos were being canceled all over the country. The war certainly had brought life as she knew it to a halt. Traveling to other rodeos—if they were being held—was probably out of the question. Jake wouldn't want to waste their farm allotments for gas.

"All tricked up and no place to go," she lamented to Jake and Neil at supper. "There must be something I can do."

Jake mopped up his gravy with a chunk of bread. "Put one on yourself."

"How? We don't have the money. Nobody could get the gas to come to it."

"You'll figure something out," Jake assured her.

Jake and Neil came in one evening, a couple of weeks later, in high spirits. "This wheat crop is one of the best I've ever seen. And they told us we'd never be able to farm this land," Jake chortled. "With the military buying up Montana wheat, we could make some real money this year."

"Hey, I think that calls for a celebration." A bubble of excitement rose in Nettie's chest. "Let's put on a neighborhood rodeo after harvest. Just like we used to do when I was a kid."

Jake stroked his chin. "Hmm. Hadn't thought about those in awhile. Sure, why not?"

"Are our corral and pens big enough?" Neil asked. "And we don't have a chute."

"We'll make it work," Nettie assured him. "We could bring in steers from the pasture and ask the neighbors to bring their green or unbroke horses." Nettie resisted the temptation to squeal like a little girl.

"Yeah. Maybe somebody even has an ornery bull." Jake grinned.

"Not for you to ride!" Nettie put her hands on her hips.

He laughed. "Okay, okay, no bull ridin'. And no steer bustin' for you either, little gal! But you and I could team rope, son."

Neil nodded. "Sure, Dad. And afterward, how about a dance in the barn?"

Nettie clapped with delight. They'd be a great team—making her idea come true.

—～—

For the next week, while the men were finishing the harvest, Nettie rode each day to visit their neighbors and announce the rodeo. They all greeted the idea with enthusiasm and offers to contribute. Then Neil and Jake went to work on the corral and fence around the holding pen.

"What are we going to use for a chute?" Neil stuck a booted foot on the lower rail of the corral one morning.

"Aw, we don't need one." Jake reached for his cigarette fixings. "We just used to form a ring with our Model Ts back in the twenties. Nothin' fancy back then."

Nettie chuckled. "Yeah, that's the kind of makeshift arena I rode my first steer in when I was fourteen."

"I would like to have seen that, Mom. I'll bet you were a cute little cowgirl." Neil grinned at her.

"Well, I don't know about 'cute' but I sure did stay on 'im till he quit bucking. I bested him." Nettie felt a warm glow of pride flush her face.

"Oh, that's right. No eight- or ten-second whistle then. Wow, Mom." He turned to his dad. "I'd like to build a chute. It wouldn't be that hard."

Jake furrowed his brow, pulled in a draught of his smoke, and exhaled through his teeth. "It's gonna cost money."

"I can use boards from that old homestead shack out in the pasture. For free."

"Won't ever use it again."

"Then I'll take it down."

Nettie was proud of Neil for keeping his temper, and willed Jake to agree.

Jake threw down his cigarette butt and ground it out with his boot heel. "All right. Do what you want." He left for the barn.

"Good idea, Neil," Neil muttered when Jake was out of earshot. "Great plan. Let me help, son."

Nettie rubbed his shoulder, wishing she could forever banish the father and son's disappointment in each other.

◆━━◆

The day before the rodeo, several neighbors trailed yearling steers and young broncs over, and Neil and Jake brought in steer calves for the kids to ride. The animals in the small pasture next to the corrals filled the night with a symphony of bawls, snorts, and squeals.

Early the next morning, the Millers, Scotts, and Gibsons arrived, the women bringing casserole dishes and pies. Soon Clyde and Alice Easterday from the Oasis Bar in Ingomar rode up in a horse-drawn buggy and unloaded several bottles of whiskey for the evening's festivities. Then Nettie welcomed Bill and Mary Smith and Tom and Jean Murphy from the other side of Ingomar, who also came with food offerings.

"What a fine-lookin' chute you've added there," drawled Chet Miller. All the men gathered around to admire the new addition.

"My boy Neil built that," Nettie was amazed to hear Jake say, and Neil's surprised look gave way to a gratified smile.

"It's convertible to a loading chute," Neil showed them all, "when we want to take a critter somewhere in a horse trailer or a truck."

Jake patted Neil on the back, wearing a look of pure enjoyment with the men's admiration of his son's handiwork. Nettie loved them both, but she would never understand why they had to spar and butt heads about *everything*.

"Okay, everybody, gather 'round." Jake held up a hand. "Here's what we've got: steer calves for us to rope and the kids to ride, and we've even got a coupla sheep for you kids courtesy of the Murphys, steers and broncs for anybody else. Just put your John Hancock down on this paper and let me know what you want to do."

Several young boys and girls flocked around, clamoring to ride, and Nettie helped them sign up. Other than Neil and his friend Art, who had received his deferment because he was the only male on his ranch, and the Gibson boys who weren't yet eighteen, the men were all older.

She smiled at the youngest Gibson child as she signed up to ride a sheep. *Oh well. We're here to have fun and celebrate a great harvest.*

— · —

The late August day was a perfect eighty-five degrees, the sky clear, and a buzz of energy filled the air. The women deposited the food in the refrigerator, telling stories about pooling their sugar rations or coming up with substitutes to bake their treats.

"I used a couple packets of Jell-O in my rhubarb pie," Mrs. Scott shared. She cut a small slice and all the women took a bite, with exclamations of how tasty it turned out.

Nettie gave each of them a hug. "What do you say we women and kids saddle up and have a little parade?"

Zelda's face lit up. "That can be our contribution to the rodeo, since we don't ride rough stock," she glanced at Nettie, "anymore."

Nettie smiled at her friend and agreed those days were long gone.

They all mounted up and paraded from the barn, around the corrals and holding pens. Nettie led with the American flag, Zelda riding behind her with a Montana flag. Ruthie and Lilly-Anne stood atop their horses and waved at the men, and a couple of kids held up a war-bond poster they'd found in town.

"Good show!" Jake whistled and the men applauded. "Now let the ridin' begin."

The youngsters rode the sheep and steer calves. While some cried when they were bucked off, others lifted their hats in the air with the same pride as a grown-up after a successful ride. Hoot Gibson, just a couple of years younger than Neil, rode a big steer and a bronc to the shrill sound of the policeman's whistle Buck had brought. Several other teenagers tried to give Hoot a run for his money, but landed ingloriously in the dust.

Jake and Neil and the older men spurred on the competition with steer roping, their small audience enthusiastic with whoops and applause.

Ruthie came out on foot, twirling her rope, and executed her new tricks. Nettie's eyes widened as Neil strode out to join her with his rope spinning. *When have they been practicing together?* Then the girls gave a trick-riding exhibition, with their "around the world" spin, hand-stands, and under-the-belly moves that ended the day on a high note. Neil led the applause with loud whistles and whoops.

Jake and Neil set up an old door on sawhorses for a table and the women brought out the warmed casseroles, fried chicken, salads, and desserts. Everyone piled their plates high and found seats on the porch steps or on the ground.

Nettie smiled as she watched Ruthie and Lilly-Anne approach Neil and Art. The boys leapt up, Art spread his chaps on the ground, and Neil took their plates while the girls settled themselves, chattering and giggling.

As dusk descended around them, Neil brought out his fiddle, Art his guitar, and Hoot pulled a harmonica from his pocket. Jake lit lanterns in the barn, Nettie hung up the flags, and everyone gathered, sitting on sweet-smelling straw, to listen to music and dance. At first all the little kids rushed out on the rough wood barn floor, whooping and jigging. When the boys played a waltz, a few of the husbands and wives ventured out.

Jake took Nettie's hand and spun her around the floor. They looked at each other and grinned, seeing Ruthie and Lilly-Anne sitting near the musicians, their eyes on every move. After awhile, Ruthie approached Neil. He blushed and scuffed his toe, but finally set down his fiddle, nodded at Art and Hoot, and joined Ruthie for a slow dance. Ruthie beamed up at him and then rested her head on his shoulder.

Nettie leaned into Jake and hummed with the music. *Ah, young love.* Neil was smooth and confident with a rope or a fiddle in his hands, but he held Ruthie like she was made of glass.

Midnight saw everyone mount up for the ride home. Art was staying overnight and the boys grabbed one last slice of pie in the kitchen. Nettie took a cup of tea for her and Jake out to the porch. Stars punctured the ebony sky like fireflies and a cool breeze caused Nettie to pull a sweater around her shoulders.

Jake reached over and squeezed her hand. "It was a good day."

"I'll never forget the look on Neil's face when you bragged about his chute."

"He did a good job," Jake conceded.

"So did you." Nettie kissed his stubbly cheek.

❦

One Sunday afternoon a few weeks later, Neil came home from church and dinner with the Millers. He joined Nettie and Jake at the barn where they were cleaning and repairing tack.

"Hi, honey. How was the service?"

He sat on an overturned bucket. "Good."

Nettie glanced at him polishing his glasses on his shirttail. "What did the Millers have for dinner?"

"Fried chicken." Neil put his glasses back on and fidgeted. "Uh, Mom, Dad, I have something to talk to you about."

Nettie's stomach contracted. What could it be? Was this about Ruthie?

Jake grunted. "Yeah, son, what is it?"

Neil expelled a breath. "Well, I, uh, I've been talking to Reverend Tormaehlen after church." He paused and licked his lips. "And I've decided I want to go to seminary and become a pastor."

Jake held the tin of saddle soap and stared at his son.

Nettie was speechless too. A pastor? Silence enveloped the three of them like heavy fog. Finally, Nettie found her voice. "Well. That is quite a noble dream." She cleared her throat. "Where would you have to go for that?"

Neil looked down at his scuffed boots. "Minnesota."

"There's nothing closer to home?" Nettie could barely breathe.

Jake carefully put the lid back on the tin in his hands. He stood up and put away the saddle he'd been working on.

"Say something," Neil said.

Jake turned to him. "How long has this consarned fool idea been rattling around your addle-pated brain?"

Neil looked back at his father, his match in height and will. "I feel . . . strongly about this. I feel I am being called."

Jake snorted. "You wanted to play music. Then you wanted to go to college. Study agriculture. Then it was engineering. Now God's calling?"

"Yes, I feel He is."

"You're hearing voices? That's loco."

Nettie recoiled, sour bile rising in her throat. "Don't, Jake," she warned.

"Don't say what I think?"

"Don't say something you'll regret."

Jake stood his ground. "Having a sissy son is what I regret."

Neil grunted as though he'd been punched. "Thanks, Dad. You've made this a lot easier." He kissed Nettie's cheek, then turned and stalked out of the barn.

As if in a dream, Nettie heard the pickup door slam, the engine roar to life, and the gears grind as Neil drove away. "What have you done, Jake? What have you done?" She beat her fists on his chest.

"Now, little gal—"

"Don't 'little gal' me! You've just made the biggest mistake of your life!" She turned and rushed from the barn, tripping over a cat she couldn't see through her tears.

CHAPTER TWENTY-TWO

Nettie ran blindly to the pasture where Pigeon nickered a welcome and approached, undoubtedly looking for a handout. Without thinking, Nettie swung herself onto Pigeon's bare back, grasped her mane, and urged the horse to run. "Faster, faster, go, go!" Nettie screamed, the echoing roar of her collapsing family filling her ears. The mare loped through the coulees and then broke into a gallop over the maize-colored prairie. Nettie squeezed her legs against the horse's barrel, leaned forward, and urged her on. The wind blew the hairpins from Nettie's bun and her auburn hair mingled with Pigeon's gray mane.

Finally Pigeon came to a halt atop a butte, Nettie's favorite vantage point. The mare's sides heaved and a sheen of sweat covered her withers. Nettie slumped onto Pigeon's neck, as drenched and wrung out as if she had been sprinting over the hills. Sobs wrenched from her body, her legs and arms trembling with the effort. Unable to hold on any longer, Nettie slipped from the horse's back and crumpled in a heap in the coarse, dry grass.

Pigeon nuzzled her neck with a velvety nose and stood over her protectively. Nettie turned her tear-stained face to the horse. "Oh, Pigeon." No matter what she did to protect Neil, she wasn't able to prevent Jake from driving him away. Renewed sobs wracked her body and she cried until her stomach muscles cramped and she finally slept.

When she woke, the sun was setting over the horizon, sending out its dreadful burnt-orange rays. She sat up from the chilling ground. Her back ached, her shoulder sent shooting pains up to her head, and her legs were stiff. Pigeon grazed nearby and lifted her head when Nettie called, "Come here, girl."

The horse blew softly through her nostrils and came closer. Nettie eased herself to standing. She had to go home. But the thought of facing Jake infuriated her. She would say things worthy of regret. Her anger bubbled to the surface. *Heck, he ought to be scared of me!*

"Well, I can't stay out here all night." She grasped Pigeon's headstall and led her to a rock, where Nettie was able to mount. She rode home slowly, dreading her arrival.

No lantern lights shone from the house or the barn. The pickup was not there. Jake's horse Stranger was gone.

Nettie gave Pigeon some oats and dragged herself to the house. Her stomach roiled at the thought of food. She lay down on the couch, numb and alone.

Sometime during the night, Nettie heard Jake fumble the door open and stumble through the living room into the bedroom. She smelled whiskey and turned her face to the back of the couch.

———

The sun's morning rays streamed through the front window and woke Nettie. She padded into the kitchen and automatically poured water into the pot, then added coffee grounds, deliberately keeping her mind blank. She stared at the pot on the stove until it boiled, then poured a cup and sat at the table, resting her head in her hands.

Nettie didn't know how long she'd sat there, but the sound of the pickup's engine made her sit upright. Neil! Her heart pounded. Her hands shook.

Jake came out of the bedroom, his gray-flecked sandy hair awry. "Neil back?"

Nettie went to the door. Neil strode up the porch steps. "Morning, Mom." His jaw was set and his face serious. He gave her a kiss on the cheek.

"Neil, honey." Nettie's voice was choked.

Jake cleared his throat. "Son. Listen, I'm sorry—"

Neil slapped a set of papers on the kitchen table. "I've enlisted in the Army. I'm going to pack a few things now and Art is coming to take me to the train. I report to Fort Douglas, Utah, in five days."

"No!" Nettie's breath expelled from the steer-kick blow to her midsection. She doubled over. "Oh, honey."

Neil put his hand on her shoulder. "I'm sorry, Mom. This is for the best." He turned and clomped upstairs to his room.

Jake sat hard in a chair, his shoulders slumped. His elbows on his knees, he held his head in his hands and moaned.

Nettie climbed the stairs. This couldn't be happening. Maybe he could still back out. She stood in the doorway of Neil's room, hoping the frame would hold her up. "Oh, honey," was all she could say. Her voice cracked.

Neil looked at her with a liquid brightness in his eyes.

"What about Ruthie? I thought . . ."

He sighed and zipped his duffel. "She's too young, Mom. I'm not ready. This is for the best," he repeated. He put an arm around her shoulders and they walked downstairs.

Jake stood. "Son—"

Neil stuck out his hand to shake. "It's okay, Dad."

Jake took his offered hand. "I'm sorry. I didn't mean—"

"It's okay." Neil turned and gave Nettie a hug. "I love you, Mom. I'll write."

Art's big farm truck sputtered to a stop outside, and then Neil was gone.

Nettie stood at the window and watched the truck pull away in a cloud of dust. Neil didn't wave.

As her son disappeared, she ran her hands through her hair and pulled, the pain welcome. When Jake wrapped his arms around her, she pushed him away. "I don't know if I can ever forgive you for this."

She dressed in a fog and stumbled down the little rise to the corral where Pigeon waited, saddled her, and rode out into the hills again.

Nettie needed the muscular comfort of a horse beneath her, the sun to bake the tears out of her, and the wind to blow her fears away. *Sissy.* With one word, life had been changed forever.

After a week, a lone postcard came from Neil. "Arrived at camp. Doing fine. Love, Neil." Nettie's heart retreated from the piercing pain.

Her days and weeks followed a similar pattern. She and Jake moved cautiously around each other, like cats ghosting their prey. They didn't talk. She set out food at mealtime, took a plate out to the porch, and picked at it until Jake left to go for a smoke or back to the barn.

Ruthie rode over, her freckled face tear-streaked and her eyes red and swollen. "Oh, Mrs. Moser. How could he leave like this? He didn't even say good-bye." She wailed and Nettie held her, unable to find words of comfort.

Most days she rode Pigeon, galloping farther and farther into the hills, seeking solace in the lonely treeless prairie, no one around except an occasional sage hen or a gopher. She watched hawks dive from the sky, spearing mice in their talons, and swoop back up into the blue nothingness.

She rested on rocks scooped out like easy chairs by eons of wind and rain, plucked dry stems of wheatgrass and chewed on them. What would happen to Neil? Where would they send him? Would she ever see him again? Clouds formed on the horizon, the daylight waning as fall approached. Nettie let the wind whip at her, relishing its coldness and the pain of the first snowfall stinging her face.

She came home only when it became too dark to see. Her body numb from the cold, she trudged, shivering, into the house, where Jake had already built a fire in the coal stove in the living room. "You're soaking wet. You'll catch your death." He led her to the bedroom where Nettie sat limp and let him peel off her clothes and help her change into her flannel nightgown and robe. Jake wrapped a blanket around her and settled her into her rocking chair by the fire. Her teeth chattered and her body trembled. Jake brought her hot tea and fed her spoonfuls of soup, hovering near.

He smoothed her tangled hair away from her face. "I love you, little gal." His voice was husky, his eyes red, his face lined with anguish. "Please. I can't lose you too."

Nettie rocked, staring at a blank spot on the wall. Her father's wizened face, her mother's shrunken body, Neil's shocked look flashed across her blurred vision. "You don't know anything about loss." She grabbed the blanket and staggered into the bedroom.

⌒⌒

Nettie woke in darkness, shivering uncontrollably. *Need . . . another . . . blanket. . . .* She slipped her legs over the side of the bed and tried to stand. Lights flashed behind her eyes. The room whirled. Nettie crashed to the floor.

"Nettie! Honey! Talk to me." Jake's voice came from afar.

"C-cold," she moaned through clattering teeth.

Jake lifted her back into the bed, piled another quilt on, then scooted in next to her and wrapped his arms and legs around her to add to the warmth.

Chills tremored through her body until Nettie thought she'd shake right out of the bed. Jake stroked her hair and murmured softly next to her ear. Finally, she slept.

In her dreams, dark figures came and dragged Neil away. She screamed, but no one came to help. Mama and Papa hovered in the fog, calling something she couldn't make out. Gradually, as she drifted in and out, it sank in. Neil was gone. Mama and Papa were gone. She was a hollow shell and had no one left. Except Jake.

She was aware of throwing off quilts, drenched in sweat, then shaking with cold again. *Where's Neil?* She struggled to remember, fog clouding her brain. The chills, sleet, riding in the dark. It was too much. She drifted off.

Nettie was vaguely cognizant that Jake was holding her hand, and he talked to her softly, telling her about the horses and how the cows were doing since the snowstorm. He had brought the rocking chair in from the living room and stayed close by, feeding her warm broth when she woke, bathing her forehead, and stroking her hair. "I love you, little gal," he whispered over and over.

When Nettie woke, late afternoon sun slanted through the curtains and she was again drenched in sweat. She threw back the covers. "Why do I have so many quilts on me?"

Jake came running in. "You're awake."

Nettie tried to sit up. "What's wrong with me? I'm so weak." She lay back on the pillow.

"You've been very sick, honey." Jake dipped a washcloth in a bowl of water and gently sponged her face and neck.

Nettie looked at the window, frowning. "How long did I sleep?"

"You've been pretty much out of it for two days." Jake dried her with a soft towel. "I called Doc Tarbox in Forsyth, and if your fever hadn't broke by today, I was going to take you to the hospital."

"Oh my." She lay there, feeling as though everything—muscle and sinew, blood and emotion—had been drained from her body.

She thought of Pigeon, who hadn't been ridden in days. And Neil in boot camp—how was he doing? Did he miss home? Her anger at Jake. But it no longer boiled inside. Her body and mind were depleted. Neil was an adult now. He would be all right. *Not doing him any good wallowing in self-pity.* She had to let him go.

One morning Nettie awakened, feeling stronger and more clear-headed than she had in a long time. She sat up and swung her feet over the side. "I think it's time to get my lazy bones out of this bed."

"I'm so relieved you're feeling better, honey. I'm so sorry . . ."

Nettie put a hand on his cheek. "I'm okay."

Jake dragged the rocker back out to the living room and helped her walk. He tucked her in with blankets and a footstool. "Do you feel up to eating some flapjacks?"

"Yeah, I think I do." Her growling stomach felt concave.

The savory pancakes and strips of bacon tasted like slices of heaven. Nettie felt strength flowing back into her limbs. "I think I'd like to take a bath. I must smell like a sheepherder."

Jake laughed. "I'll get the tub and warm some water for you."

After he had lovingly helped her bathe and dress in fresh night-clothes, Nettie went back to the rocking chair. Jake brought her book and another pillow to rest it on while she read. "Do you think you're feeling good enough that I can run into town and pick up the mail?"

"Oh, sure. I'm good enough to go wrangle a steer." She gave a weak smile. "Well, maybe not quite. No, you go ahead. I'll be just fine."

Nettie read and dozed by the fire. She saw a young Jake, lovingly building a fire in the abandoned homestead shack after they'd been caught in a hailstorm before they were married. That's when she knew she loved him. All the places they'd moved in the '30s. How she'd almost given up on him then. But she had always loved him enough to go on with him. Did she still?

The pickup engine woke her and she heard Jake stomp snow off his boots before he came in. He stuck his head around the door to the living room. "Oh good, you're awake." He came to her, holding an envelope. "I think this is something you've been waiting for."

Nettie reached out and looked at it. Neil's handwriting. Her fingers trembled as she tore the end open and tapped the letter out.

Dear Mom and Dad,

Sorry I haven't been able to write sooner. We have been on the go from pre-dawn when we're awakened with Reveille until we fall into our bunks at midnight. We've marched miles upon miles with heavy packs. I'm thankful for the hard work I've done on the ranch. Stacking hay, wrestling calves, and riding has put me ahead of many of the new recruits.

*I am also sorry I left on such a downbeat. I hope you'll under-
stand that I have to make my own way in the world. I will be
earning decent pay in the Army and I will be able to forge a future
for myself.*

*Don't worry about me, Mom. I can take care of myself. Be your
strong cowgirl self.*

Love, Neil

Tears blurred Nettie's vision, but she smiled as she handed the
letter to Jake. "He's okay. He'll be okay." She repeated those words
silently while Jake read, to convince herself.

When Jake had finished, he took her hands in his. "He will be.
Our boy has become a man."

Nettie couldn't speak for the thickness in her throat. She nodded,
relief flooding her heart. Jake finally saw Neil as she did.

The Scotts invited Nettie and Jake for Thanksgiving. Mrs. Scott had
cooked a wild turkey with stuffing, potatoes and gravy, green beans
she'd canned, and a pie made with pumpkin from her garden and wild
honey.

Lilly-Anne chattered a bit about trick riding but skirted around
the subject of Ruthie and Neil, and although her grandmother tried
to make small talk about gardening and recipes, the atmosphere was
subdued. Nettie managed to get through the meal without tears, in
spite of the men's conversation that centered around the Russians
recapturing Kiev in the Ukraine and the recent British air attack on
Berlin.

Nettie picked at her turkey. Where would Neil be shipped? Would
he be on the front lines? And where was Gary? Neither she nor Margie had heard anything from him in months.

Christmas approached and the unknown loomed as heavy as the
snow clouds. Nettie helped Jake feed the cattle every day, neither

saying much more than was necessary. Periodically, one of them would whisper "He'll be okay" like a prayer, and the other would nod bravely.

Finally a Christmas card arrived from Neil, postmarked Fort Douglas, telling them he was being shipped out to England. The short note looked hastily scrawled and again ended with "Don't worry, Mom."

Nettie chewed her bottom lip. He might as well tell the sun not to shine. What did going to England mean? Would he be assigned to combat duty? She buried her face in Jake's chest, trying to find comfort.

Nettie tried to make Christmas festive, cooking a ham and baking a "Honey Spice Cake" from the ration cookbook, *Recipes For Today*. "At least the hens are still laying," she told Jake as he brought in the day's collection.

"Good thing, too, otherwise we'd be having chicken stew." Jake grinned and gave her a kiss on the cheek.

They ate alone—Jake asking for seconds of the cake—and afterward turned on the radio to hear news of the Russian offensive on the Ukrainian front. Jake got out the World Atlas and they traced the movements of the Allied troops.

"If Neil is going to England, maybe he won't be involved in anything big," Nettie said, with a hopeful note.

Jake nodded. "Probably not."

But Nettie knew the American troops were being sent out into the European battlefront from England. Her dinner congealed to an icy lump in her stomach. How could she have eaten so much when Neil might be hungry? *Please, Lord, keep him safe.* All she could do was pray.

CHAPTER TWENTY-THREE

January brought the inevitable blizzards. Nettie and Jake had moved the cows into the pasture closest to the barn, which had a deep coulee where they could find shelter from the icy wind. Jake also strung a rope from the house to the barn, a lifeline to find his way during the dense snowstorms.

The first day, Nettie sat in her rocker by the fire, wrapped in a quilt, reading an old Agatha Christie novel, *Murder on the Orient Express*, while the wind rattled the windows. Jake lit a lamp in the middle of the day against the storm-induced darkness, stretched his long legs out from the couch, and caught up on newspapers and magazines.

The second day, he pushed his chair back after breakfast. "I'd better see if that rope's still connected to the barn and at least check on the horses and milk cow."

"I'll come with you." Nettie stacked their plates in the dishpan.

"No. No need for that. I'll just do a quick check." Jake put on his heavy wool sweater, then his canvas coveralls, and pulled his overshoes over his boots. He topped his outfit with a wool cap and thick mittens.

Giving Nettie a peck on the cheek, he then opened the kitchen door to a gust of wind and snow and disappeared into the swirling flakes.

Nettie busied herself washing the dishes and sweeping the floors. She kept glancing at the clock. Surely if the rope had broken, Jake would turn around and come back. The walk to the barn, which normally took two minutes, would take much longer, maybe twenty minutes. Then to feed and water the horses, another half hour, and then twenty minutes back. He should be back soon.

But she remembered the story from her childhood about a neighbor who had frozen to death only a few yards from his front door. The horror she'd felt then nearly paralyzed her now. She looked at the clock again. Only thirty minutes. *It's okay.* Nettie grabbed a dust cloth and paced the house, swiping at the stair banister, lifting up a vase and setting it down again. Forty-five minutes passed. *Not time to worry yet.* She jumped with every gust of wind that thumped against the house. *Why isn't he back by now?*

After an hour and a half and no Jake, she couldn't stand waiting for one more minute. Nettie pulled on her warm clothes and coveralls. The wind threatened to grab the door from her hands when she opened it, but she managed to push it closed. She took hold of the rope and set out into the whiteout. Hand over hand, she pulled herself along, the wind buffeting her, every step through the deepening snow labored. Breathing hard, she stopped to rest, then trudged forward again.

It seemed like hours until she finally saw a dark shape loom just in front of her. The barn at last! Nettie let go of the rope and forced the door open, nearly falling inside. The humid, sweet, musty scent of hay and horses welcomed her. Pigeon whickered. Stranger and Blue echoed her greeting.

"Jake!" Nettie called. "Where are you?" No answer. She walked through the barn, checking every stall. The horses had been fed. Maybe he was out at the well, breaking ice to bring in water. She stepped to the back entrance, opened the door a crack and peered out. Nothing but white. The icy flakes bit at her cheeks. "Jake!"

Nettie stared into the blankness, willing Jake to appear. Then she heard a muffled shout and saw his shape materialize, carrying a bucket of water.

"Little gal, what are you doing out here?"

Nettie melted into his arms, warm relief flooding her body. "I got worried when it took so long."

"That figures." He grinned at her, his eyebrows crusted white. "Well, I am glad you came. There's some cows up against that near fence and I want to carry them a little hay. I got a rope strung to the well, and I can get to them from there."

Jake grabbed a roll of heavy string and climbed up into the loft. "I'm going to make some bundles to carry."

"I'll help." Nettie crawled up the ladder. Together they tied bunches of hay and threw them to the floor below.

Then each grabbed a bundle in one hand and headed out into the blizzard. Nettie held on to the hem of Jake's coat and followed him through the deepening snow, holding a bundle in her other arm. Immediately the hairs froze inside her nose and her eyebrows became heavy with snow. She pushed her neck scarf up over her mouth and nose with her shoulder, afraid to let go of her guide. The wind knocked her back and Nettie nearly fell.

Finally they reached the fence and threw their hay bundles over it to the waiting cows. Jake led them back to the well, where they could grab the icy rope with their gloved hands and follow it to the barn. They rested and warmed up for a few minutes before venturing out again. Time after time, Nettie picked up another bundle and waded through the storm behind Jake, who carried two bundles.

Her feet and arms felt like lifeless stumps, her eyes burned, and her heart pounded with the effort of putting one foot in front of the other. The cows pushed against the fence and gobbled up the hay as fast as Jake and Nettie could deliver it.

"Are we doing any good at all?" she panted during one of their rest stops inside the animal-created warmth of the barn.

Jake shook his head. "I don't know, but I have to try to get them something." He pounded his legs with his fists and swung his arms. "Why don't you stay here and get thawed out? I'll make one more trip. It's starting to get dark and we'll have to head back to the house soon."

"No, I'm coming with you." Nettie stood and stamped her feet, trying to bring feeling back. She would only worry herself sick if he was out there by himself.

After one more seemingly endless trip out and back, they checked the horses again and Jake milked the cow. Then they slogged their way back through the drifts to the house, following that blessed rope.

~⦿~

As winter wore on, Nettie and Jake plodded through their daily chores, with forced conversations about nothing. Nettie cooked meals every day, mindless of what she was serving or eating. Neil was always on her mind. Upstairs in his room, his clothes still hung in the tiny closet, and his bed was still rumpled as if he'd made it in a hurry. She could still feel his presence there and couldn't bring herself to change the bedding. She baked cookies for Neil and Gary and sent them to the APO address she had, hoping that somehow they would reach her boys.

Spring had never been more welcome to Nettie than it was that year. The warm smell of new grass filled her soul. She felt like a kid again when Ruthie and Lilly-Anne came over to visit one afternoon and rode out with her to the nearby pasture to check on the newborn calves.

"What do you hear from Neil?" Ruthie asked in a small voice.

Nettie glanced over at the girl's expectant eyes. "We've only had a few letters from him. It takes so long to get mail by boat." Nettie tried to take the sting out of the fact that her son was not writing to her little friend. "I know he was sent to England and his job is driving trucks and doing mechanic work."

Ruthie blinked rapidly and turned her head away.

Nettie was making excuses for her son, but what else could she do?

"Mrs. Moser," Lilly-Anne chimed in, "we want to plan another neighborhood rodeo this year. That was so much fun last fall. Maybe we can get even more people to come."

Nettie watched Ruthie make herself cheer up, her smile too bright. "Yeah. I've been practicing my rope tricks on Ginger now. She's getting used to it and I'm getting better."

"She is, too," Lilly-Anne agreed. "And we've been working on some new tricks together."

"Well, that sounds like a dandy plan." Nettie grinned at her girls. Rodeos took everybody's mind off their troubles. "I wonder if they'll have a Fourth of July parade in Forsyth this year. Maybe we could even do an exhibition there."

Ruthie bounced in her saddle, more like her old self. "Let's do it!"

"I'll have my dad find out about the parade and see if he'll help," Lilly-Anne volunteered.

Buck later confirmed that plans were indeed underway for a patriotic parade and the Forsyth town fathers would welcome an exhibition rodeo.

Jake took up the spirit, too, and said he'd ask Buck or Chet to rope with him. Neither he nor Nettie mentioned that Neil was missing, though his absence never left either of them.

Excitement grew as Nettie and the girls made plans. They all sat down to write letters to anyone they could think of who might be able to participate, making suggestions on how people could pool their gas rations and travel together.

— ⁓ —

One early June day, as Nettie cooked dinner, she turned on Jake's new shortwave radio to listen to the dulcet tones of Harry James and his orchestra. Then the music stopped abruptly. A somber announcer's deep voice broke through the static. "The following communiqué has just been issued by the Supreme Headquarters of the Allied Expedition: Under the command of General Eisenhower, Allied Naval

Forces, supported by strong Air Forces, began landing Allied armies this morning on the northern coast of France."

Nettie's hand suspended over the hot kettle, the ominous tone sending cold fear through her. Jake came in from the living room, wide-eyed and ashen.

As they ate, they continued listening to the radio, including a report from NBC correspondent John W. Vandercook from London. "The invasion of western Europe has begun . . . " His voice rose and faded with the airwave static. " . . . promised by Churchill is now a reality . . . what General Eisenhower has called 'the Great Crusade' will bring about the destruction of the German war machine."

Was Neil involved? Or Gary? Nettie's stomach knotted. The dishes clattered in her trembling hands as she cleared the table. Maybe it would've been better not getting the radio. She heated water and scrubbed plates as if her life depended on it.

They listened for every scrap of news, as if they might learn something about their boys. They listened until the station went off the air for the night, and Jake turned off the static. Silence filled the room. There were a hundred things Nettie should say, but words would not come. How long would they have to wait to find out about their boys, about the success of the invasion, about whether the war might really end?

Jake came over and put an arm around Nettie. "I think these dishes are clean enough."

She buried her face in his chest. "He has to come home," she said through her tears.

Jake's embrace was her haven. "He will, little gal," he whispered. "He will."

—◆—

The next day, Ruthie and Lilly-Anne showed her a comedy routine they were working up for the exhibition. Dressed in clown costumes, they attempted mounting their horses, falling off the other side with exaggerated swoops and arms wind-milling.

Nettie laughed until her sides ached. She assured them their antics would be the hit of the exhibition.

Two weeks later, Nettie was just packing a lunch to take to Jake in the hayfield when she saw a pickup turn up their drive. She went out on the porch to wave at the visitor, but froze when she saw Horace Beam with the dreaded yellow telegram in his hand.

All the air seemed to leave her lungs. The glaring sun burned bright spots into her eyes. Wind roared through her ears.

Horace caught her as she slumped against the porch rail. "Mrs. Moser. C'mon now. Don't you faint on me." He eased her into a chair and patted her shoulder. "I'll go in and get you some water."

The cold liquid soothed her throat and revived her. The roaring stopped and Horace came into focus. "The . . . t-telegram," she choked out.

"Oh. Yes. I'm sorry, Mrs. Moser." Horace handed the envelope to her.

She tore it open with shaking hands.

GARY KILLED IN ACTION NORMANDY STOP.

It was signed by Glen, Margie's husband.

Not Neil. For a moment relief flooded her, then horror. *Oh, dear God. Margie.*

"Are you all right, Mrs. Moser?" Horace peered at her.

"It's my nephew. He was in the D-Day invasion." Her head involuntarily shook from side to side. "Oh, dear Lord, how do we abide it?"

Horace's eyes blinked behind his thick glasses. "Bringin' sad news sure ain't somethin' I want to do, Mrs. Moser. Time for us to win this war and get done with it."

Horace went to find Jake for her.

She sat, numb. Mama. Papa. The boys in town. Now Gary. Who else would this terrible war take from her?

She heard Jake cussing a blue streak as he and Horace clumped onto the porch. " ... consarned Huns ... oughtta go over there myself ... blow 'em all to kingdom come." Jake pushed open the door with a thump.

"Nettie, honey. Are you all right? Oh, Lord, this is terrible." His voice filled with anguish, he knelt by her side.

Nettie looked into his face, crinkled with sorrow, laid her head on his shoulder, and gave in to her tears.

<hr>

Nettie and Jake continued to devour the news that crackled over the shortwave. Because of that D-Day invasion in Normandy, the Germans were being pushed back for the first time since the Nazis had overrun France four years ago. After defeating the German beach defenses in that first attack, the Allies expanded their beachheads, and their air dominance hindered German reinforcements, delivering a psychological blow to the German occupation of Europe. Although the death toll was estimated at twenty-five hundred, the nation's leaders remained optimistic.

President Roosevelt delivered a prayer that touched Nettie's heart:

My fellow Americans: Last night, when I spoke with you about the fall of Rome, I knew at that moment that troops of the United States and our Allies were crossing the Channel in another and greater operation. It has come to pass with success thus far.

And so, in this poignant hour, I ask you to join with me in prayer. Almighty God: Our sons, pride of our nation, this day have set upon a mighty endeavor, a struggle to preserve our Republic, our religion, and our civilization, and to set free a suffering humanity. ... We know that by Thy grace, and by the righteousness of our cause, our sons will triumph. ... Some will never return. Embrace

these, Father, and receive them, Thy heroic servants, into Thy king-
dom. . . . With Thy blessing, we shall prevail over the unholy forces
of our enemy. . . . Lead us to . . . a peace that will let all of men live
in freedom, reaping the just rewards of their honest toil. . . .

Nettie closed her eyes, gripped Jake's hand, and prayed along with
the president.

A week later, Margie stepped off the train in Miles City, her eyes red
and swollen, her face white and drawn. Nettie enfolded her sister in
her arms. They rocked together, Margie clutching tight to Nettie, as if
trying to draw in strength to take the next step. Jake silently took her
suitcase, and together, he and Nettie held Margie's arms and helped
her to the pickup.

Back home, Nettie paced the floor while Margie slept, wondering
how she would be able to comfort her.

When her sister was ready to come downstairs, Nettie tucked her
in the rocking chair in front of the living room window, so Margie
could look out over the green prairie and watch the calves frolic in the
pasture nearby.

"I had to get away." Margie finally began to talk in fits and starts
over tea and cookies. "Glen just went crazy. Broke windows. Tore the
door off the hinges."

Nettie folded Margie's hand in hers.

"Then he left." She blotted her eyes with a hanky, edged in delicate
lace—one Mama had made.

"Lola was there. And the girls. But they hovered, even though they
have their own families to take care of." Margie sniffled. "I need time
to myself."

"And that you shall have."

"We don't know if we'll even get his . . ." Margie gulped. " . . . get
Gary back to bury."

Nettie held her sister while she cried, tears washing her own cheeks.

As the days unfolded, Margie spent long hours sitting in front of the window or going for endless walks. Nettie stood back as much as she could, aching for her sister and holding in her own empty sense of loss. Her nephew had seemed to see inside her soul. Much like her older brother Joe had been when they were growing up. Much like Neil in so many ways, strong yet sensitive, courageous yet caring. *Neil. Where is he today? Please, Lord, keep him safe.*

Jake went into Ingomar nearly every day to check the mail. Nettie waited on the porch, pacing until he came home, shaking his head. No letter today.

Finally one arrived, postmarked after D-Day. Neil was still alive. Nettie breathed a little deeper and her shoulders relaxed. His letter was cheerful. He mentioned the mechanic work he had to do to keep the supply trucks running, and rambled on with descriptions of the lush green European countryside without saying exactly where he'd been.

Ruthie and Lilly-Anne, pale and solicitous, came to visit and offer condolences. Ruthie even brought molasses cookies she'd baked herself.

"Girls, I'm sorry, but I can't go ahead with our plans for the exhibition this summer. I hope you understand. Margie needs me." Nettie held her hands out to the girls. "But you go ahead. I think you should."

Ruthie frowned and shook her head. "It wouldn't be right without you."

"I can't, Ruthie," Nettie repeated.

Since Margie had never enjoyed riding, Nettie took long walks with her, arms entwined, leaning on each other. Sometimes they walked for hours without saying much at all.

Sometimes Margie would suddenly smile and get a faraway look on her face. "One time when Gary was only about four, I'd had a terribly difficult day and was sitting there in my rocker, fighting not to cry. He came up to me and said, 'You're the best Mama in the world,' crawled onto my lap, and laid his little head next to mine." She turned to Nettie with a cautious, tender smile. "That made everything in the world right again."

Nettie put an arm around her sister's shoulders. "I know. When Marie was killed and I was feeling so low, everybody was urging me to get back out there and ride. Nobody understood the fear I had. Except Gary."

"He was so patriotic and had such a strong conviction to do his part for freedom against the likes of Hitler. He couldn't wait for us to get involved in the war, so he went to Canada to enlist." Margie hugged her arms to herself. "I'm so darned proud of him."

"Me too." Nettie's words choked past the thickness in her throat.

After about a month of sleeping, walking, and healing talks, Margie stood up from her chair by the window in the living room one afternoon with a sharp exclamation. "Oh!"

Nettie ran in from the kitchen. A dark sedan approached the house.

"It's our car." Margie's hands fluttered over her hair, smoothing wayward strands. "It's Glen."

Margie's husband got out of the car, moving almost painfully. His shoulders hunched like an old man, he shuffled up to the house and mounted the porch steps, stopping a moment on each one. Margie stood at the door, her hands over her mouth, her eyes blinking. Nettie felt Glen's pain radiating across the expanse of the porch. Finally, he gained the top step and looked up at Margie with sunken, bloodshot eyes.

Margie gasped. "Glen!" She threw open the screen door and enveloped him in her arms. He stood as if he were made of wood. Then he slowly raised his arms to encircle his wife.

Nettie pulled back into the shadows of the kitchen as the couple sobbed together.

After it was all over—the long trip to Cut Bank, the disappointment of not getting Gary's body, the excruciating ordeal of the memorial service, the memories, the condolences, the long, sad faces—Nettie came home to throw herself into work. She helped Jake rake, gather, and stack hay. She drove the truck as he harvested the grain, and then helped gather the straw. She rode the pastures every day, counting each cow and calf, hunting relentlessly for any missing animal, checking the fences for missing staples or downed wires.

When Nettie walked through the door of the house, the reminders of Gary's death and Neil yet in danger hit her with the force of a steer's kick: seeing the red-and-white banner with the blue star in the window, the pictures of Neil and Gary on the wall. She went upstairs to Neil's room, pulled an armful of shirts from his closet, and lay on his bed, clutched them to her chest, and wept.

When Jake brought home the mail, she pawed through every piece, looking for a letter. When one finally came, it was short and cheerful but gave her only a little comfort.

In the evenings, they listened to the short-wave and tried to make sense of what was happening in Europe. Newspaper reports often conflicted with BBC reports, adding to the sense of confusion. Nettie tacked a map on the wall, trying to follow the Allies' advancement.

In August, they heard the Allies had liberated Paris and the Soviets had taken Bucharest, and in September the announcement came that US troops had reached the Siegfried Line in western Germany. Neil's occasional letters gave them no enlightenment about where he actually was. Censors looked over everyone's shoulders now.

In mid-December, around Nettie's thirty-ninth birthday, for days the radio programs were filled with reports about the Battle of the Bulge, a surprise German offensive in the snow-packed Ardennes mountain region of Belgium, France, and Luxembourg. The casualty reports from this long, bloody battle kept Nettie awake at night.

When Nettie couldn't stand it any longer, she put on her heavy winter coat and went outside. She shivered in the bitter cold as she crunched through the snow to the barn to visit Pigeon and the other horses, thinking of the soldiers in such weather conditions. Was Neil there? Was he warm and fed? She swept stalls and replaced straw beds, carried water, fed the chickens, and gathered the eggs. When the afternoon light waned into purple dusk, Nettie took the eggs back to the house and sat down to write an insistent letter to Neil: "We need to know where you are and if you are safe."

The news turned more positive as the Allies beat back and overcame the German offensive. Nettie and Jake tried to prepare for a festive Christmas by inviting the Millers for dinner.

In January 1945, a thin letter sheet finally arrived from Neil, postmarked in November at the central APO in England.

Heard the terrible news about Gary. Am very sad. Wrote to Aunt Margie and Uncle Glen. I'm doing fine. Still busy keeping trucks running. Hope this reaches you by Christmas. Happy birthday, Mom.

They still didn't know where he was, but he was alive and well.

"He's okay," Jake would assure her sometimes, out of the blue, as if he, too, needed that reminder.

"He's okay," she would murmur to him before they fell asleep at night.

As few and far between as they were, each letter proved he was still alive, and Nettie read and reread them until the thin paper was creased and worn.

～～

"Let's have a party next week on Jake's birthday," Zelda suggested over coffee one mid-February day.

Nettie glanced out at the sun glistening on the white-quilted prairie. The Zelda she'd first met would never have made a suggestion like this. Now that the kids were older, she seemed much less frazzled.

"Let's," Nettie agreed. "I think he's having a hard time with turning forty-seven. He needs something to lift his spirits . . . we all do."

"I'll bake a cake!" Ruthie jumped up and grabbed the ration cookbook. "What kind does he like?"

"Let me take a look." Nettie thumbed through. "He liked the Honey Spice Cake last fall. If your hens are still laying."

Zelda sipped her coffee. "We get a couple now and then. We'll start saving now and we should have enough."

"I'll save mine, too," Nettie said, and the three hatched plans for a celebration and how to keep it secret.

On the evening of the twentieth, Jake and Nettie drove to the Millers, who had invited them for dinner. Arriving to inviting lamplight spilling out of the windows, they crunched through the snow to the house, where Chet opened the front door. "Howdy. C'mon in where it's warm." He stepped aside and gestured them in.

"Surprise!" A living room full of people shouted and held up their drinks in salute. "Happy birthday."

Jake stopped in midstride, a flush rising up his neck, at a complete loss for words.

Nettie clapped her hands. "Gotcha," she teased, delighted that he'd been totally surprised.

"Got me good," the birthday boy agreed with a grin.

Chet poured him a glass of whiskey. Nettie wandered into the kitchen and found Ruthie putting the finishing touches on the cake with a brown-sugar frosting.

"We found this sugar way in the back of the cupboard, hard as a rock. But we got it softened up. It took awhile, but it worked." She stood back to admire her handiwork.

Nettie put her arm around the girl. "A lovely cake. Thank you." She'd never thought something as simple as sugar icing could make her so happy. Surely the war would be over soon. Rationing would end. Neil would come home.

Zelda bent over the oven to remove a venison roast. "We're ready to eat, if you want to gather everybody around the table."

Chet carved the roast and Buck Scott raised a toast. "To our good friend, Jake. Here's to luck, and hoping God will take a likin' to ya."

Someone else chimed in, "May your well never run dry."

And another. "May the rocks in your field turn to gold."

"And we'll walk hand in hand, till we meet again," Nettie murmured. Jake beamed at her, and she beamed back.

The hearty meal continued with warm and lively conversation, the men making plans for spring crops and summer harvests and the women comparing the recipes they would make when they could buy all the sugar they wanted.

CHAPTER TWENTY-FOUR

Several days after the party, a postcard from Neil arrived.

Happy birthday, Dad. Doing okay. Still tinkering on trucks. Love, Neil.

Jake grinned. "That's my boy. He'll be a darn fine mechanic when he gets home."

Nettie breathed easier until each new battle report resounded from the radio. She shut her mind to her worry and concentrated on the daily chores of getting through the winter, sheltering new calves during a late snowstorm, and enjoying the freshness of spring when it finally arrived. The war would be over soon.

One sunny spring day, Nettie was delighted to receive a letter from Trixi.

Just returned from touring with the USO to England and France with Slim Pickens and Bob Hope. My, what an experience! The GIs really appreciated our show and my rope tricks brought whistles and cheers. It's so good to be able to help those boys forget the horrors of war for a few hours.

I understand your frustration. Nothing much going on in rodeo in the western part of the state either. When I can, I ride into Missoula to put on a show or just round up a few old-timers for a shindig in Ovando.

I'll be traveling with the USO again later this year, I think. Tell Ruthie and Lillie-Anne hello and not to give up on their dream!

With warmer weather drying up the mud, Ruthie and Lilly-Anne resumed their rigorous training schedule, and Nettie rode over to coach them whenever she could.

Nettie watched the girls swooping on and off their horses, their moves smooth and practiced. "Good goin', girls. Keep up the great work. Now let's do that switch-up again, and concentrate on the balance that comes from your gut." As she helped them with new tricks, she was surprised to find she was learning too.

"You know what we should do?" Nettie told them about Trixi's letter. "We should do a show for the VFW in Miles City, entertain the veterans from the Great War and anyone who has come back wounded from this one."

Ruthie bounced up and down in her saddle. "Oh, yes! Let's!"

Lilly-Anne agreed and they began to plan their routine.

Another letter came a few days later from Vivian White, lamenting the lack of rodeos.

With this war, there just aren't many men around anymore to produce shows. I think we women will have to jump in to fill the gap. I've been fighting with the RAA to let us ride rough stock again ever since Madison Square Garden in '41.

The war. Nettie shook her head. So much destruction, so much pain and heartache. Mama died because of the shortage of drugs, caused by the war. The Germans had not only killed Gary and other young boys, but the war had also killed rodeo. She balled her hands into fists. And she feared for Neil every single day, not knowing where he was or when he'd come home.

She went to the pasture, saddled Pigeon, and went for a ride. The breeze in her hair and the muscular movement of the horse soothed her. She stopped to watch the new calves frolicking in the sun, their red bodies and bright white faces vivid against the green grass and the huge, intense blue sky. Nettie smiled, her heart filled with the Creator's artistry. That same sky watched over Neil. How could she remain sad with so much beauty and peace around her?

All through April 1945, news reports were filled with accounts of Allied victories as they advanced into Germany. On the last day of April, a radio bulletin announced the suicide of Adolf Hitler.

Jake slapped his knee and cheered. "May he rot in hell."

"Does this mean . . . ?" Nettie was overcome with all her hopes.

"We won the war," Jake assured her. "We've all but won the war."

They spent the following days sitting close to the short-wave, listening as the German Reich fell. On May 2, German troops surrendered in Italy. Nettie held her breath. Was Neil there to see this happening?

On May 7, regular programming was interrupted by the BBC. Prime Minister Winston Churchill's sonorous voice came over the crackling airwaves. " . . . unconditional surrender to the Allied forces . . . Tuesday the eighth of May . . . we will celebrate Victory in Europe Day . . ."

"Neil will be coming home!" Dizzy with the news, Nettie danced with Jake and laughed until tears ran down her face. They finally collapsed, breathless, into their chairs. "This calls for a celebration." He grabbed her hand and they raced to the pickup to join their friends in rejoicing at the wonderful news.

At the Scotts', the celebration paused in reverence as Buck raised the American flag. Grandma Scott held the younger kids' hands, and Ruthie and Lilly-Anne stood with palms flattened over their hearts. As the red, white, and blue unfurled, the girls led the recitation: "I pledge allegiance to the flag of the United States of America, and to the republic for which it stands, one nation, indivisible, with liberty and justice for all."

Cheers and applause erupted. Everyone hugged and the little kids ran around the yard shrieking. Nettie began to believe the peace was real. Even the men had moist eyes.

"C'mon in. I got a special bottle to break open for just such an occasion," Chet called out, "and wine for the ladies."

Glasses clinked, the men made toasts to "the future and prosperity," and the women laughed while they helped Zelda prepare an impromptu feast. Toward evening, they all piled into vehicles and headed to the Oasis in Ingomar to continue their celebration.

The bar was packed with farmers and ranchers, cowboys and housewives, all hooting and hollering and hugging each other. A lively tune blared from the player piano as someone pumped the pedals. Couples danced in a small cleared space, tables pushed back to the wall.

"Hip, hip, hooray for the USA," someone shouted. "Drinks all around."

Nettie downed her glass. This was a day never to forget. This was the start of the rest of their lives. And as her eyes watered from the whiskey, she knew exactly how to honor the past and build a future that should be.

━◆━

A couple of weeks later, a letter on the familiar paper as thin as an onionskin arrived. She held her breath as she tore the seal and read it aloud to Jake.

Hi Mom and Dad,

The war with Germany is over! Hallelujah! Much celebration going on in Europe right now. Allies are dividing Germany. I can tell you now I will be part of that occupation in the western part. Don't know when I'll be coming home. Hoping it will be soon.

See, Mom, you didn't need to worry about me!

Love, Neil

"He knows you too well." Jake grinned at her.

Nettie's pent-up breath released, and she sat up straighter, as if a huge weight had been lifted. Neil was safe. The war was over.

Jake scanned the letter again. "He *is* okay." His Adam's apple bobbed as his words came out husky and choked. Tears pooled in his blue eyes, and he hugged Nettie. "Our boy made it."

—◆—

With a giddy sense of weightlessness, Nettie rode to the Scotts'. She whistled back at the meadowlarks and giggled as her loping horse frightened a sage hen from the brush. "Run, little chicken, run," she called out.

Ruthie and Lilly-Anne were in the corral, saddling their horses. "Hi, Mrs. Moser," Ruthie called out, "I think we're almost ready for our exhibition. When do you think we should do it?"

Nettie dismounted. "Well, first I have good news." She told them about Neil, and the girls clapped their hands with glee.

"We can still do our exhibition," Nettie went on, "but something Vivian said about the lack of men to put on rodeos got me to thinking. Why couldn't we put on an all-girl rodeo in Miles City?"

Ruthie shrieked. "That's a great idea, Mrs. Moser! I'll bet Trixi and Margaret and Thelma would come!"

"Yes!" Lilly-Anne's face lit up. "We could plan it for the Fourth of July."

Nettie clapped her hands, caught up in the girls' excitement. "I'm sure they will want to celebrate the end of the war with a parade anyhow. And what better way to introduce you girls and your new tricks to the community."

Over the next couple of weeks, Nettie and the girls wrote letters, designed posters for the "All-Girl Rodeo," and drove to Forsyth and Miles City to put them up. Nettie talked to the mayor and convinced him that although their boys were still gone, the event would honor the troops for all the sacrifices they had made.

On the morning of the fourth, Nettie stepped outside her tent at the fairgrounds to a glorious display of pink, lavender, and gold splashed across the horizon. "Time to get up, girls. We've got a lot to do today!"

Ruthie and Lilly-Anne tumbled out of their bedrolls, yawning and giggling, then shrieking as they splashed cold water on their faces. Trixi and her friends, Thelma and Margaret, joined them for breakfast. Then Birdie wandered over. Jake kept serving flapjacks as one young woman, then another, and another showed up, asking Nettie if they could ride in the rodeo.

"I'm going to ride a steer," one said.

"And I've been practicing calf roping," chimed in another.

"Trick riding."

"Bronc ridin'."

Overwhelmed by the response, Nettie wrote down all their names and told them where and how to sign up. Then they all rode downtown to begin the parade.

Nettie approached the mayor to ask where she and the girls should line up. He greeted her with a hearty handshake. "Mrs. Moser, so glad to see you. What a wonderful idea you've had for our festivities today!"

"Thank you, Mr. Mayor."

"I would like to offer you the honor of being parade marshal and leading the parade with all your girls in the color guard."

Nettie's jaw dropped. Why her? "Parade marshal? Surely there are more-deserving people, someone home from the military, perhaps."

"No, no." The mayor reached around behind his viewing stand and brought out a large American flag on a pole. "The council voted for you." He handed her the flag and gestured to the girls. "I have flags for all of you."

Nettie mounted and Jake helped her position and secure the bottom of the flagpole on her stirrup, then went to help the girls.

Pigeon pranced beneath her as the band began John Philip Sousa's "Stars and Stripes Forever." The July sun shone warm on her back and a breeze rippled the flag above her. She glanced back at her entourage, a sea of red, white, and blue above proud, smiling faces.

Nettie urged her horse forward. The war in Europe was over, Neil was safe, and he would be coming home soon. She grinned over at Jake, following along the sidelines. It couldn't get much better than this—as she helped these young girls fulfill their own dreams, Nettie's dreams were also coming true.

Afterword

My first two novels, *Cowgirl Dreams* and *Follow the Dream*, are based on my grandmother, Olive May "Tootsie" Bailey Gasser, who rode steers in Montana rodeos in the 1920s. While *Dare to Dream* does follow a historical timeline and many true family incidents, this is more a work of fiction than the first two.

The 1920s were the heyday of rodeo, when the cowgirl was as much a part of the festivities as the cowboy. The first cowgirls learned to ride out of necessity to help on their family ranches. At an early age they learned to ride horses, rope cattle, and stay in the saddle atop an untamed bucking bronco. They competed with the men in those early ranch gatherings and continued to do so at the organized roundup events.

In 1929 Bonnie McCarroll died in a fall from a bronc at the Pendleton Round-Up and Marie Gibson was killed in a freak accident after a successful ride in 1933. Several other women were also killed during rough stock competition. As a result of these incidents and the formation of the all-male Rodeo Association of America, cowgirl bronc riding became increasingly rare in the West, leaving only beauty pageants, relay racing, and some exhibition riding open to women competitors during the 1930s and '40s.

I have no information that my grandmother mentored young riders or that she was involved in the cowgirls' movement to form the Girls' Rodeo Association in 1948. But I would like to believe that she would have, if she'd had the chance. She and Grandpa bought me my first horse when I was eight, and Grandma did help teach me to ride. She died when I was twelve.

ABOUT THE AUTHOR

Heidi M. Thomas grew up on a working ranch in eastern Montana. She had parents who taught her a love of books and a grandmother who rode bucking stock in rodeos. Describing herself as "born with ink in her veins," Heidi followed her dream of writing with a journalism degree from the University of Montana and later turned to her first love, fiction, to write her grandmother's story.

Heidi's first novel, *Cowgirl Dreams*, has won an EPIC Award and the *USA Book News* Best Book Finalist award.

The second book in the Dare to Dream series about strong, independent Montana women, *Follow the Dream*, is a WILLA Award winner.

Heidi is a member of Women Writing the West and Professional Writers of Prescott, is also a manuscript editor, an avid reader of all kinds of books, and enjoys the sunshine and hiking in north-central Arizona, where she writes, edits, and teaches memoir and fiction writing classes.

Married to Dave Thomas (not of Wendy's fame), Heidi is also the "human" for a finicky feline, and describes herself primarily as a "cat herder." Visit her at heidimthomas.com.